DESIRE'S HOSTAGE

VIKING LORE, BOOK 3

EMMA PRINCE

BOOKS BY EMMA PRINCE

Viking Lore Series:

Enthralled (Viking Lore, Book 1)

Shieldmaiden's Revenge (Viking Lore, Book 2)

The Bride Prize (Viking Lore Novella, Book 2.5)

Desire's Hostage (Viking Lore, Book 3)

Thor's Wolf (Viking Lore, Book 3.5)—a Kindle Worlds novella

Highland Bodyguards Series:

The Lady's Protector (Book 1)

Heart's Thief (Book 2)

A Warrior's Pledge (Book 3)

Claimed by the Bounty Hunter (Book 4)

A Highland Betrothal (Novella, Book 4.5)

The Promise of a Highlander (Book 5)

The Bastard Laird's Bride (Book 6—Reid Mackenzie's story) coming Fall 2017!

The Sinclair Brothers Trilogy:

Highlander's Ransom (Book 1)

Other Books:

DESIRE'S HOSTAGE

VIKING LORE, BOOK 3

~

By
Emma Prince

Desire's Hostage (Viking Lore, Book 3) Copyright © 2016 by Emma Prince

For Scott. Always.

1

808 A.D.

"Farewell!"

Alaric's twin sister Madrena leaned out past her ship's wooden sides, waving furiously at the docks.

Eirik waved back with one hand, the other wrapped protectively around his wife. Laurel held little Thorin in her arms as she, too, waved.

Even from this distance, Alaric could see that tears shimmered in Laurel's dark eyes. He could only imagine the barrage of emotions she was experiencing as she watched her friends set sail for her former homeland.

"We shall see each other again soon!" Alaric shouted over the ever-increasing span of water. He intentionally spoke in Laurel's native tongue despite the fact that she'd quickly learned the Northland language upon arrival in Dalgaard.

Laurel grinned widely. "Aye, I know we will!" she called back in her language.

Even before he'd learned that it would be vital to him, Alaric had asked Laurel to teach him her language. Though Alaric had only been charged with leading this voyage since last fall, he'd sensed long ago that a knowledge of the lands to the west would serve him well. That mist-shrouded, green terrain had called to him ever since he'd first laid eyes on it two summers ago. By some whisper of the gods, he knew his fate lay there.

Eirik and Laurel, along with the other villagers from Dalgaard who'd gathered to see the voyagers off, shrank to specks as Alaric and Madrena's longships drew farther out into the fjord. Still, Alaric let his eyes linger on Dalgaard as it faded.

Home.

Would he ever see Dalgaard again? Would he ever see Laurel, Eirik, and their son Thorin, whom he thought of as a nephew, again?

He always spoke confidently in front of his crew and even shielded Laurel from the worst of his fears. But when he and Eirik talked quietly within Dalgaard's long-house through the long, dark nights of winter and into the spring, they spoke the truth.

Alaric and his crew might never return, for this voyage bristled with dangers of every manner.

Aegir the sea god could frown on them at any point during the sennight-long voyage. They could be sunk, or blown so far off course as to never see land again. And if they did somehow manage to make it to those mysterious lands to the west, battle, disease, or simple starvation could await them.

But he could not let his dark thoughts rule him. The time of his death may be in the hands of the gods, but his fate was his own to make. Yet the new weight of responsibility sat heavy on his shoulders—there was more at stake than his own glory in the eyes of the gods.

At last, Alaric turned his back on the village. The breeze barreling down the length of the fjord whipped his hair around his head. He glanced to his left and found Madrena's longship skimming past his. Even over the roar of the wind, he could hear her urging on her rowers.

"A race, then?" he shouted over the expanse of water separating their longships.

Madrena snapped her ice-blonde head to him. Her pale gray eyes sparked.

"To the mouth of the fjord!" she called back.

"And the prize?"

She chuckled, but the sound was snatched by the wind. He knew his sister well, though.

"Honor before the gods, of course," she yelled.

But Alaric didn't need reminders about honor from Madrena. He was the leader of this voyage. Its success or failure rode on him.

He nodded, but before he could explain Madrena's game to his crew, his sister's ship darted forward.

"To the mouth!" Alaric barked to the men already plying their oars with a good deal of effort. He didn't have to say more, for his men could see for themselves that Madrena was pulling away. A spark of competitiveness instantly ignited within the longship. Alaric's men threw their weight against their oars, shouting encouragement to each other.

Without hesitating, Alaric took up a seat on his sea chest and snatched an unmanned oar. With practiced ease, he fell into rhythm with the others as they pulled against the dark fjord waters.

It felt good to have the oar's wood under his hands.

This was something he could control.

His strength, plied against that of Aegir the sea god's.

His will against the fates that swirled unknowably.

His determination against the mysteries held in the lands to the west.

Alaric's longship surged alongside Madrena's. Even as she redoubled her urgings to her crew, they fell behind, spent from their initial burst. As the arching dragon prow on Alaric's ship plowed into the open waters of the North Sea, he let his triumphant laugh drift on the wind to Madrena.

His sister scowled fiercely, crossing her arms over her chest. Alaric's crew slumped in victorious satisfaction as Madrena's ship glided alongside it.

"Unfurl the sails," Alaric ordered, a merry smile still stretching his face. Both his and Madrena's crew began stowing the oars and raising the sails, all the while shouting barbs and fresh challenges across the water at each other.

"I think my second in command has learned her lesson," Alaric said once both ships were prepared to set out into open waters.

Madrena dared to stick her tongue out at Alaric. He could only laugh again.

Without him needing to give the order, Madrena moved to her ship's stern. He did the same and guided the wooden tiller to the right. When the wind caught their red and white striped sails, they'd be thrust westward, into the unknown.

Alaric drew a deep breath of cool, salty air.

They were off.

2

———

The only warning Elisead had was her father's hands closing tightly around her arms. Then she was yanked to her feet, her carver's pebbles scattering in the dirt.

Her father spun her so that she faced him. His face was mottled red with anger beneath his gray-copper beard.

"If I've told you once, I've told you a hundred times," he bit out. "You are not to carve unless it is on your bride gift."

He snatched up one of her hands by the wrist, bringing her fingertips close to his face. At the calluses there, he cursed.

"You are the daughter of a chieftain, not some common mason," he barked, waggling her fingers in the air between them.

"Masons are not common," she said, drawing her

hand away. "At least not ones who can do this." She gestured to what she'd been working on, keeping her head level. Though she normally didn't dare talk back to her father, the crisp air of the summer morning had intoxicated and emboldened her.

In the dappled shade beneath the spreading oaks overhead, she'd found the perfect rock. It jutted tall and proud from the forest floor as if it had already been shaped and smoothed from the quarry. She couldn't help herself. The rock spoke to her, whispered of its ancient past. She'd begun carving a leaping deer first, then a bird taking flight. With each new design and image, the stone came more alive.

Her father glanced dismissively at her carvings. "What good does it do to etch woodland creatures on a stone no one will ever see?"

She'd heard the like from him before, but it still stung. Explaining how she felt never moved him, so she remained silent, lowering her head.

His hand closed around her arm once more, giving her a little shake. "I'm only trying to protect you," he said, his eyes narrowing. "Carving is meant to elevate God. This," he gestured behind her to the entwining animals and patterns used by her people for generations, "this smacks of the old ways."

What he spoke was true, but Elisead didn't care. "No one knows it is my work."

"And who else learned to carve stone when that cursed mason came through all those years ago?" her father snapped. "Who else slips away from the fortress into these woods with a pouch full of pebbles and a chisel and hammer?"

"There is no one to enforce the punishment for a trespass into the old ways," she tried again.

Her father paused at that. Though Christian priests occasionally visited them from Torridon, they were as rare in these remote hills as the skilled masons who traveled the land, leaving their exquisite carvings behind. In fact, the last time a priest had been to their little corner of Pictland, Elisead had already learned the secrets of carving from Una.

"No daughter of a chieftain, and certainly not my only heir, will coarsen her hands on stone," her father said, planting his feet and crossing his arms.

That was the true reason he'd forbidden her from carving—it always came back to himself. No daughter of Maelcon mac Lorcan, chief to a small but proud clan of Picts, would debase herself with labor. Except for the bride gift she'd been ordered to make.

"And the bride gift?"

She knew the answer, but some small spark of rebellion still burned within her—'twas the forest that made her so bold. She wanted to make him defend himself.

Her father harrumphed. "At least some good can come of your obsession. Your skills should be put to use on that stone, for God and for your future husband, not out here for the spirits."

He didn't seem to notice, but he'd just let slip that like so many others, he still believed in the old ways just as much as the new. Her people were slow to change generations' worth of trust in the ancient spirits, especially when that change came from the outside.

Her heart softened ever so slightly toward her father, who still gripped her arm and glared at her under lowered eyebrows. He was a hard man and had grown even more obstinate since his injury, but what he did, he did for his people. He wanted a good future for her, even if it meant peddling her skills to the son of the King who'd nigh forsaken them.

The old, familiar longing bit into her heart once more. How she yearned to please her father, to gracefully bend to his plans for her. But some unruly seed within her had taken hold from the first, too deep to be uprooted. He wanted her to remain within their fortress, sit quietly in the dim light, and wait for her impending marriage.

But she wanted to run through the forests, to roll in the damp soil and fragrant greenery. And most of all, she wanted to speak to the stones, to draw out their innermost whispers.

"I could make you stop, you know," her father said, but suddenly he sounded defeated. He'd tried ordering her. He'd tried locking her behind the thick stone walls of the fortress. He'd even tried redirecting all the longing within her toward the stone she was to carve for her future husband.

Naught would work, and they both knew it in that moment.

"Come on, then," she said, bending to gather the pebbles of various sizes that had spilled earlier. She dropped each one, more precious to her than gold, into a pouch on her leather belt. Silently, her father led her back toward the fortress.

With one last stolen glance over her shoulder, she made a promise to her beloved stone.

I'll come back, no matter what.

3

Alaric rubbed the scruff on his jawline. His gaze swept once more over the rocky coastline. Though it was coated in a thin blanket of emerald green moss, the land was rugged and treeless.

He burned to land his longship against that narrow coast and explore—climb every jagged, jutting rock, trot along the cliff-like edge overlooking the North Sea, and proclaim the land his.

But nei, he couldn't think of his own simmering desire for adventure now.

The responsibility of his task had pulsed continuously in the back of his mind—through the storms, through the surging seas that had threatened to swallow their little crafts, and through the first thrill of spotting land yesterday.

What had looked like a solid landmass had proven to be a series of chain-like islands. Alaric had been eager to explore them, but as his ships had drawn nigh, the distinctive shapes of Northland sails and shallow-hulled longships had materialized.

Eirik had told him the tales of other Northlanders not simply raiding these lands to the west, but actually settling on them over winter.

Now Alaric knew they weren't just rumors. Other Northmen had reached those islands and had claimed them for themselves. Though Alaric would have paid a dear price to exchange stories with those voyagers, his mission tugged incessantly at him.

Eirik had tasked him with finding a suitable place to make a settlement, which meant that the land had to be good for agriculture. They would need plenty of timber and stone to build dwellings. The last thing Alaric needed was to compete with other Northlanders over what was proving to be a sparse, bare landscape.

"Will we land, brother?"

Madrena's call drifted on the breeze to where he stood at his ship's stern, one hand on the tiller. Her ship trailed his as they made their way south down the rugged coast.

"Nei, not yet," he responded, never taking his eyes from the shoreline.

How different it was from the terrain they'd seen two summers ago. Eirik had managed to convince his uncle, then the Jarl, to form a raiding party to the whispered-about lands to the west. When they'd arrived, they were met with soft, rolling hills, lush grasses, and, further inland, forests as far as the eye could see.

But that was a land called Northumbria, according to Laurel. Alaric and Eirik had decided to aim further north, for Laurel claimed Northumbria was a more populated region. Above it, however, she'd said only a few tribes of half-wild men roamed, a thorn in the Northumbrians' side, but little trouble for a band of Northland warriors two score strong set on claiming land.

Laurel had clearly never laid eyes on these bare northern reaches. Alaric's stomach sank like an anchor. He'd seen his ships through storms and sailed past other Northlanders without issue, but those triumphs would be for naught if he couldn't find arable and forested lands on which to settle.

His hand tightened around the tiller until his knuckles were white. He would not be bested so easily. These rocks would prove impossible for farming, but perhaps if he could go deeper into the land's heart, beyond this cursed shoreline…

He squinted into the sun as his gaze traveled southward down the coast. Lifting a hand to shade his eyes, he focused on a green-brown mass taking shape ahead.

But the mass jutted out into the sea, and water shimmered on both sides of it.

An inlet.

"There!" he called, pointing. "We sail there!"

The crew must have picked up on his sudden burst of energy, for several spoke in excited tones as they adjusted the sail's ropes to capture the wind most advantageously.

As they drew closer to the inlet, Alaric's heart squeezed with hope. Sure enough, the landmass he'd spotted jutted from the mainland in a peninsula, sheltering the bottom side of a fjord-like bay. The oval of sea water narrowed suddenly on its western side, where dense, shadowy green promised a lush woodland.

With a whistle and a gesture, he motioned for both longships to enter the mouth of the inlet. The waters within were calm and deep, and the longships glided soundlessly over the smooth surface.

At another whistle from Alaric, the ships' crews lowered the sails and took up their oars. Now the silence was broken by the oars' rhythmic lapping of the bay's water.

At last they reached the narrowest point of the inlet, where water flowed from a river into the bay. The river was wide and slow-moving, perfect for a settlement.

A quick glance told Alaric that he could have sent the longships up the river's soft bends, for their keels were shallow enough to float in water that was barely knee-deep. But the stretch where the river met the shel-tered bay was too perfect to pass up. Instead, he guided his ship toward the shore.

As the two longships glided onto the bay's sandy shoreline right at the river's tail, Alaric let his eyes drink in the sight before him.

This land was hilly, to be certain, but the jagged ridges of the coastline farther north had smoothed somewhat. Perhaps tucked within these hills were lands flat enough to plow with an ard. Best of all, his initial assessment of the shadowed woods he'd seen from afar had proved good. Just beyond the shoreline, the land was covered in dense forests of oak and pine.

In the shelter of the bay, he wouldn't have to fear

that his ships would be blown away in a storm. And with the river draining into the salty inlet, they'd never lack fresh water.

Though his crew likely wasn't considering the strategic benefits to this location, as he must, they were nevertheless awed into silence. Tearing his gaze away from the green expanse before him, he glanced at Madrena's ship, which had come to rest against the shore alongside his own.

Even his twin sister, who had a knife for a tongue and wits to match, stood in slack-jawed amazement at their surroundings.

"This will do," Alaric said softly under his breath. A sudden and deep swell of pride jolted through him. This land promised a bounty unknown in the Northlands. Here lay his future as leader to these Northland explorers turned settlers.

Alaric launched himself over his ship's gunwale and landed with a splash in the shallow water. He waded toward the shoreline, eager to be the first of the North-landers to touch dry earth. Several more splashes sounded behind him as the others made their way after him.

Just then, a flicker of movement in the trees ahead had Alaric jerking his head up.

The shore rose into a small but densely forested hill. A flash of red stood out amongst all the greens and browns.

An animal? The reddish color blurred as it darted away. What strange beasts might inhabit these woods? Laurel hadn't mentioned any creatures so different from what he'd encountered in the Northlands. And the red blur had moved more like…

The woods were still once more. The splashes of his crew and their excited chatter drowned out any sounds drifting out of the forest.

Unease trickled down Alaric's spine. Were they being watched? Surely if there were other people living in these parts, they wouldn't have had time to form an attack.

Alaric nearly impaled his sister when she placed a hand on his shoulder. He quickly shoved his half-drawn sword back into its leather scabbard before he spooked the others, but Madrena's pale eyes were too sharp.

"What is it?" she said, her posture suddenly matching his. Madrena was one of the most skilled shieldmaidens—nei, *warriors*, male or female—in the crew, and perhaps in all the western Northlands. She'd already reached for the sword belted on her hip, her eyes searching Alaric.

"Naught, I'm sure," he said levelly, trying to soothe his unease. "A trick of the light. Or an animal. This new land simply has me…on edge." He kept his voice low so as not to alarm the rest of his crew.

Just then, Rúnin stepped to Madrena's side. His sister's mate had just as sharp an eye as Madrena. Though Alaric trusted his sister unquestioningly, he was even more confident that Rúnin would warn them if he sensed another presence in these woods. Rúnin's long years as an outlaw had forged him into a man who seemed to instinctively know when others were nigh—his life had depended on it.

"All is well," Alaric said before Rúnin could ask. "I don't want the men panicking."

Rúnin's bright blue eyes narrowed on Alaric slightly, clearly comprehending Alaric's implication. All might not be well, and they should keep a keen eye pointed toward the woods, but 'twould be best not to raise an alarm just yet.

The crew had busied themselves in pulling both longships more fully onto the narrow beach. Though they were all strong Northland men—plus a strong Northland woman, Eyva, who was training to be a shieldmaiden under Madrena's guidance—they struggled with the large ships. Each longship could have held twice as many sailors, but Alaric had wanted a small crew, partly to have enough room for all the equipment they'd needed, and partly to keep Eirik's risk of losing so many able warriors from Dalgaard low.

At last the ships were secured, and the crew eagerly began streaming onto the beach where Alaric, Madrena, and Rúnin stood.

"Let's head up the river and look for a good place to make camp," Alaric said lightly to his men. Even still, the others followed his lead as he withdrew his round, painted shield from the side of one of the longships.

The river cut a wide ribbon through the hills on either side. There was enough of a flat, sandy bank to allow the Northlanders to walk two by two with Alaric in the lead. Madrena and Rúnin walked on silent feet behind him, their postures relaxed but their eyes restlessly scanning their surroundings.

At a bend in the river, a wider, sandy expanse

spread out between the water and the trees. A scattering of rocks and sticks littered the sand, but those would be cleared away easily enough. Alaric trotted ahead of the others to scout the area, his apprehension at last dissipating. This site might as well have been handed to him by the gods, for he couldn't imagine another spot more suited to his purpose.

"'Tis perfect!" he shouted over his shoulder to the others. "We'll gather the tents from the ships and—"

The words died in his mouth as his eyes landed on what he'd thought a moment before were a few scattered rocks and sticks.

His boot crunched down on a skull.

A human skull.

Blackened bones jutted from the sand, which was stained gray long ago by ash.

His abrupt halt must have drawn the attention of the others, for suddenly he was surrounded by Northmen, their weapons unsheathed and their shields held at the ready. Alaric hardly registered their battle-readiness, however. He tore his eyes from the dozens of charred bone fragments and tried to pierce the forest with his gaze.

Leaves and branches rustled, teasing him. The woods were withholding their secrets. Awareness honed his senses, though. His eyes darted with each flicker of movement in the boughs and underbrush.

"Alaric!"

Madrena's voice was taut with unease. His gaze snapped to where she stood frozen at the edge of the forest. Her sword was drawn, but her eyes were focused on a large stone at waist height.

He sprinted to her side, unsheathing his sword as he went. When he skidded to a halt next to her, his eyes locked on the rock she was staring at.

Upon its weathered surface, two Northland runes had been carved. One was the symbol for man, and the other for ash.

'Twas a crudely rendered message, for runes aligned with different sounds and were not representational. But the meaning, simple as it was, came through clearly.

This was a place of death. Death for Northlanders.

Ice stabbed Alaric's belly.

He opened his mouth to give an order to his crew to move back to the ships, but a flicker at the edge of his vision once again had him snapping his head around.

Another flash of red.

This time, Alaric didn't hesitate. He exploded into a sprint toward the figure lurking deeper in the woods.

Noise erupted as Madrena bolted after him, though he didn't bother waiting for her. Alaric distantly heard her calling to Rúnin and the others over the pounding blood in his ears.

The red blur was indeed a human. A fleeing human. Though the figure moved swiftly and with a familiarity for these woods, Alaric was like an angered bear crashing through the forest. Naught would stop him, he vowed, and he hurdled himself through the trees.

He was drawing closer despite the fleeing figure's agility. The figure cut suddenly and sharply to the right, darting back toward the river.

He couldn't have set the trap better himself. He followed, but made a less severe angle. He'd pin the lurking observer between himself and the water. Then he'd have his answers.

Alaric's legs and lungs burned, but he pushed harder. At last, he struck. He darted more fully to the right, knowing there was nowhere for the runner to go.

Just as he reached the tree line where the river's sandy bank opened, he skidded to a halt. He felt his jaw slacken in stunned silence as the red blur at last froze and turned to him.

It was a woman.

A beautiful woman.

A terrified woman.

Her small frame heaved with labored breath. Berry-red lips parted as she gasped for air. Her wide eyes darted desperately, searching for a way to escape, but they found none. At last, those large eyes settled on him, and his sharp inhale had naught to do with the chase he'd just given her.

Deep pools of liquid amber held him, begging silently for release. Her golden eyes were set off all the more dramatically by her auburn-red hair.

This wild forest spirit was the red blur he'd seen earlier. But she wasn't a spirit. Nei, she was a flesh-and-blood woman.

Slowly, Alaric lowered his sword and shield. A quick glance at her lithe form and empty hands told him she bore no weapons. At his movement, slow though it was, she started and tried to take another step back. But her heels were flush against the lapping river and she was forced to remain in place.

His gaze once again slid over her, and despite himself, Alaric's blood stirred with lust.

Her ragged breathing caused her breasts to press against the finely made woolen tunic she wore. The garment was elaborately adorned with delicate needle-work along the collar, wrists, and hem, which fell to her booted ankles.

Her slim waist was belted with a braided leather band that had a pouch dangling from it. With her legs braced apart in preparation to flee, he could make out the outline of her gently curved hips and slim but shapely legs. Her delicate yet womanly form caused something primal to twist deep in Alaric's belly.

Suddenly, shouts sounded in the forest behind him. His crew was closing in on them. A look of utter horror stole over the young woman's face, and all at once he was drowning again in her amber eyes as they pleaded with him wordlessly.

"Go," he said, choosing the Northumbrian tongue. He had no idea if this girl would understand, but based on the look of terror she'd given him, she certainly wouldn't be familiar with the Northland tongue.

Impossibly, her eyes widened even more as disbelief and comprehension warred over her soft features. So she *did* understand him.

Alaric glanced over his shoulder to gauge how far away his crew was. When he turned back, the girl had already darted away. He watched as she dashed along the sandy shoreline, then slipped into the trees.

Why in Hel's realm had he let her go? He needed answers—about the charred bones, about her presence in these woods, and if there were others.

But something about the desperate fear in those enthralling amber eyes had been his undoing. She might have died of fright if she'd seen forty armed Northmen explode from the forest behind him. Even still, he cursed himself for losing an opportunity to question her.

"What in Odin's name—" Madrena crashed through the underbrush, sword raised and breathing heavily. When her eyes landed on Alaric, unharmed and with his blade and shield lowered, she stilled.

"'Twas a woman," Alaric said, loud enough for the others to hear as they caught up with Madrena.

"And she got away?" Madrena snapped, her eyes flaring in outrage.

"I let her go."

"Alaric, why in—"

He held up a hand to silence his sister. His gaze roamed once more to where the auburn-haired beauty had stood a moment before. Her small boot prints trailed through the sandy riverbank, then cut into the shadowed forest.

Alaric gritted his teeth. He had a responsibility to Eirik, his crew, and all those counting on him back in Dalgaard.

"We'll follow her. If there are others who live in these woods…well, we'd better introduce ourselves."

4

Elisead dared to risk another glance over her shoulder. Even though there were no sounds of pursuit, she would never trust a band of wild Northmen.

Especially not their golden leader.

Her already hammering heart squeezed painfully. She stumbled to a halt, her legs no longer able to keep up her frantic flight.

Elisead leaned against a rowan tree as she struggled to catch her breath. By all the gods, old and new, what had just happened?

She'd slipped from her father's fortress in the wee hours of the morning. As she had done countless times in the last few years, she'd let herself wander the dense woods unperturbed. How peaceful they'd been that morning. The birds seemed to be relishing the sunshine and fresh air. The leaves and boughs overhead had rustled softly in the gentle breeze blowing in from the North Sea.

Elisead had inhaled a deep breath of the salty air and had decided to make her way toward the bay where the river met the sea. When she'd crested a rise to get a better view, however, it was as if she'd stepped into a waking nightmare.

Two rectangular red and white sails had torn the perfect blue sky. Those long, dragon-prowed ships sliced through the water like knives. And then a horde of Northmen had spilled forth into the water and onto the beach.

She'd been frozen in place, the air turning to ice in her lungs. But then one of the Northmen, the first to jump into the water, had looked upward and pinned her with his eyes. Even from a distance Elisead could see that they were vibrant green. His golden hair had ruffled past his shoulders, his square jaw dusted with dark gold stubble.

He was huge—tall and broad with muscle. And he moved like death itself.

After what felt like a sickening eternity, she'd sucked in a breath and bolted. The fastest way to get back to the fortress was to follow the river. But that had meant traveling past the site that still haunted her sleep.

She'd vowed never to return to that horrible spot where the Northmen's bones still lay. Even though she knew her mind was playing tricks on her, she'd imagined the stench of burning flesh clinging to her as she'd skirted that terrible place.

But the Northmen came again.

They moved like wolves along the river, a deadly pack bristling with swords and shields. And the golden

Northman, the one with the sparkling green eyes, had seen her once more.

As he'd hunted her through the forest, she considered simply laying down and letting him slash her open with the shining sword he wielded. What chance did she truly have in outrunning a Northman, hardened by battle and honed for killing?

But that old spark inside wouldn't let her give up. If he was going to slaughter her, he'd have to catch her first.

And he had.

But then he'd let her go.

And he'd spoken in a thickly accented Northumbrian tongue. None of it made any sense. Northmen were unpredictable in how they doled out their terror and death. Her people had learned that last time, which was why she had to send up an alarm.

Elisead pushed herself away from the rowan tree she'd been leaning on and forced her legs back into a sprint. As she reached the outskirts of the village, she gasped for a deep breath.

"Northmen!" she shouted. "To the fortress!"

Even though her lungs burned, her cry was enough. Those moving calmly about the village immediately stopped what they were doing. Some dove inside their thatched huts to gather their loved ones, while others simply bolted toward the fortress.

Elisead tore through the village and propelled herself up the sloping hillside upon which her father's fortress sat. The high stone walls towered overhead as she ran alongside the other villagers.

One of the guards standing watch on the wall must have seen the frantic stream of villagers making their way toward the fortress, for Elisead could hear the creak of the wooden gate being opened from the inside and the groan of the iron grille as it was ratcheted up.

Nay, it will not be like last time.

Fear threatened to steal what little breath she had, but she forced herself onward. She had given the warning, which was far more than they'd had seven years ago. All would be safe—at least she prayed so.

At last she crested the hill. Only the flattened expanse of soft grass at the top of the hill stood between her and the fort. She pushed herself harder until finally she slipped under the iron grille and between the gates along with the others.

She was safe—for now. She slowed her burning legs and gasped for breath. But she only allowed herself a few pants as the grille was lowered and the gates closed tight behind her. She had to warn her father.

Elisead made her way through the throngs of panicked villagers now filling the open yard between the high stone walls and the great hall. Her father must have heard the commotion, for just then he emerged from the great hall, his mouth turned down behind his red-gray beard.

"Father!" Elisead plowed through the frightened villagers.

"What has happened?" Maelcon's brows lowered as his gaze locked on her. She must look a fright. She'd fled so swiftly and recklessly from the Northmen that she'd torn her tunic in several places. Her hair was a tangled mess atop her head, and she had no doubt there were leaves and twigs knotted in it.

"Northmen," Elisead breathed. Those around them who'd overheard gasped and cried out in fear.

Her father's eyes rounded. "Into the great hall." He grabbed Elisead's elbow and dragged her into the dim wooden structure, villagers streaming in behind her.

"Triple the guard on the wall," Maelcon said over his shoulder as he strode swiftly across the open hall and toward the small chamber he used to hold meetings in private. Drostan, her father's best warrior, nodded at his chieftain's order and departed for the wall.

"We are safe here," Maelcon said loudly, turning to the terrified villagers who'd followed them inside. "Our walls are impenetrable and our warriors strong. Rest easy while I learn more from my daughter."

With that, he continued on to the corridor at the back of the hall where the smaller chamber sat, all the while gripping Elisead's elbow.

"Now, tell me what you saw," Maelcon snapped as he closed the heavy wooden door behind them.

"Northmen," Elisead panted again. "Two ships. They sailed into the bay, then began making their way upriver on foot."

Maelcon cursed and brought a fist to his mouth. "How many?"

"Perhaps two score."

Elisead squeezed her eyes shut under her father's string of curses. When Northmen had landed on their shores seven years ago, there had been half that many.

And even though they had managed to beat them back, it had come at a terrible cost.

Maelcon began pacing before her, his limp a subtle reminder of that nightmare seven years ago.

At last her father's cursing and pacing halted. Elisead looked up to find him staring hard at her.

"What were you doing out there, Elisead?" he snapped.

"I…"

She was saved from fumbling for an answer by a swift rap at the door. Drostan let himself in without waiting for a reply. The warrior and her father frequently used this room, furnished only with a few chairs and a table, to discuss the village's safety.

"The wall has been fortified, Chief," Drostan said. The man's deep brown eyes quickly scanned Elisead. "What do we face?"

"My daughter has seen forty Northmen approaching from the bay," Maelcon said, seeming to gather his wits in the presence of his right-hand man.

Drostan's fists reflexively clenched at his sides. "We must strike swiftly, Chief. Else—"

Elisead swallowed hard. Seven years ago, she'd been little more than a girl, but she remembered vividly how the golden giants from the north had set upon them like wolves on a flock of lambs.

Before that terrible time, she'd heard whispers of the scourge from the north, but their little village was isolated here in the heart of Pictland. None had truly believed the Northland destroyers would reach them. But when they had, she'd seen Hell with her own eyes.

"We are safe within the walls," Maelcon said firmly.

"But if we were to attack, and attack now, before they've gotten their bearings—"

"They speak the Northumbrian tongue," Elisead blurted out.

Both Maelcon and Drostan rounded on her, Drostan's eyebrows shooting up and her father's mouth falling open.

"What say you?" Maelcon asked.

"They spoke—or one of them did. They may not be strangers to this land. They may have planned to land here, to strike the fortress."

The thought sent a shiver of fear down her spine, but it was information her father and his most trusted warrior needed to have. Even in these remote parts, almost everyone could speak both the Pictish tongue and the Northumbrian one. They'd been at war with their neighbors to the south too long not to have learned their language.

"*You were close enough to hear them speak?*" Her father closed the distance between them and was suddenly shaking her hard. "Foolish girl!" he roared. "What have you done?"

Drostan stepped to Maelcon's side and laid a firm hand on his shoulder. "Now isn't the time," he said simply.

Drostan had long known of Elisead's propensity to slip from the village and wander the woods. She knew that if her father had ordered him to, Drostan would have followed her at all times, even though such a task would have been an insult for the clan's greatest warrior.

Even still, Drostan knew well the private struggle for freedom between the chieftain and his daughter.

Maelcon's grip on Elisead's arms eased. "Tell me the whole of it. What did you see and hear, girl?"

Before she could speak, a second knock sounded at the door. Another of her father's warriors stuck his head inside.

"Forgive the intrusion, Chief, but one of the lookouts has spotted a band of warriors approaching —Northmen."

Her father cursed again. Drostan's jaw clenched.

Elisead felt like she was going to be sick. At least the villagers had made it behind the walls. Even still, the nightmare from seven years ago was threatening to start all over again.

Maelcon strode out of the chamber, leaving Drostan and Elisead to trail after him. He made his way through the great hall, not bothering to address the villagers gathered there. Elisead broke into a run to reach his side as he crossed out of the great hall and into the yard.

"They saw the site of the pyre for their people," she said hurriedly. "Perhaps they don't mean to stay, now that they know we've bested their kind before."

Her father didn't acknowledge that he'd heard her as he began ascending the crude stairs made of stacked stones along the inside of the wall. No one knew who had originally built this stronghold, for it had been passed down through generations of Pictish chieftains. Now it was all that stood between them and the approaching Northmen.

Elisead followed after her father, knowing that the

extra stones mortared to the top of the wall would provide her cover. Drostan followed as well, though he gave Elisead a disapproving look. She shouldn't have been up there with them, but her father was too distracted to send her back to the relative safety of the great hall.

When she peeked over the lip of stone behind which she crouched, her heart flew to her throat. A horde of Northmen had broken the tree line and were weaving through the still and empty huts at the base of the hill.

Strange, Elisead thought distantly. When the Northmen had come before, they'd attacked the village mercilessly until naught had been left of it but burning rubble and broken bodies. Those behind the walls had been forced to watch helplessly until at last the Northmen had run out of ways to desecrate her people's homes.

But these Northlanders didn't seem to have any interest in the empty huts. Perhaps it was because there was no one down there upon whom to sate their blood lust.

Just then, she caught sight of the leader, the golden Northman who'd held her with his emerald gaze and then inexplicably let her go.

Her breath caught in her lungs. He moved with deadly grace, every inch of him hard and honed for battle. He walked at the front of the group, sword drawn and shield at the ready, his eyes trained on the fortress.

She ducked her head back behind the stones, letting out a shaky exhale. Something about his elegant lethality shook her to the core.

Her father and Drostan stood, their heads and shoulders exposed as they took in the sight before them.

"Hail, fortress!"

Was that the leader, the golden-haired giant? The voice was the same deep timbre and heavily accented Northumbrian as the one word he'd spoken to her.

Both Drostan and Maelcon seemed taken aback at first. But her father recovered quickly from the sound of the Northumbrian tongue in a Northman's mouth. From where she crouched, she looked up at his face, which was set hard and unyielding like the chieftain he was.

"Hail...warriors," Maelcon called back in Northumbrian. "I am Maelcon mac Lorcan, Chief of this village and this land."

"I am Alaric Hamarsson," came the voice again. "Of the Northland village of Dalgaard."

That confirmed it—no matter that he spoke the Northumbrian tongue, he was not of this land.

"How dare you trample across my land and threaten my people thus, Alaric Hamarsson?" Maelcon bit out.

A deep laugh drifted over the wall, burning Elisead's ears.

"I have yet to threaten anyone, Maelcon mac Lorcan," he called. "I had hoped only to talk."

Drostan snatched Maelcon's elbow and spoke lowly in his ear. "Why haven't we attacked yet, Chief? The longer these Northman stand talking, the more time they have to enact whatever scheme they've come up with."

"Perhaps a few of my people can enter your fine

fortress and discuss the future," the Northman's voice said levelly.

"'Tis a trap!" Drostan hissed. "We must strike now before they do."

Her father considered for a tense moment as Alaric waited for a response. "The archers," Maelcon said at last under his breath.

Dread knotted Elisead's stomach. A battle was about to erupt nigh at her feet, and there was no telling who would survive.

5

Drostan turned and gave a low whistle. Several warriors who had gathered in the yard below them hustled to mount the stairs. They nocked arrows and partially drew back their bowstrings as they moved into position along the wall, crouched low like Elisead.

Drostan suddenly threw a fist into the air. As one, the archers straightened.

"Shield wall!" someone shouted from below, a mere breath before the air was filled with the sound of thwacking bowstrings and whirring arrows.

Elisead bit her knuckle on a scream as the sickening thunks of the arrows hitting solid matter rang in her ears. But distantly she registered that there were no howls of pain from the Northmen below and the arrow strikes made a hollow, reverberating sound.

"Again!" her father shouted, his voice tight with frustration. The archers unleashed another hail of arrows, but again there were no screams of agony.

Once the archers had spent their second round of arrows, an eerie silence hung in the air. Elisead glanced up at her father, who was frowning as he looked down upon the Northmen at the base of the wall.

Another low chuckle drifted up from below. The fine hairs on Elisead's arms stirred as the dark sound seemed to lance right through her. She gripped the top of the wall's lip and risked raising her head above it.

In the grassy expanse between the wall's base and the downward slope of the hill upon which the fortress sat, the Northmen had transformed into a tight ball of shields. They looked like some primeval creature, their painted, round shields stacked together like scales. The shields bristled with dozens of arrows, but there were no fallen bodies on the ground.

"Thank you for providing us with such a fine collection of arrows," that same silky, deep voice said. "You've saved us the trouble of having to whittle and fletch our own."

Drostan's hands turned into fists where they rested on the top of the wall's lip. He ground them into the rough stone until blood oozed from his knuckles. Maelcon cursed under his breath, but Elisead was familiar enough with his oaths that she knew this one wasn't borne of pure anger. Nay, it was spiked with fear.

"Now, to return to the subject of discussing our future." A slit appeared in the wall of shields. The face of the golden leader appeared. A small smile played around his mouth, but his eyes were hard.

"We could open the gates and attack them straight

35

on," Drostan said, barely loud enough for Elisead to catch his words. "Face them sword to sword in combat."

"They outnumber us," Maelcon hissed. "And you know better than anyone what happened last time, even when we matched them in number."

"You would genuinely consider letting them within the walls?"

At Drostan's urgent whisper, Elisead shuddered with memory. She'd already seen what Northmen were capable of when they'd set upon the half-full village seven years ago. What would these ones do if given access to the fortress, which was filled with innocent villagers?

Elisead ducked behind the wall once more, her gaze now searching the yard below. Her eyes fell on Feitr, who lurked in the shadow of the great hall. His white-blond hair was braided back from his face in the Northland style, as he'd worn it every day in his captivity since he was taken as a slave seven years ago.

The flood of memory brought on by the sight of Feitr stung Elisead's eyes. For the second time that day, she struggled against the stench of burning flesh that rose unbidden to her nose.

It had been considered a mercy for Maelcon to take Feitr, then just a lad barely older than Elisead, as a slave instead of simply killing him. Slavery was a common enough fate for an enemy's survivors. But Feitr's icy eyes and pale, braided hair was a constant reminder of the Northland devils—his presence never failed to send chills of unease through Elisead.

Elisead's attention snapped from Feitr to Drostan and her father.

"You cannot think to simply attack, Drostan."

The hardened warrior clenched his teeth as her father's words, no doubt seeing insult in them. Though Drostan was indeed mighty and skilled, Elisead's thoughts ran with her father's. Would it not be suicide to open the gates and send their men, outnumbered as they were, into battle with these invaders?

"There are two ways this can go," the male voice from below cut in. "If we had wished to take your fortress, we would have done so already."

'Twas a bold boast, and from their expressions, both Maelcon and Drostan found it farfetched.

"Is that so?" her father shouted in response.

"Ja, that is so." Now Elisead was certain the man was losing his patience. "Shall I tell you how?"

Without waiting for a response, the golden leader went on. "We'd have our choice, of course. Most obviously, we could simply wait you out, though I like that option least of all because I notice the river runs behind this hillside. If you are smart, and I am granting that you are, you would have dug a well within your walls so that you'd at least have fresh water for however long a siege lasted."

Drostan snorted, his eyes narrowed on the speaker below, but Maelcon remained unmoved.

"I hate waiting, so another option would be to advance behind our shields even if you chose to keep firing upon us. There are enough of us to provide cover from your arrow fire while the others lift that grille you have lowered in front of your gate."

Could they truly do that? From her father's tightening mouth, she had to assume so. The grille was solid iron, and even with the pulley system they had, it took several of her father's men to ratchet it up. But these Northmen were terrifyingly large and no doubt strong.

"The route I am favoring at the moment, however, would be to have some of us use our shields to launch the others up to the top of the wall," the one called Alaric said casually. "It is really quite easy. We've done it before, in fact, in the Northlands. You might imagine that you'd be able to pick us off one at a time as we arrived on the wall, but what if ten of us were launched at once? Or fifteen? I count ten archers on the wall currently, and perhaps you have more warriors behind them, but judging by the size of your village, I doubt you have more than a dozen or so families here, which means only a score or so of warriors in addition to your archers."

A wave of fear and helplessness washed over Elisead. How could they possibly hope to survive? These Northmen were not only the most dangerous warriors known in the world, but they were clever, too? How could he have guessed with such accuracy just how strong their force was?

A long silence stretched as her father stood motionless, looking down on his attackers.

"You said you wish only to talk. What is it you want to discuss?"

"The future—yours and ours. I have a feeling they are intertwined."

"You hope to steal our future, is that what you mean?" Maelcon bit out.

What could these Northmen invaders want if not to raid, loot, rape, and murder until there was naught left of Elisead's home and people?

"Nei, that is not why we are here. As I said, we can discuss this further within the walls."

"I beg of you, Chief, do not trust these Northmen," Drostan whispered, but Maelcon had already resigned himself to his choice, judging by his slow exhale.

"Very well," Maelcon said, suddenly sounding weary. "But only you will be allowed in."

The silence that followed was only broken by the soft whispers of the Northmen below. Now they spoke a rolling, guttural language that must be their own. The whispers rose, and discord filled several voices, but Elisead quickly picked out the deep, smooth voice of the leader, Alaric. He snapped something, which seemed to settle the conversation, and all fell quiet again.

"Two others will accompany me," the golden leader said. His demand brokered no negotiation. "The others will move back down the hill while you admit us. If we do not return to them by the time the sun approaches the horizon, they will attack."

"You'll leave your weapons and shields behind," Maelcon responded.

"Very well."

Truly, these Northmen had no fear. They would walk unarmed into the fort, surrounded by warriors ready to kill them? They must have trusted that the rest of their small army would finish the job if harm befell them. They clearly weren't afraid of death. That thought sent another shiver down Elisead's spine

The air filled with clanging, and she dared to peek over the wall once more. Three enormous warriors were separating themselves from the wall of shields. The golden leader handed his shield and sword to one of his men and even unstrapped a long dagger from his boot. A dark-haired giant next to him was doing the same.

As Elisead's eyes shifted to the third warrior, she inhaled sharply.

A woman.

With her pale blonde hair braided away from her face and flowing down her back, she looked like a goddess from the old ways. But she bristled with weapons of every variety and size. In fact, it took her the longest to disarm herself.

At last, the three strode forward and away from the safety of their shields and companions. With a gesture from the leader, the others began to retreat down the hill, but they still faced the wall in case the three warriors were set upon.

"Get into the great hall," her father suddenly snapped at her.

Without hesitation, she bolted for the stairs and hurried toward the hall's double doors. Behind her, she heard the groan of the iron grille once more, but this time it was being ratcheted up to allow the Northlanders entrance.

She dared one look behind her as she slipped into the great hall.

As the wooden gates widened, the golden-headed Northman strode boldly through, flanked on either side by the dark-haired man and the woman warrior.

Something tightened in her belly. Had she imagined it, or had his green eyes landed on her just as the great hall's doors closed behind her?

6

Alaric set his face in the easy almost-smile he so often wore. He forced his body to remain loose and relaxed as he crossed through the fortress's wooden gates, but his insides clenched as he took in the greeting they received.

The wall was lined with archers, all of whom had arrows pointed at them as they strode into the fortress's yard. Almost as soon as they had crossed under the iron grille meant to protect the wooden gates, it was let down with a ground-shaking thud. Several more warriors, swords and spears aimed at them, stood waiting.

Before him sat a wooden structure not unlike a Northland longhouse. The long, high-ceilinged building had a wooden roof, though, rather than thatching.

As his eyes took in this building in the middle of the fortress, he saw that same telltale flash of red. The woman from the woods was slipping inside.

Alaric's stomach unknotted ever so slightly. She'd

made it back safely. For some reason that knowledge was a relief.

He didn't have time to consider the woman's fate, however, for just then Maelcon mac Lorcan spoke from behind them.

"We could simply kill you now. At least then your force would be down three warriors."

Alaric turned and shrugged with practiced ease, though he didn't relish the thought of dying without a weapon in hand.

"You could. But then you'd never know why we are here and what we want from you."

He'd already made his strength clear by detailing the several ways he could lay waste to this stronghold. Now he'd try to appeal to this man's curiosity, for clearly he didn't know what to make of Alaric and the other Northlanders.

The chieftain grunted, but the man at his side, clearly a warrior, crossed his arms over his chest and assessed the three of them. Alaric felt Madrena stiffen at his side, but she knew better than to make a move in that moment.

"You wished to talk, so let us talk," Maelcon said at last.

"It is customary where we are from to welcome visitors with food, drink, and a comfortable seat," Alaric said levelly.

He thought the tall, dark-haired man at the chieftain's side might lose his eyes, for they bulged in indignation at Alaric's bold words.

"You are not our guests," the chieftain said tightly.

"You came uninvited and threaten us with your very presence."

"As I said before," Alaric responded with studied calmness. "I have not threatened you, nor will I—unless you choose to make things difficult."

The chieftain seemed to finally run out of patience for their cautious meeting. "Are you not Northmen?" he barked. "And do not Northmen come to our lands to raid and slaughter?"

The chieftain's warriors tensed at their leader's flaring temper, and also no doubt at the reminder of what Northlanders did best. By Odin, Alaric had an uphill battle in front of him to convince these people to let him settle here. But he had to try. The heft of responsibility sat squarely on his shoulders.

"As I said, I am Alaric. This is my second in command, Madrena. She also happens to be my twin sister."

The introduction seemed to catch everyone off-guard enough to ease the tension for a moment, so Alaric went on.

"And this is Rúnin, Madrena's mate and a trusted warrior under my command. We have been sailing for more than a sennight, so we ask forgiveness for not being as clean as we'd prefer on entering your home."

Several jaws slackened at that.

"We appreciate any hospitality you are willing to extend, for I am sure we have much to discuss. Though if you would prefer to stand here all day, very well."

Alaric squinted up into the midmorning sun as if calculating how long they'd be standing under it. He'd learned long ago that catching people unawares with humor or politeness often worked just as well as a show of strength.

And this latest attempt proved him right once again. The chieftain grunted for a second time, but at last he gestured toward the building.

Though he hated to turn his back on all those archers, let alone Maelcon and the warrior standing at his side, Alaric forced his feet to pivot and made his way toward the long wooden structure. He opened one of the large doors and motioned for Maelcon to lead the way, giving him the honor of crossing the threshold first.

In the structure's dim interior, Alaric was met with the terrified stares of several dozen villagers. They shied away from him, Madrena, and Rúnin like frightened sheep stuck in a pen. Maelcon didn't seem concerned, though, so Alaric strode on behind him.

The chieftain guided them to a large wooden table surrounded by chairs that sat atop an elevated platform. Again, Alaric was struck by how this village, its people, and its longhouse were not so different from Dalgaard. He'd have to stress that point when trying to explain his plan to Maelcon.

They all sat, and Maelcon gave an order to one of the villagers in a strange tongue. So, Northumbrian wasn't the only language these people used. Alaric's gaze trailed after the man Maelcon had spoken to, tensing for some sort of trap, but then the man returned with several cups of ale.

As they settled themselves at the table and took the ale from the villager, Maelcon raised his cup and ceremonially poured some of the contents into Alaric's. Alaric did the same, showing all who watched that he and their chief drank the same liquid—no poison would be laced there.

"You speak the Northumbrian tongue well," Maelcon said, raising the cup to his bearded face and taking a long sip.

"Thank you. I was taught by a Northumbrian woman who was captured by my Jarl two summers ago."

That seemed to send tension back into the already wary chief, so Alaric went on. "But I take it we are not in Northumbria, for you have your own language as well."

"Nay, you are not in Northumbria."

"Then what do you call this land?"

"You are in the heart of Pictland," Maelcon said, watching as Alaric took a long drink from his cup.

"And what do you call yourselves?"

Maelcon shifted his gaze to the villagers gathered in the hall, and Alaric's eyes followed. They looked on, some still unabashedly terrified, while others, like the warriors who'd filtered in quietly, bore expressions filled with suspicion or hostility.

"Outsiders call us the Picts—the Painted Ones, for it is our way to paint ourselves before going into battle."

Alaric scanned the warriors once more. They must not have had time to prepare for the Northlanders' arrival, for none were painted. "And what do you call yourselves?"

"We are the People of the Ancestors, descendants of the Ancient Ones—but to you we are Picts."

Alaric rubbed the sennight's worth of stubble on his jawline. Maelcon certainly wasn't going to make this easy. He'd best lay forth his purpose before he lost this sliver of opportunity.

"Let me speak plainly," he said. "As I have assured you, we are not here to raid or raze your lands and people. We are here to settle, to make this our new home. Though I had initially sought an uninhabited area for my people, I am coming to consider the benefits of joining a village of locals—Picts, you say—and combining our peoples."

Alaric was rewarded for his declaration with an audible gasp from those gathered, and the swinging jaw of Maelcon mac Lorcan.

The chieftain sputtered for words for several long moments. At last he managed to regain his wits—mostly. "You...you are settling here?"

"Ja. I was sent by my Jarl to find a suitable plot of land on which to build a settlement. Others will likely be joining us next summer, and perhaps more after that. Those who have arrived with me will build huts, work the land, and raise animals."

"And...and you want to...*combine* our peoples?" The chieftain was beginning to redden behind his rust-and-gray beard.

"This is a fine fortress you have here. It would take us years of hard work—work better put toward farming and defending against outsiders—to build one for ourselves," Alaric said calmly.

Madrena was growing impatient by his side. She tapped her foot and rolled her eyes in annoyance as Maelcon struggled and sputtered over what Alaric was saying. Her preferred approach was to demand what she wanted—usually at sword-point. But Alaric wouldn't simply threaten these people into becoming his allies. Nei, that would never work. He had to remain composed as he and Maelcon worked through this plan —'twas what a true leader would do.

"You know this land and how to work it," Alaric went on. "You also know the dangers of this place. You know whom to trust among your neighbors—and whom not to."

"And you simply want me to surrender my fortress, my village, my farmlands, and my knowledge to you?" Maelcon's knuckles were growing white where he gripped his wooden ale cup.

"Nei, not surrender them. I wish for you to…see the benefit in aligning yourself with my people," Alaric said carefully.

"And what benefit is there to me?" the chieftain bit out.

"Think on it. Have you had problems with raids in the past?" Alaric's mind instantly skittered to the pile of burnt bones and the crudely rendered warning etching in runes—death to Northmen.

He gritted his teeth against the urge to demand an explanation from Maelcon. Now wasn't the time. His goal was to open negotiations, not remind everyone present of their divisions.

Maelcon set his cup down and brushed his beard

absently. "I see your line of thinking," he said at last, his voice grudging. "So you offer your protection for the privilege of our lands and fortress?"

"Now you are understanding," Alaric said, flashing an easy smile.

"And how do I know that you will not simply destroy us if I give you the chance?" Maelcon said, his temper flashing to life once more. "Or that you will not renege on your agreement? Or that you are lying as you speak?"

Alaric kept the smile on his lips, but turned it wolfish. By Thor, he was walking a knife's edge. If he came out all threats and bluster, he'd call forth Maelcon's instant defensiveness—and risk an all-out war with the people he was trying to align himself with. But if he approached the wary chief with charm and promises of mutual benefit, Maelcon might not realize that he had no choice in the matter. Alaric had to flex his might just enough so that Maelcon knew how things would be, but not so fiercely as to scare the chieftain away.

"Let me make a suggestion," Alaric said, leaning back in his chair disarmingly. "These negotiations have opened promisingly. No blood was spilled. No insults given. I think we are beginning to understand each other."

Slowly, reluctantly, Maelcon nodded.

"Then I propose we continue these negotiations in the coming sennights—and fortnights, if necessary."

At another wary bob of the head from Maelcon, Alaric went on.

"In my land, it is customary to exchange hostages

during an extended negotiation to ensure…mutual cooperation."

Maelcon tensed slightly but spoke, albeit cautiously. "It is the same in these lands. Though normally the hostage must be someone of great import."

"I offer myself."

The tall, dark-haired warrior who'd been at Maelcon's side earlier stepped forward from the crowd of villagers and warriors below the dais. In one easy leap, he hoisted himself onto the dais, which made him tower over Alaric, sitting as he was.

"I am Drostan, Chief Maelcon's best warrior and trusted advisor. I will be your hostage."

Alaric considered the man for a long moment, then shifted his gaze back to Maelcon. The chieftain's bushy gray eyebrows were drawn down over bright amber eyes. Eyes so much like…

A sweep of red hair caught the corner of Alaric's vision. He turned to spy tucked amongst the other villagers the flame-haired woman whom he'd cornered by the river. Her liquid amber eyes were riveted on him, wide though less frightened than before.

He glanced back at Maelcon, and something clicked into place in the recesses of his mind.

He pointed at the girl, and skittish villagers fell away until only air remained between the end of his finger and the auburn-headed forest spirit.

"Nei. I want *her*."

7

The great hall felt like it was spinning. Only the golden warrior's green eyes pinned her in place.

Suddenly Elisead couldn't breathe. Her chest felt like it was being squeezed of every wisp of air, and still his gaze held her.

She heard her father shout something in the distance, but she couldn't understand the words. It was some sort of denial. He would never turn over his daughter to a band of savage Northmen. As her father continued to fume and reject Alaric's demand, the Northman's eyes felt as though they were eating away at her, gnawing right down to her bones.

At last he freed her from her captivity and turned to her father.

"You said yourself that the hostage must be of some importance. Who better than the chieftain's daughter?"

Her father sputtered. "She is engaged to another— the son of the King of Picts himself. She is innocent.

There is no way, by God, that I would send her into a camp full of Northmen!"

Alaric's eyes darted back to her, and once again she couldn't breathe. His brows drew together as if she suddenly displeased him—or the news of her engagement displeased him.

A laden silence stretched as the golden warrior continued to assess her.

"And what if I could promise that she will remain untouched, as pure and innocent for her intended as she is now?" Alaric said, his gaze traveling over her just as it had when he'd trapped her between himself and the river.

"How could you promise such a thing?" Maelcon snapped.

Alaric's relaxed air suddenly vanished, and he sat forward so swiftly in his chair that Drostan, who stood next to Maelcon, jumped and reached for his sword.

"A man's honor is the only thing he truly has," Alaric said icily. "It is the only thing that matters in the eyes of the gods, and the only thing he can control. Do not call mine into question."

The woman who sat at his side gripped his arm, urging him back into the chair. They exchanged a look that seemed to bear much silent communication. The act was not lost on her father. Suddenly his amber eyes were sharp on the two Northlanders.

"And who could you possibly offer in exchange as a hostage? Who could rival the importance of a chieftain's daughter?"

Alaric seemed to consider for a moment, but when

he spoke, his air of coolness had returned. "I offer my twin sister, who is also my second in command. That should suffice."

Now it was the Northlanders' turn to erupt in refusals, or what Elisead took for refusals, for the woman and the dark-headed man spoke rapidly in their own tongue. To her surprise, it was the dark warrior on Alaric's other side who seemed most agitated at the suggestion.

At last Alaric put a stop to the debate with a hand raised for silence. The woman, his sister, gave a curt nod despite the black looks the other warrior was giving her.

"Very well," Alaric said to Maelcon. "Your daughter in exchange for my sister. Both are to remain completely unharmed—in any way. Their safety is what binds us together as we move forward in these negotiations."

Elisead shook her head slowly. "Nay, Father," she breathed, but he was already grudgingly extending his arm toward Alaric. As they clasped forearms, Elisead had to swallow hard not to choke on the bile rising in her throat.

She would be the golden Northman's captive.

She would be alone in a violent, nightmarish camp surrounded by savages.

It was all too much. The room once again spun wildly. The ground swayed beneath her feet, and then suddenly it was rapidly approaching.

She slammed into something hard, but the ground was still a hand-span away. Through fuzzy eyes, she looked up to find Alaric looming over her. The hardness encasing her was his body. His arms bound her like iron bands to the rock wall of his chest.

He'd caught her just before she'd slammed to the floor in a faint. But how had he moved so quickly from the dais? And how were his eyes so vividly green?

She shook her head, trying to clear it of her addled thoughts. Alaric lifted her with ease and propped her upright, his hands lingering on her shoulders to steady her. Unbidden, her own hands rose between them and gripped his linen tunic for balance. The hard expanse of his chest was warm beneath her curling fingers.

Then her father and Drostan were by her side, and Alaric's hands dropped away instantly.

Maelcon shot a dark look between the two of them.

"Prepare yourself, daughter," he said at last. "For you are to go at once."

8

Alaric waited in front of the now-open wooden gates. Madrena and Rúnin stood off to the side, talking quietly. His hostage had yet to emerge from what he'd learned the Picts called a great hall.

Apparently, much like a longhouse, there were private chambers built off a corridor along the back for the chieftain and his family. The chieftain's daughter, now Alaric's hostage, was there now, readying herself to depart.

He sent up another round of thanks to Odin, Thor, Freyja, and all the other gods that the girl had proven to be the chieftain's daughter. It had been a risk to insist that she be his hostage, an impetuous move that could have sent his whole mission crumbling if it had failed.

The needlework he'd noticed earlier on her long tunic set her apart from the other Picts he'd seen gathered in the great hall. She was different—he'd sensed it from the first.

But it was more than her finely made clothes that had marked her as the chieftain's daughter. There was a likeness in the golden-amber eyes of both father and daughter. Some shared intelligence and nobility lingered there. Some proud spirit flickered in their depths.

Taking her as his hostage meant that he'd have leverage over Maelcon—but it had also meant that he had to risk his sister. He'd catch Hel's wrath from Rúnin for such a move, but it was the only way to show Maelcon that he was serious about negotiating for the Northlanders' settlement.

Just then, the doors on the stables built against the wall to the left of the great hall slid open and a stable lad emerged pulling a donkey. The donkey was harnessed to a small wooden cart, which the animal drew behind him.

Before Alaric could ask the stable lad a question, the great hall's doors opened and the girl emerged. She was dressed for winter, though it was a balmy summer afternoon. Over her tunic now draped a thick wool cloak, fastened at the neck with a pin.

Behind her, a few young men filed out carrying a chest of her personal effects. As the lads loaded the chest in the front of the cart, several others emerged from the great hall struggling under the weight of an enormous stone slab. They grunted and groaned as they shuffled toward the cart. When they slid the stone onto the wooden planks, the whole cart sagged low.

"What in..."

"My daughter is a skilled stone carver," Maelcon said as he emerged from the great hall. "She is making a fine carving for her betrothed as her bride gift. I do not wish for her to fall behind on her work while our… discussions continue. She will be married at the end of the summer, which is barely two moons away."

The words were spoken coolly, as a pointed reminder to Alaric of her betrothal—and his promise to leave her untouched. He gritted his teeth against a sudden frustration that sprang into his body.

The chieftain's daughter climbed into the cart and sat upon her chest of belongings. Madrena and Rúnin seemed to take that as a sign that their time to separate had come, for they embraced for a long moment, whispering unheard words into each other's ears.

Alaric waited until Madrena had untangled herself from Rúnin before stepping to her side.

"Take care of yourself, sister," he said. Though he attempted lightness with his voice, the words sounded too ominous.

She barreled into him in a hard embrace.

"I'll be fine, brother," she said. "I'm more worried about you."

He drew back slightly. Leave it to his brave, fierce, shieldmaiden sister to be a hostage in a strange fortress and be worrying about him.

"I hope you know what you are doing," she went on. Her pale gray eyes flickered for the briefest moment toward the chieftain's daughter.

Something twisted deep in Alaric's belly at the sight of the girl, her auburn hair glinting in the sun and her eyes wide with fright for what lay ahead.

Odin's breath, what had he gotten himself into?

57

~

Maelcon stood on the wall and watched as his daughter was carted away by the two Northmen. As they descended the hill and wended their way through the deserted huts, he caught sight of the rest of the band of Northmen warriors approaching them from the woods.

"I hope you know what you are doing." Drostan stood by his side, a deep frown on his face. But if there was anyone in the world who'd stand by Maelcon's decision, it was Drostan, his loyal warrior.

"Aye, I do."

"How can you be so calm when your daughter is in those bastards' hands?" Drostan said, his voice tight.

"Though you are too proud to admit it, they could have slaughtered us all." Maelcon tugged on his beard absently. "We should both be thanking God that those Northman wish to settle instead of raid."

"But they are still animals," Drostan persisted. "How can you trust——"

Maelcon rounded on Drostan, his patience at last worn out. "There is a reason I am Chief and you obey my orders, not the other way around. I am thinking about my people—not just today, not just tomorrow, but for countless generations. Our fate rides on this moment."

Though Drostan stood nigh a head taller than Maelcon, the warrior bowed slightly in acquiescence to Maelcon's authority.

"The Northumbrians will never cease to threaten

the borders of Pictland, no matter how many times we drive them back," Maelcon went on, lowering his voice though none dared to eavesdrop on the Chief and the leader of the warriors. "And even though we count Causantín mac Fergusa as our ally today, there is no telling which direction the winds of his favor will blow tomorrow."

"Even when Elisead marries Causantín's son?"

"Aye, even then. These Northmen will never stop coming, and like as not, more will wish to settle, like these ones, rather than just raid. Hell, Dál Riata has been swarmed with them. Though Causantín hopes to put Domnall on the throne in the west, the King of the Picts may not have that option if the Northmen have their way."

Drostan squinted over the wall into the sun. Maelcon's eyes followed, catching the last sight of Elisead's cart as she and the Northmen around her were swallowed by the forest.

"And you think that aligning yourself to these Northmen will provide you some…protection?" Drostan said, his voice calmer now.

"Aye," Maelcon replied, clenching his fists against his powerlessness. "From Causantín, from the Northumbrians, and from other Northlanders, when they come—and they will come."

Maelcon descended the stairs and made his way toward the great hall. He would wait to send word to Causantín mac Fergusa, King of the Picts. News of these Northmen's arrival, their desire to settle, and Elisead's role as their hostage would only threaten the betrothal between Elisead and the King's son, Domnall. Everything hung in a delicate balance, and one wrong move, one rash decision or early jump would destroy it all.

Even still, he wasn't going to sit on his hands until the Northmen contacted him again. He would need their camp watched. And mayhap the Northwoman, Alaric's sister, could provide information.

He approached the strangely-clad woman, eyeing her where she stood in the yard as if poised for battle.

"I'll show you to my daughter's chambers. You may be here a while, so you'd best make yourself comfortable."

The woman—Madrena if he remembered Alaric's introduction—tilted her head in such a way that she acknowledged Maelcon while still looking down her nose slightly at him. She was unusually tall, but it was more than that. She carried herself with a regal, arrogant air. Maelcon gritted his teeth against the foul taste in his mouth at the predicament he found himself in.

"Very well," Madrena said, with that same thickly accented Northumbrian tongue as her brother.

As Maelcon guided Madrena toward the great hall, his eye snagged on a flash of white in one of the shadows.

Feitr.

Perhaps the Northland slave would finally prove more valuable than the labor to be wrung from his body.

Maelcon's mind swirled even as he plastered a kindly smile on his face for Madrena's benefit.

9

As the Northmen emerged from the woods to meet the cart, Elisead had to bite the inside of her cheek to keep from screaming.

It was already terrifying enough to be mere feet behind Alaric as he walked with a hand on the donkey's harness, guiding it away from the safety of the fortress and everyone in the world she knew.

She watched, nigh spellbound, as he strode with an easy gait that belied his swiftness. Even now, her body hummed at the memory of the hard expanse of him wrapping around her, protecting her from the floor. Her shoulders tingled where his hands had lingered for a breath longer than necessary when they'd steadied her.

The one called Rúnin walked behind, setting the hairs on the back of her neck to stirring. And as the cart was surrounded by the warriors nigh two score in number, her skin crawled with unease.

But these were her keepers now. She tried to remind

herself that her wellbeing was in their best interest as well—if what Alaric had said in the great hall was true.

Many sets of eyes, mostly shades of blue and green, darted to her as Alaric spoke in that lilting tongue. A moment later, he was guiding the donkey into the trees.

Elisead jerked her head around and caught one last glimpse of the fortress before pine boughs obscured it. Her heart hammered in her chest, her stomach sinking like a rock in a pond.

She was alone with these Northmen now, with no stone walls or chieftain father to protect her. Her father had seemed all too quick to agree to Alaric's terms. As usual, he put his people's safety above his daughter's happiness and wellbeing. If it had been anyone else in this situation, she would have seen the wisdom in it. But as it was, she wanted to scream at him for her freedom from these Northmen.

"What is your name?"

Elisead's head snapped back around at the rich, silky voice right next to her. Alaric had let one of the other Northmen take the donkey's harness and he now strode slowly by her side.

She swallowed. "Elisead."

"Elisead." He tested the name. It sounded different, foreign on his tongue. For some reason, goose bumps rose on her arms despite her heavy cloak. She'd worn it just in case the Northmen left her out in the elements. For all she knew, she might have to sleep on the ground in the open, and the sea breezes turned cool even in the summer.

As if reading her mind, Alaric shifted his gaze to the cloak. "Cold?"

"Nay," she said quickly, feeling heat rise to her cheeks. "But…I know not how long I will be forced to remain with you."

She dragged her gaze up and held his eyes boldly, a silent challenge in them. She must make it clear early on that she would not be pushed over like a reed in the wind. She was not here by choice, but she would maintain her dignity in the process. She was a chieftain's daughter, and soon to be a King's wife.

"You are engaged."

Again, it was as if Alaric could see into her mind and discern her thoughts with ease. But unlike his question about her cloak, which had been subtly playful, now his eyes were dark and searching.

"Aye."

"To whom?"

He seemed slightly annoyed at her lack of ready information. *Good.* Elisead had no desire to make life easier for this intimidating Northman.

"To Domnall."

He raised a golden eyebrow at her. "And who is Domnall?"

"The son of Causantín mac Fergusa."

"And who is Causantín mac Fergusa?"

She chewed on her bottom lip for a moment, considering any other possible evasion. "He is King of the Picts," she said at last.

This had both brows shooting up and a slow exhale escaping from Alaric's lips. Her gaze lingered there for a moment. His lips were most expressive. They curved playfully, or wolfishly, or they compressed into a hard line that conveyed an unbending will.

"Your father must be very interested in negotiations if he would risk such a valuable…asset." His eyes roamed over her, as they had by the river, and she felt heat once again move up her neck. Though his gaze wasn't lewd, something about it sent a knot into her belly.

Elisead silently cursed herself for giving up that piece of information. In truth she didn't understand the whole of her father's reasoning. Perhaps Alaric had already deduced more about her father's position wedged between the Northmen and the Pictish King than she had.

"Don't punish yourself overmuch," Alaric said, that easy smile creeping back to his lips. "You fought valiantly to make that information hard-won."

She stiffened. "It is not my place, nor my wish, to help you in any way. I will just have to work harder to avoid inadvertently aiding you."

Alaric snorted softly. "You need not see me as the enemy. You are a hostage, not a captive."

"What is the difference?"

"As you likely very well know," Alaric said, holding her gaze, "if you were a captive, you would not be sitting in that cart. You'd be over my shoulder."

Elisead inhaled sharply. Then unbidden, the tingling started in her body where she'd come in contact with her as he'd scooped her up in her faint.

"But as a hostage, I must look out for your wellbeing as if you were my own flesh and blood."

A dark promise that Elisead didn't fully understand flickered in Alaric's bright green eyes. All she knew was that it was wrong—wrong of him to insinuate aught, and wrong for the knot to tighten hotly in her stomach at the glint in his gaze. Nevertheless, she straightened her spine so that she sat rigidly on the swaying cart.

"I want naught to do with you barbarians. The sooner these negotiations are over, the better."

Alaric chuckled, drawing the eyes of some of the men who walked alongside them.

"Very well, little spirit."

"What did you just call me?"

His eyebrows drew together for the briefest moment, as if translating from his native language to Northumbrian. "Do you not have forest spirits in this land?"

She was so startled by the question that her lips parted wordlessly for a long moment. "Aye," she managed at last. "We have forest spirits. Or at least we did—in the time of the ancient ways."

"And do not your forest spirits run through the trees, hair unbound, luring strange men deeper into the woods?"

He took a tangled lock of her auburn hair between his thumb and forefinger and rubbed it boldly.

Elisead jerked back, freeing her hair from his gentle grasp. Of course, if he had wished to maintain his hold, he could have—and might have even yanked out a few strands given Elisead's swift jolt. But he let her hair slide between his fingertips and then dropped his hand.

She floundered for a long moment, trying to come up with something to say in response to his teasing question. She must have looked the fool, for he chuckled again.

"You are quite safe, little spirit," he said, though his smile began to fade. "My honor, the life of my sister, and the future of my people depend on it." By the time he finished speaking, his jaw was clenched and his emerald eyes were stormy.

Though he was a Northland savage, strangely she believed that she wouldn't have her throat slit in the night or her skull split with an axe. Yet heat continued coiling deep within her as he shook away the tension that had crept into his strong features and flashed her another wicked smile.

At last, he turned away and fell into pace with the one called Rúnin. The two spoke quietly in their own tongue.

It wasn't long before she caught a whiff of salt air among the pine and soil scents of the forest. The trees thinned ahead and the two longships came into view. Their curved dragon prows, painted red and baring their teeth, send renewed apprehension through her.

She was in the belly of the beast now.

10

———————

Alaric watched Elisead's face as she took in the sight of the longships moored along the bay's sandy shoreline.

Did she know just how expressive her amber eyes were? He doubted it, for she'd seemed surprised at how easily he'd sensed not only her changing moods but the shifting thoughts and fears behind them.

Alaric forced himself to tear his gaze away and return his attention to where it belonged—on his crew, and on the camp that needed making. A quick scan of the area helped get his thoughts in order.

"We'll make camp there." He pointed to a level patch of ground slightly elevated from the bay's shore. The trees were sparser on that sandy expanse before the forest rose and the land sloped into a series of hills.

His crew set about unloading the two longships. They formed a line and passed down chests and beams of wood that had been tucked along the ships' sides.

Alaric was about to take up a spot at the end of the chain when he heard Elisead shifting in the cart behind him. Before she could awkwardly struggle to the ground, he spun and captured her waist in his hands.

Even through the thick material of her cloak, he could feel the supple trimness of her waist in his grasp. She gasped but automatically placed her small hands on his shoulders as he slid her to the ground.

Involuntarily, he inhaled. He hadn't gotten the opportunity earlier when he'd caught her in her swoon, but now he took full advantage of her nearness. She smelled like sun-warmed pine boughs and something sweet and subtle, perhaps her own skin.

When her feet reached the ground, he quickly removed his hands lest he forget how to control himself. Even still, he lingered. Alaric's pulse thrummed as he stared down at Elisead, those liquid gold eyes enthralling him.

By Thor's bloody hammer. He spun on his heels and took his place at the end of the line.

'Twas an innocent touch, he told himself firmly. Naught to berate himself over—and certainly naught that warranted the heat coursing through his veins.

He flexed his hands in preparation to take the large wooden chest being passed down the line. He'd only promised to leave her a virgin, not forego assisting her in any way that put them in physical contact.

As he piled chests, tent beams, weapons, and the rest of their supplies on the ground, he kept one eye on Elisead. She stood awkwardly to the side, watching them all work. Perhaps his sister had been more astute in her caution than even she knew—perhaps he would have to tread carefully with Elisead, else his own interest in the girl distract him from his mission.

JUST AS THE sun dipped behind the western hills, Alaric straightened, wiping the sweat from his brow. They'd erected a dozen tents along the shoreline where the river flowed into the bay. Most of his crew had already made their sleeping arrangements and were carrying their sea chests into the tent of their choosing.

His tent was by far the largest and finest. It had been a gift from Eirik in honor of this voyage. Alaric stood back and admired it for a moment as the sea breeze cooled him.

Two thick wooden poles leaned against each other, crossing well over Alaric's head. The top ends of the poles, which stuck out above either side of the tent, were carved with the same dragon heads as the prows of his ships. A rafter pole nestled at the point where the heads sprouted and extended nigh ten paces back, resting on another set of poles propped together. Finely spun but stout wool, the same as they used for their sails, provided the roof and walls, with a slit in the front for a door flap.

'Twas a tent fit for a Jarl—and in a way, Alaric was the Jarl of this voyage, the Jarl of this new settlement. Pride at his responsibility swelled as he gazed upon the tent.

"What are you going to do with her?"

Rúnin emerged from the back of the tent, where

he'd been fastening the woolen cover to the poles.

Alaric didn't need him to clarify the question. Elisead stuck out like a sheep among wolves amid the Northlanders. She'd stayed next to the cart the entire time they'd worked, not making a sound.

"Since my sister isn't here, I'll share your tent. She can have mine."

Rúnin scowled at the reminder that Madrena was with the Picts. But instead of arguing further with Alaric about the wisdom of his plan, Rúnin silently hefted Alaric's sea chest, which lay nearby, and carried it the short distance to his own smaller tent.

Alaric approached Elisead as the blue light of the summer evening began to settle around them.

"You will have the use of my tent for the duration of the negotiations."

Those amber eyes widened in horror, and it took Alaric a moment to understand why.

"I will be sleeping elsewhere," he said quickly as realization struck him. "As I promised, you will go untouched within this camp."

She nodded quickly, lowering her gaze. Reaching into the cart, he lifted her wooden chest and hefted it on one shoulder.

"This way."

She walked with him toward the tent but faltered when he held back one of the flaps for her to go inside. She stared for a long moment at the dragons carved into the tent's poles and a visible shudder went through her.

Something tightened in Alaric's chest at that. Surely she had every right to be frightened of the situation she found herself in. The runes carved next to the burned bones revealed that whatever Northlanders had landed here before, their contact with the Picts had been violent. He'd have to ask her what had happened—not tonight, though. This day had been trying enough.

There was just enough light filtering in from the open flap that she could pick her footing toward the back of the tent. To his pleasant surprise, he found that Rúnin had set up the bed that had been part of Eirik's gift. A thick mattress stuffed with goose down sat atop a wooden crate. A few furs covered the mattress. The bed was fit for a King—or the daughter of a Pictish chieftain.

Alaric set down the chest at the foot of the bed with a grunt. Even that sound made Elisead jump. It would be quite the task to get her to relax and truly believe she was safe here.

"What do you wish to do with your…stone?"

Maelcon mac Lorcan had called her a skilled stone carver. Alaric hadn't gotten a good look at it, but the stone must be important for the father to send it with the daughter into Northmen's hands.

"I'd have it brought in, if that is all right."

All her hardened bluster from before seemed to have withered away. He could tell from her eyes that she was coming to learn the seriousness of her situation.

Alaric nodded and stepped out of the tent. He motioned several men over and they retrieved the enormous slab of stone, even longer than he was tall and as broad as his shoulders. They shuffled into the tent and lowered the stone to the ground.

In the dim light, Alaric could make out a few swirls and divots in the rock's surface. Yet another thing he'd have to ask Elisead about—in the morning.

"We'll have a fire going shortly," Alaric said as the others filed out of the tent. For some reason, he found himself lingering in her presence yet again. "You are welcome to warm yourself by it. There will be food and drink as well."

"Nay," she breathed. "I would rather…be alone."

"Very well. I'll have some nourishment sent in, all the same."

She nodded, and suddenly he felt like he was being dismissed from his own tent. She was the daughter of a chieftain, after all. Alaric forced his feet toward the slit in the tent's front, then dropped the tent flap closed behind him.

Just as he was about to step away, however, he heard a muffled cry from inside. He almost barged back in, sword drawn and ready to face any danger that threatened Elisead. But then the noise came again, and he realized it was the sound of her weeping.

She must have buried her face in the furs, or perhaps her cloak, for each cry was barely audible. An unfamiliar twinge of guilt twisted in his chest. He didn't relish causing the fire-haired beauty pain, but he had responsibilities greater than tending to her worries and sorrows. Elisead—and Madrena—bore the consequences of his plan, but the stakes were higher than the two of them.

He willed his feet away at last, distancing himself from her sobs.

11

———

Elisead woke with a pounding headache that was no doubt the result of her childish tears the night before.

True to his word, Alaric had sent a blond-headed lad, who was perhaps of an age with Elisead, to her tent with a horn of ale, a package of dried meat, and a somewhat stale round of flatbread.

But more than his word to send her food, he'd kept his promise that she'd be safe all night. Except for the young lad, who blushed so deeply in Elisead's presence that she had a hard time imagining that he was a danger even to a midge, no one had disturbed her.

Even still, she'd slept poorly. Every snort or shifting body beyond the walls of the tent sent her jumping. Considering all the tales she'd heard about Northmen and what she'd seen for herself seven years ago, it was a miracle she got any sleep at all.

As the sounds of the camp rising and starting the

day filtered into the tent, she lingered behind the woolen walls. At last, the sun was high and strong enough that the tent was filled with soft light. She removed a comb carved out of bone from her chest and set into the tangles in her hair.

When that task was done, she still didn't feel ready to face the Northmen—especially Alaric, whose gaze seemed to tease and yet cut into her every time he looked at her.

With naught left to do, she sat down in front of the stone that was to be her bride gift. She'd already discarded her heavy cloak and so was able to reach into the pouch at her belt unimpeded.

She fingered the pebbles that sat at the bottom of the pouch. Though an untrained touch would be hard-pressed to distinguish between them, she knew the shape and size of each with a brush of her fingers. She considered the stone for a moment, then withdrew a pebble of medium size. She wouldn't do the most detailed work just yet—she didn't trust her nerves, or the still-soft light filling the tent.

Elisead placed the pebble atop a small hole she'd already made in the stone. Then she glided the pebble toward another of the holes, then another. As she worked the pebble between the string of holes, a groove formed in the stone that connected the little marks. The groove would eventually turn into the outer edge of a twisting vine winding around a stag.

As the pebble rolled under her callused fingers, a sense of calm stole over her. Though this project was one she'd been ordered to complete by her father, carving of any kind never failed to soothe her. Gradually, she took to humming in time with each stroke of the pebble against the stone's surface.

Suddenly, harsh light flooded the tent as the door flaps were drawn back. The song in her throat turned into a scream. The pebble fell from her fingertips as she whipped around, squinting into the sun at an enormous figure outlined in the doorway.

"Easy, Elisead." Alaric's deep, rich voice sounded like he was trying to calm a spooked animal. And she supposed she was behaving like one.

His bright green eyes flitted past her to the stone, and he squinted at the area she'd been working on.

"Your father said you were a carver, but I don't think I understood his meaning until now."

Alaric fastened one of the tent's flaps back, allowing the bright morning sun to continue streaming in. Whatever his original purpose for entering the tent, he now seemed completely transfixed by what she was doing.

"You...you did all this?"

Alaric crouched next to her, and suddenly her heart pounded hard in her chest. But not from fear—nay, for strangely, she felt both unsettled and safe in his presence. How could that be? She pushed the thought aside as she watched his battle-roughened fingers trace over the band of curling vines and forest creatures she'd been carving around the edge of the stone.

"Aye," she managed at last. Her voice sounded small in her own ears.

"'Tis too fine to have been done with a chisel," he said absently, his fingertips caressing the stone.

"Do you…do you truly wish to know?"

He looked at her then, mirth around his mouth but his eyes sharp. "You think me a barbarian, a savage. And to your mind, savages must not have any interest in or appreciation of art."

It wasn't a question, but rather almost an accusation. Elisead's cheeks heated under his scrutinizing stare.

"My people have faced Northmen before. We know your brutal ways. You are no better than wolves, preying on God's children and devouring everything in your path."

Though she'd spoken bravely, she had to swallow hard once the words were out, for at her declaration, Alaric's smile dropped and his eyes darkened. Suddenly she felt like she was face to face with a real wolf.

Was this a glimpse of the Northman's true character? Was he just like the others who'd ravaged her lands and people?

Alaric glanced down at the stone again, narrowing his eyes. When he returned his gaze to her, understanding flickered there.

"The runes next to the burned bones. You carved them, did you not?"

She swallowed again. Was she as safe as she'd come to believe over the course of one undisturbed night?

"A-aye."

"Come with me," he said, standing suddenly. He lifted her by the elbow, and although his grip wasn't meant to inflict pain, it was firm enough to make it impossible to break free.

Before she could ask where they were going, he

guided her out of the tent. She had only enough time to cast a brief glance around the camp.

A low fire burned near the bay's shore, and a few of the Northmen lingered around it with their morning meal. Others were moving about the little tent village they'd erected last night. A few glanced at Alaric and Elisead, but none seemed concerned at their leader's grip on his hostage.

Alaric made his way along the bank of the river, Elisead in tow. Realization struck her even before the dreaded site came into view. He was taking her to the carved runes—and the remnants of all those incinerated bodies.

"Nay!" She struggled harder against his hold, but his grip didn't falter.

Her leather-clad feet sank into the soft sand of the river's bank where it widened. The sand was gray here. Seven years of rain, snow, and wind hadn't removed the ash. In fact, they seemed only to drive the ashes deeper, like a stain on the earth.

At last Alaric halted in front of the stone with the two runes carved into it.

"You did this."

"I...I carved them, aye." There was no point in lying. She'd always been told her face betrayed every thought and flicker of emotion.

"How did you learn these symbols?" Alaric's eyes, like his voice, were hard and flat.

"There was...a boy. He was with them." She gestured vaguely at the field of bones, unable to look.

The stench assailed her again. Although she knew it

wasn't real, only a product of her imagination, it still made her insides twist.

Alaric didn't seem to notice, though, for he frowned down at her. "What boy?"

Perhaps if she told him all, he would release her and she could flee this terrible place. "His name is Feitr. He came with the others. Now he is my father's slave."

The sickening pops and crackles of burning flesh rang in her ears. If she didn't get away soon, she would be sick.

"How long ago was this? And who were these other Northlanders? Did they have a distinctive color or pattern to their sails? How many of them were there?"

She swayed in his hold. "Please…" She wasn't above begging now. Blood darkened the sand in her mind's eye. Screams tore through the air—the screams of her people as they fell under the Northmen's blades.

Elisead looked up to find a blurry Alaric gazing down at her, his brows drawn together. The sun glinted off his golden head, so sharp it was almost painful to her eyes.

"What is the matter?"

The harsh edge to his voice was now replaced with genuine concern, but she didn't trust herself to open her mouth to respond, lest she become sick right there and then.

She pointed to the tree line behind him. Without hesitation, he guided her swiftly away from the carved stone and into the protection of the trees.

Elisead inhaled deeply of the fresh, piney air, trying to rid herself of the burnt smell lingering in her nostrils.

Inadvertently, she caught his scent. 'Twas surprisingly clean—lye soap mixed with wood smoke and plant life.

"I do not wish to bring you harm or distress you," Alaric said at last, his voice low. "But I must have answers. What ails you?"

Taking another steadying breath, she met his searching gaze. "I become…overly sensitive at times."

'Twas embarrassing to discuss it with him. Her father and those in the village knew she was odd, but to explain it to this outsider made her feel ashamed. "I… feel things intensely. Sometimes I faint if I become over-whelmed."

His dark gold brows winged as his eyes widened slightly. "Were you cursed? Or hexed by a witching woman perhaps?"

Elisead repressed a sigh. That was what some in the village thought—that she was to be pitied at best and feared at worst because sights and sounds overwhelmed her at times, and an unexpected touch or a powerful scent could send her swooning. Even memories could be so strong as to cause her panic and tears.

"Nay, I have always been this way."

In truth, it had gotten slightly better when she'd learned how to carve. Even though the world's intensity still left her stunned at times, carving always an escape, a relief.

Alaric's eyes searched her for another moment. Then his gaze softened. "You are touched by the gods, then."

"What?"

He shrugged but considered his words, likely picking

79

them carefully in the Northumbrian tongue. "Our gods deign to grant a select few a sliver of their powers. You've been touched, albeit lightly."

It sounded like something from the old ways. But she and her people were Christians now. They only had one God, and her sensitivity was certainly not a favor granted by Him.

She shook her head. "It does not feel like a gift most of the time."

"Perhaps your people do not understand your true value."

Alaric lifted his hand as if he would brush a lock of her hair behind her ear, but then hesitated, his fingers suspended in the air between them. Her mind shot back to how she'd pulled away from his touch last afternoon. Suddenly she felt a stirring, barely a flutter, low in her belly. Would his touch be as soft as it had been before?

"Your eyes are the color of amber." His voice was like a silky caress, intimate and dark.

"Aye, so I have been told."

"Amber is a most precious stone where I come from. Its beauty is held in the highest regard, its value unmatched."

The flutter turned into a knotted warmth deep in her core.

"Aye?" It was barely more than a whisper, for suddenly her throat was dry as he held her gaze for another long moment.

At last, Alaric dropped his hand, and the spell seemed to break. Elisead shook her head a little to clear it.

"I have a great many questions," he said. "And you have been less than forthcoming."

He softened the critique with a quirk of one side of his mouth. "I do not wish to drag answers from you. Surely you can see how providing me with the information I seek will have you settled back in your home with your father and people all the sooner."

"Nay, I suppose I don't see." Now that she had recovered her senses, she forced her feet to take a step back from Alaric's large frame.

"The better I understand your people and their ways, the easier it will be for my people to join yours and get on with the process of making our home here."

"And you truly wish to settle amongst us?" Though she'd heard him proclaim it in the great hall, she still didn't fully believe that a Northman wished to do more than plunder and destroy.

"Ja," he replied, slipping back into his own tongue, though from the fervency of his tone and the clear, stubborn set of his face, she understood his meaning well enough.

She hesitated for a long moment, considering all that had transpired since yesterday morn.

The Northmen had landed upon their shore, armed and prepared for battle. They'd reached her father's fortress and demanded admittance.

But they had never attacked, even when her father's archers had fired on them. Since then, they'd built a temporary camp but hadn't made another move against her people or the fortress. And of course before all of that, Alaric could have killed her by the river, but instead had let her go.

And here she stood with the man now, alone and far enough away from camp that no one would hear her scream if he tried to harm her.

Perhaps it was all some elaborate plot to lure her father into letting his guard down, then striking. They'd already managed to earn enough trust—or mayhap simply leverage—to gain the chieftain's daughter as their hostage.

But from what she'd heard of Northmen and what she'd seen for herself seven years ago, they weren't known for their patience or their elaborate plots. Nay, they normally took what they wanted when they wanted it, life, limb, and property be damned.

Mayhap Alaric and his men were different than the other Northmen. Should she believe the little voice in her head that said she could trust him?

"I suppose I can answer your questions...in the interest of ending my sentence as a hostage."

It was a lie, the soft voice whispered in the back of her mind. If not a lie, then an untruth by omission. For though she longed to free herself from the role of hostage, more than that she wished to trust the tall, golden man before her.

What was happening to her? What powers did this pagan barbarian have over her?

She didn't dare consider the answer.

12

"And that one there?"

"Rowan."

Alaric was familiar with the properties of the tree, for they grew in the Northlands also, but he didn't have the Northumbrian word for it.

"Rowan," he said, letting the word sink in.

He and Elisead had been playing a game of sorts. He'd led her farther into the woods and away from the site of the bones. The distance from that spot seemed to instill an ever-spreading calmness within her. He hadn't asked further about the bones and the other Northmen yet. She needed time to relax, time to trust him.

Alaric ran a hand absently over the rowan's bark. This land was not so different from the Northlands. Yet it was softer somehow, more fertile.

He'd already asked Elisead about what kind of crops her people grew. As in Dalgaard, they harvested oats, barley, and some rye. But when Alaric had left Dalgaard a little over a sennight ago, it was still considered early summer. The farmers on the outskirts of the village had only just begun sowing their crops, for though the summer was intense in the Northlands, it was all too short. Elisead had said that villagers around the fortress had begun laboring in the fields nigh two moons ago.

Alaric let his gaze shift to Elisead. Indeed, this was a lush, ripe land.

She was toying with a small rock she'd found on the forest floor.

"You must know a great deal about the quality of stone here," he said, watching her fingers stroke the rock.

"Aye," she replied, her amber eyes lighting.

"How did you come to learn how to carve those patterns?"

The flicker in her gaze dimmed somewhat, but she answered him. "Many of the great stone masons travel throughout Pictland, sharing their gift and honoring God with their carvings."

Why might that piece of information cause her to become ever so slightly guarded? Alaric kept his air easy as he bend to retrieve a stone of his own from the ground.

"And such a mason came here."

"Aye, her name was Una, and she was truly gifted."

Again, she answered with restraint.

"*Was*?"

The question was enough to draw her gaze to his. "She is well, I am sure," she replied. "But she was only able to stay with us for a season. And…"

Alaric longed to prod her, but instead casually tossed his rock into the air, then caught it.

"…And it was a dark season."

"You mean winter?"

"Nay, I mean…it was just before the Northmen arrived."

Unwittingly, he'd stumbled once more upon the very topic he was trying to avoid. She was like a frightened doe, especially when it came to the subject of Northlanders.

It was important to him that she grow more comfortable around him—only because it would aid his mission in negotiating a place for his people on these lands, he told himself firmly. It had naught to do with wanting to see Elisead's eyes light up and a soft smile curve her rosy lips.

He fumbled for something to say to put her at ease once more, but she surprised him by going on unbidden.

"Needless to say, we were all very…distracted. But she taught me well in what little time we had."

"And is it normal in this land for women to become great stone masons and travel the countryside? Is that what you will do some day?"

Unexpectedly, she erupted in laughter. The sound was like the most delicate waterfall. Alaric's stomach twisted into a knot of heat.

"Oh, nay!" she said between giggles.

He couldn't help but smile at her sudden merriment. "Is what I said so preposterous?"

"Aye, it is!" she blurted. At last she got her laughter under control. "Una was special, indeed. 'Tis very rare here for women to be allowed to become artists. But Una's skill was undeniable."

"Then yours must be, too, for your father encourages you to carve that enormous stone he sent with you."

A shadow passed over her features, and yet again Alaric wondered what he'd said wrong. He turned fully toward her, laying a hand over hers to still her absent rubbing of the pebble there.

"I saw your work myself. I have never seen its equal."

"Thank you," she said softly.

Was it his imagination, or did he feel a tremble in her hand beneath his?

"It isn't that I doubt myself, it is that…"

With her free hand, she tucked a lock of auburn hair behind one ear. "If my father had his way, I would never have learned how to carve. Now he sees it only as a way to advance our people through my marriage."

"That is why he sent you with the stone—your gift to your future husband."

She nodded, and the lock of hair, like polished copper, slipped free once more. "'Tis an honor to be able to carve such a work as that."

Yet the way she said it, the task sounded more like a punishment.

"Come," he said gently, intertwining their fingers. "You never explained just how you create such fine detail in that slab of rock."

She blinked up at him, surprise floating in her eyes. "You wish to see the stone again?"

"I wish to learn more about your skill," he corrected. The stone was a work of art, but it was the artist he was interested in.

Her hand in his, she let him lead her back toward the camp—though he carefully skirted the site of the burned bones. As they walked, he caught a glimpse of her brows knitting out of the corner of his eye.

"Is it normal in *your* land for women to become artists and travel the countryside?"

It was the first question she'd asked him about his homeland. Something swelled inside his chest at her curiosity.

"We don't have many traveling artists, except for skalds—those who recite verses," he said. "But you saw my sister Madrena. She is a fierce and greatly respected warrior. I doubt you've noticed her yet, but there is another shieldmaiden in my crew. She is a pupil of Madrena's. She wished to become a warrior, and so she has."

"And...and that is *allowed?*"

Alaric shrugged but didn't release her hand. "Life is merciless in the Northlands. If someone possesses a particular skill or a desire to work hard and help our people, we accept it."

Elisead seemed to puzzle over this for a long moment as they continued to weave their way back toward camp.

"Strange," she said under her breath, and again, something expanded in his chest.

13

The camp was buzzing with activity in the cheery afternoon sun. While he and Elisead had been away, several of his crew had applied axes to the thin, young trees growing among their tents. Now the camp was more open, which meant it would be easier to keep watch for intruders or wild animals.

A few of the men were gone, likely hunting for fresh meat. Alaric would have to tell them what he'd learned about the animals and plants of these woods from Elisead when they returned.

As he led her toward her tent, he caught sight of Eyva, Madrena's pupil, practicing her swordwork with her husband of a few moons, Tarr. He squeezed Elisead's hand and nodded toward the two as if to prove his words about shieldmaidens earlier.

Elisead watched the two spar in slow motion for a long moment. Her hand relaxed in his. He still hadn't learned what the extent of her knowledge about North-landers was, but he could surmise by her soft, curious features and bright eyes that he was changing some of her ideas.

He turned to fasten the tent flap back for her, eager to learn more about her carving, but just then a whistle tore through the air.

Alaric tensed immediately. It was the signal for an approaching outsider.

Unthinking, he pushed Elisead into the tent and stepped in front of the open flap, hand gripping the hilt of the sword on his belt.

A movement in the denser forest beyond their little clearing on the shoreline caught his eye. Alaric partially drew his sword. Elisead gasped behind him in confusion.

A white-blond head emerged from the woods, attached to a young man Alaric guessed was close to Elisead in age.

He was dressed as the other Pict men—woolen tunic to his knees over trousers and leather boots, leather belt around his waist, and a brightly colored expanse of cloth thrown over his shoulders like a cloak despite the mild weather.

But his coloring was more like a Northlander. Even from this distance, Alaric could make out the man's ice-blue eyes. His nigh white hair flashed blindingly in the sun as he stepped from the cover of the trees.

"I come with an invitation from Maelcon mac Lorcan," the man said, though he spoke in Alaric's native tongue.

"Feitr," Alaric said by way of greeting.

The man seemed surprised that Alaric knew his name, but after the briefest pause, he continued forward. Alaric eased his blade back into its scabbard and dropped his hand, though he remained between Maelcon's Northland slave and Elisead.

When Feitr reached him, Alaric noticed out of the corners of his eye that several of his crew had stopped what they were doing and watched the stranger. Some looked on suspiciously while others seemed surprised to hear their tongue spoken by the man.

"Maelcon wishes to speak with you again. He invites you to return to his fort with the man who accompanied you the first time—the dark one. And he wishes you to bring his daughter so that he can verify her wellbeing."

Rúnin was suddenly standing behind Feitr. When the dark warrior's shadow fell across Feitr, the pale man actually flinched slightly.

"And what of Madrena? How does she fare?" Rúnin asked, his voice a low threat.

"She is hale and hearty, I assure you," Feitr said, turning slightly so that he was not pinned between Rúnin and Alaric, both of whom were a hand span taller than he was.

"She'd better be," Rúnin bit out.

Alaric longed to echo Rúnin's sentiments, but as the leader he had to maintain control of this situation. He glanced at the sun. It had already passed its zenith and was heading toward the distant mountains in the west.

"Tomorrow, then," he said to Feitr. "Tell your master

that we will be happy to meet with him tomorrow morn."

At Feitr's nod, Rúnin strode away, muttering under his breath. But instead of turning to deliver Alaric's message, Feitr lingered in front of the tent for a moment.

"Do you need assistance in finding your way out of the camp?" Alaric asked Feitr sharply.

Suddenly Feitr leaned in and spoke only loud enough for Alaric's ears.

"If you knew what was best for you, you'd leave now."

Unease coiled in Alaric's belly. Feitr had waited for Rúnin to leave, and he spoke in Alaric's tongue so that Elisead, who still stood behind him within the tent, wouldn't understand.

"What do you mean, *what is best for me?*" Alaric snapped, narrowing his eyes on Feitr.

"Sail now while you still can," Feitr hissed. He darted a glance over his shoulder and noticed that some of Alaric's crew still watched them.

He stepped back from Alaric abruptly and spun on his heels. As Alaric watched, Feitr stole into the woods, heading upriver toward the fortress.

"What did he say?" Elisead asked, drawing Alaric's narrowed stare from Feitr's back.

"We will visit your father's fortress tomorrow morn," Alaric said, forcing his voice to be level and his face smooth.

Her eyes widened hopefully at that, and Alaric was

reminded that she wasn't with him by choice. For some reason the thought soured his mood further.

"And the last part? What was Feitr muttering to you?"

Alaric shook his head, but then plastered a light-hearted expression on his features. "Naught. Only that he missed speaking in his native tongue and wished to extend the conversation."

Elisead's brows drew together but she nodded.

"Your explanations about your carving techniques will have to wait," Alaric went on. "I must discuss tomorrow's meeting with my crew."

She nodded again, though he thought he caught a flash of disappointment in her eyes.

"You are free to move about the camp, though don't go beyond the tree line," he said, stepping away from the tent.

He forced down the desire to stay by her side as he walked between the smaller tents of his crew. Feitr didn't pose an immediate threat. He was just one man against a camp of nigh forty Northland warriors.

But unease still laced through Alaric's gut. Were Feitr's words a threat? A warning? Was he plotting something? Or was Maelcon mac Lorcan?

Alaric barked Rúnin's name. He needed to chew on Feitr's words before sharing them with his friend, but he felt the sudden need to release the energy burning in his veins with a sparring match. Rúnin was one of the few who could hold his own against Alaric.

Rúnin partially drew his sword, but Alaric shook his head and unbuckled his scabbard from his hip. Rúnin followed his action, comprehending wordlessly that Alaric wished to spar with his bare hands.

As he took up a readied stance across from Rúnin, Alaric's mind set to work on Feitr's words. Whatever they meant, he swore by Odin that Elisead would come to no harm.

14

_____

"You want to take my fortress?"

Even though the words weren't directed at her, Elisead flinched back at her father's tone.

Alaric sat calmly by her side at the high table, seemingly unaffected by Maelcon's outraged question.

"Nei, not *take* it. Have the use of it. Just as your own people do," Alaric said levelly.

Things had gotten underway smoothly enough that morning. Alaric had suggested that they take the cart and donkey back to her father so as not to appear to be pilfering in any way. She'd ridden in the cart, while Alaric and Rúnin, who still frightened her with his dark scowls, had walked beside it.

They'd been greeted civilly by Maelcon, with Drostan standing ever silent by his side.

Alaric's sister Madrena had rushed into Rúnin's eager arms, though she assured both her mate and her brother that all was well. She'd been treated fairly, she said loud enough for all to hear. She'd even taken up residence in Elisead's old chamber.

After Elisead had made her own assurances of her wellbeing to her father, Maelcon had led them all into the great hall for a morning meal of porridge, cream, and clay bowls full of the forest's ripest berries.

But when it came to the actual negotiations, her father's temper flared. And although Alaric wore the relaxed smile that was becoming familiar to her, when she peered down she noticed his hand clenching and unclenching under the table.

"And why ever would I turn my fortress over to a band of Northmen if not by force?"

Madrena, who sat across from Elisead, actually rolled her eyes, but Alaric shot her a warning glance.

"We've been over this, Maelcon," he said patiently.

"That's *Chief*." Drostan remained standing by her father's chair, rigid and tight-lipped.

Alaric held Drostan in his gaze for a long moment before nodding slightly in acquiescence.

"You must stop thinking of us an invaders, *Chief*, and see us as settlers."

Maelcon's cheeks turned red above his beard. "Do not invaders arrive uninvited? And do not invaders demand admittance into my home? Do not invaders simply *take* the land they want, pretense of negotiations be damned? Nay, man, you are not merely settlers!"

Alaric's fist hammered down on the table, sending the cups and bowls bouncing. Elisead jumped and stifled a scream behind her hand.

"I have said it before, but you make me say it again."

Alaric's voice was surprisingly even given his obvious annoyance. "If we had simply wanted to destroy your people and your land, we would have done so already."

"More threats from the purportedly peaceful settlers," Maelcon shot back.

Alaric leaned back in his chair, considering her father with sharp eyes. "Ja, I suppose you are right. I have threatened you in order for you to see the benefit in working peacefully with me."

Now it was Maelcon's turn to stare narrow-eyed at Alaric. "And what is the benefit to *you* of remaining peaceful?"

It was a question that Elisead had longed to ask Alaric as well. These Northmen didn't behave the way she'd expected, and though she'd spent nigh two full days in their presence, she still couldn't make sense of Alaric's motivation for leaving her people un-accosted.

Alaric smiled and casually rubbed the dark gold stubble bristling his jawline. "I fear you will mistake my motives for weakness, but I trust you know that such an error would be deadly wrong. I take it you know little of the Northlands?"

Maelcon frowned. "Only rumors."

"It is a harsh land, to be sure, made harsher in recent years by a terrible string of winters. My people are primed to thrive, yet the land seems to wish to keep us in check." Alaric shrugged. "So we seek new land."

Her father leaned forward. "That isn't an answer. I'll have your true aims out of you, for I would be a fool to trust you otherwise."

Alaric chuckled, surprising Elisead once again.

"Very well. Consider my options. My crew and I could have laid siege to your fortress. After we'd taken it, we could have slaughtered everyone within its walls. Then for sport, we might have burned down the huts outside. We'd set fire to your crops, just to make sure that your neighbors understood our ability to completely destroy them."

Both Maelcon and Drostan visibly tensed at the scene Alaric painted. The man gave no hint that what he spoke of caused him any qualms. Elisead repressed a gasp. Was he truly the same as the other murderous, destructive Northmen after all?

But then Alaric dropped his removed air and leaned forward, holding her father with his gaze.

"Setting aside the fact that such a course of action is utterly shameful and dishonorable according to my gods and my people, it would be foolish and short-sighted as well. We'd have naught to eat come winter. If we destroyed the fortress and the village, we'd have nowhere to take shelter when those neighbors whom we threatened with our very presence came hunting for us. And we wouldn't even know our enemies from our allies."

Her father stroked his beard, clearly pleased to have gotten the information out of him.

"And although I'd hoped to…encourage you toward peaceful negotiations with the knowledge that I can take away your choices," Alaric went on, his eyes flashing, "you have your reasons as well. Who would dare challenge a Chief with a band of Northmen two score strong at his back?"

"Aye," Maelcon said with a slight nod of his head.

"But that brings us to another patch of thistles. You say your men will be at my back. Does that mean I'll be their chieftain? Or would you seek to usurp my power and name yourself chieftain?"

Once again they were back to staring at each other coolly across the wooden expanse of the high table.

Suddenly, Alaric pushed his chair back and stood. "Let that be the starting point of our next discussion. I think we've accomplished enough for the day."

Maelcon stood as well, clearly not used to following another man's lead. But Alaric took command of the situation with such ease, with such self-assuredness, that Elisead doubted he ever found himself trailing after others.

As they all made their way from the great hall to the yard, her father caught her arm.

"You are sure you are well?"

Elisead knew that as she stepped into the sun-drenched yard, her blush wouldn't go unnoticed.

"Aye, Father, I am fine." Why heat flooded her cheeks, though, she could not comprehend.

She was more than fine under Alaric's care. In fact, she couldn't make sense of how safe she felt in his presence. It was simply because he needed her to continue these tense negotiations, she reminded herself firmly.

Maelcon kept a grip on her upper arm but raised his voice to ensure the others heard him as well. "Good, because these talks will only continue if you are kept unharmed and untouched."

Her cheeks flamed even hotter, for suddenly she thought of all the times Alaric had touched her. He'd held her hand, and gripped her waist as she'd stepped down from the cart, and had even caressed a lock of her hair.

They were undoubtedly intimate touches—mostly unnecessary for her wellbeing. Each moment of contact seemed to please Alaric, for his eyes glowed whenever they touched. She, too, felt a strange flutter at every touch, however brief or utilitarian.

Shame at her own reactions flooded her. He was a Northman and she a Pictish maiden engaged to another. Her body had no right to respond to his handsome features and powerful form the way it did.

"I am a man of my word," Alaric said coolly in response to her father. "I promised to keep Elisead safe, and I will."

Madrena broke the tension by moving in to say her farewells once more. Elisead had to avert her eyes when Rúnin took Madrena in his arms firmly and the two shared a lusty kiss. They whispered in their own language for a moment before Madrena turned and gave her brother a hard hug and a pound on the back, strong as any warrior.

Then Feitr approached from the stables, the same donkey and cart in tow that they had brought back that morn.

Alaric frowned. "I wished to return those to you."

"I appreciate the gesture," Maelcon said. "But when these negotiations come to a conclusion, you'll need them to safely transport my daughter and her bride gift back to me."

When, not if. And Elisead didn't miss her father's

second overt warning to Alaric in as many moments that his daughter was to remain pure for her impending marriage.

"How goes your work on the stone, daughter?" he asked as he stepped to Elisead's side and assisted her into the cart.

"It goes," she said vaguely. Truth be told, she'd barely worked on it since entering the Northmen's camp. Late summer—and her wedding—loomed ahead, yet there was still so much to be done.

Maelcon eyed her for a moment before huffing and turning away.

Feitr stepped aside as Alaric approached the donkey and cart, the slave's pale blond head lowered. But Elisead didn't miss the defiant flash of Feitr's eyes as he dared a glance up at Alaric.

Strange. Feitr had never been content as a slave in her father's fortress, but such was the fate of a captured enemy. He was not treated cruelly, only expected to work hard.

What had just silently passed between Feitr and Alaric? And what had Feitr said yestereve that had upset Alaric enough that she hadn't seen him again until this morn?

The fort's gates were pulled open and the iron grille lifted. Elisead refused to look back as they cleared the walls and began their descent to the Northmen's camp.

Nevertheless, she sensed Feitr's gaze lingering on her, and unease tingled between her shoulder blades.

15

Alaric resisted the urge to kick a fist-sized chunk of rock lying in his path.

He was the leader of forty Northlanders, selected by his Jarl to create a new settlement in this land, not some petulant child.

Still, Maelcon's stubbornness and resistance to the negotiations grated.

Alaric glanced at Elisead, who sat with her back straight, hands in her lap and looking calm despite the jostling cart she sat in. There was more at stake in these negotiations than his pride or his patience. His people were counting on him, and so was Elisead.

He felt Rúnin's eyes on him, so he quickly dropped his gaze from his hostage.

By Odin, why did she have to be so beautiful? Her auburn hair shone like polished copper in the midday sun. Her skin was pale, despite the fact that she clearly loved being out in the fresh air. And her form—she was smaller than most Northwomen, but her feminine curves were more than enough to keep a man enthralled for all his days.

And it wasn't just her delicate beauty that kept distracting him. There was something about her—some air of otherworldliness, of mystery. She might indeed be a forest spirit, for she seemed touched by a god—either hers or one of his.

Thor's bloody hammer, he was staring again. She was not his to ogle, nor would he ever break his word and risk his entire mission falling apart. His people were counting on him—desire for this Pict woman be damned.

But judging from Maelcon's continued hesitancy to trust Alaric, these negotiations could draw on for several more sennights. And that meant Elisead would be sleeping in Alaric's tent, eating around his fire, and entrancing him with her every breath during that time.

Alaric bit down on a curse. He was stronger than his desire. He had to be.

They began their descent down the sloping hillside upon which Maelcon's fortress sat. The village spread below them, and beyond that, the woods separating the fortress from Alaric's camp stood dark and quiet.

The village was still and empty, for the villagers had once again removed themselves to the fortress, just in case the Northmen had planned to lay waste to their homes rather than negotiate.

The donkey leading the cart was letting the slope of the hill do some of his work for him. He and the cart were speeding up, so Alaric took the donkey's harness firmly in hand.

Suddenly a stone came flying through the air. It hit the donkey's flank, spooking the animal.

Alaric didn't have time to glance behind him in search of the stone's thrower for the donkey bolted, ripping the harness from Alaric's hand.

Elisead screamed in surprise as she went plummeting down the hill in the cart. Alaric took off after it, Rúnin on his heels, but the donkey and cart were gaining speed.

"Hold on!" Alaric shouted to Elisead, but he wasn't sure she'd be able to hear him.

The animal, cart, and Elisead careened through the deserted huts. Just as the sloping hill leveled off, Alaric heard a snap.

The donkey was suddenly free of the cart. He sprang to the side and slowed to a trot as the cart sped onward.

"Secure the animal!" Alaric shouted over his shoulder to Rúnin. Without waiting to see if his friend did as he bid, Alaric sprinted after the cart. It had built up enough momentum coming down the hill that even now it plowed past the edge of the village and toward the dense forest.

"Alaric!" Elisead screamed. Her red hair streamed behind her wildly and she clung desperately to the cart.

Alaric had noticed immediately upon first seeing the cart that it was a simple wooden contraption. The wheels were fixed to their axles, and the axles were attached directly to the cart's bed, so that the cart couldn't turn unless guided by man or beast.

Now that knowledge sent a stab of fear into his chest. Elisead was barreling directly toward the thick forest with no way to control the cart.

Alaric pushed his legs to their limit. At last he seemed to gain some ground on the runaway cart, for the grassy earth was nigh level now. But in just seconds, Elisead would be thrown into the woods.

The cart flew between two trees, and Alaric knew he was out of time. He hurdled over a fallen log, never losing his pace, and at last came even with the cart.

"Reach for me!" he shouted to Elisead. He only granted the side of his vision to avoiding low-hanging limbs and protruding roots. His gaze was focused on Elisead, who clung to the cart as it bumped and jostled over the uneven forest floor.

She extended one arm but was nearly thrown from the cart as the wheels thumped over a series of roots.

There was no more time for delay. Alaric lunged forward, clamping his arms around Elisead and yanking her hard from the front of the cart. He lost his footing from the effort. The two of them went tumbling to the ground.

They rolled over and over again. Alaric wrapped his arms even tighter around Elisead, trying to take the brunt of the impact with his own body. Distantly, he registered a loud crack and the sound of splintering wood.

After what felt like ages of endless tumbling, they finally skidded to a halt. Elisead felt so small and limp in his arms, but he could feel her chest rapidly rising and falling against his.

Slowly, Alaric eased himself up to sitting. Never loosening his hold on Elisead, he brought her up with him.

"Are you hurt?"

She lifted her head and blinked up at him. Her amber eyes were clouded with lingering fear and confusion.

"Nay, I do not think so."

Just then, a trickle of blood slipped from her hairline and down her forehead.

Alaric cursed and wiped the blood away with the sleeve of his tunic. Careful not to hurt her, he probed her scalp and found the cut, small but flowing freely. He pressed his sleeve against the wound, drawing a wince from Elisead.

"What happened?" she asked.

Just then, Rúnin sprinted into Alaric's line of sight. Alaric waved, though he kept one arm firmly wrapped around Elisead.

Rúnin dragged the donkey, who was calm now but panting heavily, behind him by the harness.

"Are you well?"

"Ja. Though we would have ended up like the cart if I'd been a breath slower." Alaric motioned with his chin behind Rúnin, where the cart lay in splinters. It had slammed full force into an enormous oak tree.

"There is foul play afoot," Rúnin said darkly as he came to a halt where Alaric and Elisead sat.

"Speak in our tongue," Alaric said sharply in his and

Rúnin's language. "There is no need to frighten her further."

Rúnin nodded. "When I caught up to this beast, it was obvious that his harness had been cut."

Alaric stood slowly at last. His body ached from taking the worst of the impact and protecting Elisead, but naught felt broken or seriously damaged. He stepped stiffly to Rúnin's side, blocking Elisead's view of the donkey with his back.

Sure enough, the leather harness had cleanly snapped—too cleanly. Only a sharp knife taken with purpose to the harness would cause it to break in such a way.

"Who?" Rúnin said quietly.

It had been Feitr who'd brought the cart and donkey from the stables. The slave had glared daggers at Alaric. And his ominous words from the night before—either a warning or a threat, Alaric knew not which—still rang in Alaric's ears.

But Feitr was a slave, meaning that he followed orders—Maelcon's orders. Would Maelcon dare to harm his own daughter? He'd dragged his feet at every moment during their negotiations. Was the chieftain looking for a way out of their talks?

If only Alaric had been able to see who'd thrown the rock at the donkey, spooking him and causing the already-cut harness to snap.

"We have enemies at every turn in this new land," Alaric muttered.

"Ja, but this was aimed at the girl. Who would want to hurt her?"

Alaric rolled his neck, aware of the ache that was forming from his tumble. "Our negotiations with the Picts ride on Elisead's wellbeing. If she were to come to harm…"

"Then the negotiations would be destroyed," Rúnin finished.

"Ja. Who would benefit most from ending our talks and setting our peoples against each other?"

Rúnin lifted a dark eyebrow. "As you say, enemies are everywhere."

Alaric cursed and rubbed his neck. Someone—or several someones—worked against him. And whoever it was didn't mind risking Elisead's life in the process. She was now not simply his hostage. She needed his protection.

"Alaric, what is happening?"

Elisead sat on the forest floor, a fresh trickle of blood sliding down her forehead. Her brows were knitted as she gazed up at him. Gods, but there was a look of trust behind the confusion in her honey-colored eyes.

He turned away from Rúnin and extended a hand toward her.

"Naught," he lied flatly.

"But…but he said foul play was afoot," she said, her gaze flicking to Rúnin.

"Do not concern yourself. He merely fears that your father will be upset that his cart has been destroyed. But it was an accident, a freak occurrence."

His stomach twisted as he watched her absorb his lie.

He'd called himself a man of honor, but he wasn't

above lying to Elisead if it meant keeping her safe. If it was truly all an unfortunate happenstance, he needn't worry her pointlessly. Of course, he didn't believe for a second that the smoothly sliced harness was an accident, in which case frightening Elisead with the truth wouldn't keep her any safer.

When Elisead placed her hand in his, he lifted her to her feet. But when she stumbled, he scooped her up, not trusting her shaky legs to carry her back to camp.

He'd be damned by Odin himself if he gave in to these intimidation tactics. Yet the thought of Elisead being harmed for the purpose of keeping him from his mission sent a stab of fear into his belly.

No matter what, he had to protect Elisead. His mission was riding on it.

But it was more than that. Some invisible thread tugged at him, binding him to her. He would protect her with everything he had. But protect her from whom?

16

As Alaric walked into camp, his crew's activities stilled. With Elisead cradled against his chest and Rúnin pulling the cart-less donkey behind him, he was sure they made quite the sight.

Alaric felt Elisead stiffen in his arms at all the stares. His fingers dug into her soft flesh, longing to shield her from the scrutiny. Instead, he strode swiftly to the tent Elisead now used as her own. The subtle but sweet scent of her hair and skin lingered within, enveloping him as he stepped inside.

He set her gently on the mattress at the back, then turned to go. But she caught his sleeve, which was still red with her blood.

"Alaric, something goes on. Why won't you tell me?"

She gazed up at him, her pleading eyes rending him like a knife.

"As I said, 'tis naught. Rest here for the day. The cut

seems to have stopped bleeding, but you needn't push yourself."

Elisead's soft lips curved down as she continued to stare up at him. But at last, she leaned back against the downy mattress with a sigh. Her dark lashes fluttered closed as she succumbed to fatigue.

Alaric should have turned away, but it was as if his feet were rooted in place, his eyes drinking in the sight before him thirstily.

Elisead's auburn hair spread out beneath her head, wild and windblown. Her delicate features were at last easing out of their frown, though even in dismay she was stunning.

As her breathing evened, he watched her breasts rise and fall. With each inhale, those pert peaks strained against her finely made tunic, which was soiled and stained from their tumble in the forest.

What would those soft breasts feel like in his hands? Could he make her now-steady breaths catch in her throat with a swish of his thumb—or his tongue?

Alaric ripped his gaze away and stormed to the tent's flaps.

What in Hel's realm was he doing? He wasn't fool enough to deny his attraction to the Pict chieftain's daughter, but he knew better than to indulge in the kind of lust-filled musings that had nigh made him lose control just now. His manhood stirred rebelliously under his tunic. Bloody hammer, not only did he not have time for such thoughts, but they threatened his entire mission.

He yanked back one of the tent's flaps and stomped out into the bright sunlight. Several members of his crew had gathered in front of the tent, waiting for him to emerge.

"What happened?" asked Tarr, the brown-headed youth who'd worked so hard over the last several months to join this voyage. "Rúnin wouldn't answer us. He said he'd let you explain."

Alaric flicked a glance at Rúnin, who was tying the donkey to a nearby tree. He gave Rúnin a swift nod of thanks, then pushed his way through the gathered crowd.

"Naught but an accident. The donkey was spooked on our way from the fort."

That didn't seem to ease the lowered brows and looks ranging between concern and suspicion at Alaric's strange reappearance in the camp.

"And negotiations—how did your talk with the chieftain go?" Tarr probed. Though he was only a few years younger than Alaric, Tarr had an earnest determination about him that made Alaric forget just how sharply perceptive he was at times.

"Well enough. The old man still wishes to be courted—or coerced," Alaric said, which drew some chuckles.

He made his way to the makeshift fire pit set off from the other tents. Though the day promised to be warm, he tilted his hands over the banked embers from the night before. It was something to do as his mind churned over the events of the last hour.

Most of his crew began dispersing to the tasks they'd abandoned when Alaric had arrived with Elisead in his arms. Some resumed sparring along the bay's shoreline, while others took up mending their tents and clothes or tended to their weapons.

A few, however, followed Alaric to the fire pit.

"Was he amenable to giving us a portion of his farmlands?" Tarr took up a seat on a stump across the fire pit from Alaric.

"It hasn't come up yet," Alaric said through clenched teeth.

Tarr pressed his lips together but was wise enough to leave the topic alone.

Olaf, the red bear of a man, was not so wise, however. He snorted loudly as he took a seat on a stump next to Tarr.

"What is this *courting* of our enemies? Why have we not simply taken the fort from that blustering old chieftain and be done with it?"

Alaric felt his already grim mood darken. "If *you* had been placed in charge of this voyage by Jarl Eirik, the village, the fort, and all the Picts living here would be wiped away with naught to build on."

Olaf, clearly missing Alaric's dangerous tone, cracked his knuckles with satisfaction. He'd mistaken Alaric's warning for a compliment. "Ja. Wiped clean and ready for our own settlement. We are Northmen, are we not?"

In one deadly swift step, Alaric cleared the fire pit and was standing in front of Olaf. The red-haired giant jerked to his feet, meeting Alaric. Though the older man was broad, tall, and battle-proven, Alaric's sudden rage would give him more than enough strength to best Olaf if necessary. He would not be challenged.

"But you were not put in charge, Olaf Skull Splitter," Alaric said, barely maintaining control over his fists, which he clenched at his sides. "*I was*. That is because I know when to fight and when to talk. And I also know when to keep my mouth shut."

Olaf jutted out his chin, sending his red beard quivering. But at last the old bear took Alaric's meaning. He grunted, then lowered himself onto his stump once more in clear concession to Alaric.

Alaric turned to the others who'd followed him to the fire pit. Rúnin, Tarr, Olaf, and Geirr, who'd earned a spot on this voyage at the same time Tarr had, all stared silently at him.

"Does anyone else have something to say about my decision to pursue these negotiations?" Alaric snapped. He knew he shouldn't be taking his rage at the attack on Elisead out on his men, but he would suffer not a whiff of dissention among his crew. They needed to know who their leader was.

At the silence that met him, Alaric waved his hand, dismissing the men. All but Rúnin got up immediately and busied themselves elsewhere.

"Do you have something to add, Rúnin?" Alaric bit out crossly.

"You know that I, more than anyone here, appreciate the value of avoiding open conflict," Rúnin said quietly. "I stand by you."

Alaric pushed out a breath and sank to one of the stumps ringing the fire pit. "Ja, and I thank you." After nigh fourteen years as an outlaw, Rúnin had survived far worse than what Alaric was dealing with now.

Perhaps Alaric's judgement was clouded by his over-powering desire to fulfill the responsibility placed on his shoulders by Eirik.

"What would you do, knowing what you know?" Alaric asked carefully, catching Rúnin's gaze.

Rúnin exhaled slowly. "You are right to follow a diplomatic route, but I sense that is not what you're asking."

At Alaric's nod, Rúnin went on.

"You won't like my answer, but here it is. You must wait. If you suspect Maelcon is behind the incident this morning and you confront him, you'll destroy any chance for a peaceful settlement between our peoples. And if Maelcon is not responsible…" Rúnin shrugged. "If the plan was to harm the Pict girl to foil negotiations, the plan failed. Whoever is plotting against us will be forced to strike again."

Alaric narrowed his eyes at Rúnin. "You are right—I do not like your answer. So you are suggesting that I leave Elisead open to attack? That she will be the bait to lure whoever is trying to destroy these negotiations?"

Rúnin leaned forward, his voice low but sharp. "Think clearly, Alaric. It is obvious you desire the girl for yourself. I didn't want you to put Madrena in harm's way, yet despite my frustration over the situation, I understand that it had to be done for the larger mission."

Anger surged in Alaric's veins, but he clamped his mouth closed on a retort.

Ja, he'd knowingly put his sister in danger in order to achieve his aim of a peaceful settlement. But Alaric would never doubt that Madrena could take care of herself. Elisead, on the other hand, seemed so fragile, so vulnerable. She wasn't a fierce and skilled warrior like Madrena.

Still, Rúnin was right. Alaric wasn't thinking clearly, and it was because of the flame-haired beauty sleeping in his tent as they spoke.

Alaric's gaze drifted from the dying embers to Tarr, who had returned to where his wife, Eyva, had been practicing her sword work. Eyva's presence in camp was a constant reminder to Alaric that she was there at Madrena's insistence. How did his sister fare in the midst of the Pict fortress?

An idea began to form as he watched the two. They had earned their place on this voyage as skilled warriors, but he'd considered it an added bonus that they'd both been farmers before that.

"Maelcon will continue to drag his feet," Alaric said to Rúnin even as he continued to consider Tarr and Eyva. "Which means that the longer these negotiations stretch, the more danger Elisead and Madrena are in."

Without having to look at him, Alaric could sense Rúnin's displeasure. But a plan was taking shape in his mind's eye.

"Perhaps we can force his hand, though," Alaric went on.

He glanced around the camp. Their tents could be taken down and packed away in the longships on the bay's shore a stone's throw away in a matter of minutes. The only alteration they'd made to their camp was to cut down a few saplings.

"What did you have in mind?"

"Tarr, Eyva!" Alaric called, not answering Rúnin's question.

The two newlyweds stopped their sparring immediately and strode toward Alaric.

"Gather a dozen men of your choosing, and have them bring freshly sharpened axes. Bring the ards and seeds we brought to sow as well."

Tarr and Eyva exchanged a surprised look, but Alaric hardly noticed, so fast was his mind racing.

"Are we…planting fields?" Eyva asked hesitantly.

"Nei, not just planting fields," Alaric said. "We are making ourselves at home."

Rúnin snorted, which was nigh as close as the man came to laughing. But he gave Alaric a little nod. "I'll go with them. 'Twill be a relief to lean my back into something productive."

As Tarr and Eyva moved off to gather the supplies and men they needed, Rúnin paused in joining them.

"So, you'll force Maelcon's hand by beginning to settle on his lands whether he likes it or not?" he asked, lifting one dark eyebrow.

"Exactly."

"And if he sees your move of clearing land and planting fields as an act of aggression?"

Alaric felt a smile play around his mouth, and this time, it wasn't one he'd strategically plastered there. Nei, genuine excitement swelled within him now.

"As you said, we need to apply ourselves productively, even if he wishes to talk in circles all summer. He can either go along with us, or sit by while we bring in our crops year after year—without our protection at his back."

Rúnin nodded again, his blue eyes dancing. He extended his arm to Alaric, who took it in a firm grip.

As Rúnin released his hold and strode toward Tarr and Eyva, Alaric glanced down at his arm. Blood—Elisead's blood—still darkened his sleeve. He was gambling with her life as well as Madrena's.

The thought sent a stone of foreboding into his belly. He needed to think clearly, as Rúnin had said—like a leader, not a besotted lad. And to think clearly, he needed to clean himself.

A dunk in fresh water would order his thoughts. Alaric set out toward the river.

17

Elisead awoke with a start to the sounds of shouting, clanging metal, and the pounding of feet.

She bolted upright, unsure for a moment where she was. Male voices calling to each other in the guttural, rolling language of the Northmen filtered through the thin material of the tent's walls and roof.

The now-familiar interior of the tent soothed her from her initial fright. She lay atop the downy mattress and furs that Alaric had meant to use himself. Her chest of clothes and personal items sat at its foot. The enormous stone that was to be her bride gift rested untouched along the other side of the tent.

Nay, she wasn't in the middle of a Northman's siege, despite the noise to the contrary. She slipped from the mattress and crept toward the tent's door. Lifting one of the flaps slightly, she peered out.

Afternoon sun beat down on the little camp, which was swarming with activity. Some of the Northmen were lifting chests onto their shoulders, though she could only guess at their contents. Others hoisted long, flat slabs of iron the length of a man's body and began carrying them away into the woods.

Two Northmen stood in the center of it all, apparently giving orders. Except while one was a tall young man with light brown hair, the other wasn't a man at all.

It was the woman Alaric had pointed out before. She seemed impossibly small compared to the Northmen all around, but she was likely similar in size to Elisead. Unlike the others, who, except for Rúnin, had hair in shades ranging from light brown to white blond or flame red, the woman was dark-headed.

As before, Elisead had to marvel at the young woman. Even amongst all the towering blond warriors, she held herself with authority and confidence.

The flurry of activity was suddenly shifting direction. Under the man and woman's commands, the dozen or so Northmen began moving off into the woods and away from the camp.

Elisead exhaled and let the tent flap drop. Though no one had threatened her in any way, she couldn't help but feel relieved to have some space between her and all those Northland warriors.

But the interior of the tent was growing warm as the sun beat down on it. Elisead reached up to wipe a bead of sweat from her forehead, only to have her fingertips encounter a few flakes of crusted blood. She felt her scalp where she'd split it on a rock during that petrifying tumble away from the cart with Alaric.

If she let herself dwell on it, she'd have to admit that while being in the runaway cart had been terrifying, tumbling in Alaric's arms hadn't been. Or perhaps it was terrifying in a different way, for she felt strangely safe in his embrace, yet also precariously poised on the edge of danger—danger of doing something she shouldn't, feeling something she shouldn't.

She shoved the thoughts away. What she needed was a bath to clear her muddled thoughts and rid herself of the crusted blood that served to remind her of the tangle of events earlier that day.

Perhaps now was the perfect time to steal off to the river while the others at camp were away. Elisead hadn't seen Alaric in their midst, but that was just as well. He was so often her shadow. No matter where she was around camp—and she mostly stayed in his tent—she always sensed his presence nearby.

No wonder her thoughts were clouded. How could she be expected to remain clearheaded when a giant, golden Northman was constantly watching her with those piercing emerald eyes?

Elisead moved to her wooden chest and snatched a clean underdress and tunic. She tucked a piece of heather-scented soap and her bone comb between the garments' folds and stood. With a careful peek outside the tent once more, she slipped past its protection and made her way toward the river.

So lost in thought was she as she walked that she didn't hear the splashing until it was nigh too late. She jerked her head up just as she was clearing the tree line along the river's bank.

Rising from the slow-moving river like a god from the old ways…was Alaric.

Elisead's breath caught in her throat. Her chest squeezed painfully.

Water sluiced off his golden head as he emerged from the river. Little streams flowed over his bare, broad shoulders, surprisingly bronzed by the sun.

He began to turn toward the bank, the slick muscles of his arms catching the light and rippling with movement.

Barely suppressing a squeak of horror, Elisead flung herself behind a wide tree trunk. Had he seen her? Would he march over to her—unclothed—and demand to know why she was lurking like a spy in the woods while he bathed?

She held her breath, her heart hammering loudly in her ears. But instead of the sounds of approaching footsteps, all she heard was sloshing water. Mayhap if Alaric had slipped below the river's surface, she could slink away with him none the wiser.

Elisead dared a darting glance around the tree trunk, but to her dismay, Alaric's head was still above water. He'd turned more fully toward her, exposing the naked expanse of his chest.

Sunlight rippled on the water's surface, bouncing up to make little patterns across his torso. Though the shimmering, liquid light did its best to soften him, every line of his body was hard. She might as well have carved him from stone.

The thought sent heat flooding her body. Images assailed her—of her fingers running a pebble along every groove and ridge across his chest and abdomen. She sank her teeth into her bottom lip to keep from crying out with need or laughing hysterically—she wasn't sure which she'd do at the moment, so addled were her thoughts.

By every god she'd ever heard whispers of, he was a work of art—nay, he was better. He was perfection.

She ducked back behind the tree trunk just as Alaric brought his golden head up. For the briefest of moments, she saw a flash of green as his eyes caught the light.

Her lungs felt close to bursting. Clamping a hand over her mouth to quiet her breaths, she sat transfixed behind the tree. Water splashed again, and this time she was sure he'd seen her.

But his commanding voice or the thundering footfalls of his approach never came. Instead, the sound of deep, rumbling humming drifted to her. She heard the rustle of clothing, followed by a faint scraping sound.

Just when her heart was finally slowing its galloping pace, he spoke.

"You can come out now."

Mortification washed over her, but there was no point in hiding any longer or pretending she wasn't there.

Slowly, she rose to her feet and stepped from behind the cover of the tree.

Alaric crouched along the bank of the river, his back

—now clothed in a linen tunic—facing her. He was drawing a small blade over the stubble on his cheek.

Clutching her bundle of clothes to her chest, she walked past the tree line and onto the bank. Alaric glanced up at her, his green eyes dancing with merriment. Despite her embarrassment, she kept her head up, refusing to be shamed.

All at once, he erupted into laughter. Great barks of laughter. Seemingly never-ending rolls of laughter.

"You can hold your head up like a queen, girl, but that doesn't change the fact that your cheeks are bright red!"

Despite her bluster, she felt her bottom lip tremble in utter humiliation. More heat flooded her face, and she quickly looked away so as not to be blinded by his wide, radiant grin.

Suddenly his laughter cut off and he was looming over her, his golden head blocking the sun from her eyes.

"I only meant to tease you, Elisead, not cause you dishonor." His voice was a low, silky caress against her flaming cheeks.

She tried to turn her face down in order to hide the obvious sign of her guilt, but he captured her chin in one of his large, warm hands.

"You were watching me."

It wasn't an accusation, for he spoke softly. Yet his hand on her chin forced her to meet his vivid eyes.

"A-aye."

"Why?"

She swallowed hard. "I only meant to come to the

river for a bath. I didn't expect to find you here, but you were—"

"Nei, I gathered that," he said, his gaze flicking for the briefest moment to the bundle of clean clothes she still clutched against herself like a shield. "I mean, why did you continue to watch me when you found me bathing?"

"I..." Hot humiliation burned in her throat and stung her eyes. What could she say? *I kept looking because you remind me of the finest carved stone I could ever imagine? Because you are formed like one of your pagan gods?*

It was too much. Her throat closed and her lip trembled again.

Now a look of compassion crossed his once-mirthful eyes—compassion and something else much darker as his gaze dipped to her lower lip, which quivered just above his thumb.

"You've never seen a man's bare body before."

Again, it wasn't a question, but unlike before, his voice held an unfathomable suggestion in it.

She shook her head in confirmation, unable to speak.

He breathed a curse. "And I doubt you've ever been kissed before either?"

Again, she shook her head. The hot shame from a moment before was transforming into something new. It melted her insides and at the same time knotted them into a tight ball deep in her center.

Alaric pinned her with his gaze, but now all teasing had fled from his emerald eyes. He swished his thumb along her chin until he brushed her lower lip.

Elisead sucked in a breath, for though his hands were callused, his touch was feather light.

Somehow he drew even closer, despite the fact that they'd already been nigh touching. She could feel the heat of his body curling around her even through their clothes.

She squeezed her eyes shut, expecting at any minute that he'd slam into her, claiming her mouth the way that Northmen did everything—savagely. And far off in the back of her mind, she wanted him to. She wanted him to be the first to kiss her, to feel those soft, expressive lips on hers.

His thumb brushed across her lower lip again, making her jump with anticipation. Then she felt a hot breath close to her mouth. She inhaled, suddenly flooded with his clean, piney scent.

Each moment stretched as she stood suspended, unable and unwilling to move. His breath fanned over her lips once more, and she feared she would melt into a puddle along the riverbank.

Then at last his lips made contact with hers. But instead of a crushing kiss, it was the lightest, feather-soft brush. His mouth, at times so firm and at others so playful, was surprisingly gentle.

The hand on her chin slid along her jawline to the nape of her neck, holding her in place while he pressed more completely into her lips. He tilted his head so that their mouths slanted against each other, and suddenly they fit perfectly, as if their lips had always been meant to meld together this way.

She was drowning in sensation. Her scalp tingled

where his fingers entwined in the hair at her nape. Her hands turned to claws in the bundle of clothes she clutched to her chest. And her lips—her lips were singing against his, coming alive in a way she never knew possible.

It was all so much. She swayed on her feet, hardly able to tell up from down anymore. His other arm came around her back and steadied her by pulling her against the rock wall of his chest. He was so warm and yet so hard.

And then his tongue brushed her lips. She gasped at the intimacy of such an act. But in doing so, she opened her mouth, and their tongues touched.

Ever so slowly, he caressed her, the kiss turning to liquid heat. Their tongues danced and embraced in an unhurried rhythm. She let him lead, unsure of how to stretch this perfect moment, to deepen the waves of pleasure washing over her. But soon she began to understand, and she met his strokes with her own.

He groaned, and she felt the vibrations travel from his chest to their lips. His hand tightened in her hair, shooting tingles of sensation down her spine—and between her legs.

What was happening to her body? It was as if her whole being had suddenly caught fire, kindled at the point where their mouths melted together.

Suddenly, he ripped his mouth away and dropped his hands from her as if he had been burned. He took an abrupt step backward, leaving naught but empty air between them.

Though the day was sunny, the absence of Alaric's warm body sent a shiver through her.

"I...I shouldn't have done that," Alaric said. His voice was ragged and low, but his gaze still scorched her with desire.

Elisead felt her eyes widen. "Nor should I," she breathed.

What had come over her? And over him? She was to be married to another come the end of summer. And Alaric had promised to leave her untouched, else his negotiations would fall apart.

How could she let a Northman kiss her? Besides carving in secret against her father's wishes, she'd never done aught she wasn't supposed to. And surely the way Alaric's mouth had felt against hers, the way his hands had gripped her to him, the heat that had passed between them, couldn't be right.

"I'll be back at camp," he said, at last averting his gaze. "You can bathe here without fear of disturbance."

She nodded quickly and dropped her chin, once again feeling the warmth of shame touch her cheeks. A moment later when she raised her head, Alaric had vanished into the trees.

Elisead hurriedly plopped her clean clothes on a nearby rock. As she began to work the laces at the back of her tunic, her gaze darted around the silent woods lining the river. It felt as though the trees hid a thousand eyes.

Had anyone seen her kissing Alaric? Had they seen her spy on him as he bathed? What would she feel if she knew his dancing green eyes watched her now as she undressed?

Cool air fanned her heated flesh as she ripped off her tunic and underdress with one yank. She kicked off her boots even as she scrambled for the cover of the river.

At last, she sank underwater, but even with her nakedness concealed, she felt more exposed than ever.

18

"**Y**ou should be the first."

Alaric yanked his thoughts away from Elisead—her soft lips, untried until he'd claimed them, her rapid breaths, those honeyed eyes that threatened to drown him in their sweet depths.

Tarr raised a light brown eyebrow at him. Bloody hammer, was Alaric's line of thinking so obvious to the others?

"You should be the first to try the ard, that is," Tarr said. He held the ropes that led from the donkey's mended harness to the iron ard. With raised hands, he extended the rope ends toward Alaric.

Alaric needed to focus on the task before him—plowing, though not the kind his body craved. With a silent curse for himself, he shoved his lust away.

"Shouldn't one of you farmers do it?" he said, eyeing Tarr and Eyva. Unlike them, Alaric had been raised from birth to be a warrior, not a farmer.

Eyva snorted and Tarr only grinned.

"Nei, you're our leader. You should cut the first row."

"Very well," Alaric said, reluctantly taking the ropes from Tarr's hand. He snapped his wrists, making the rope thwack against the donkey's flanks.

Slowly the animal got underway. He was clearly unused to pulling the long, flat blade of metal the Northlanders used to cut rows in soil. But when the donkey finally took up a steady walking pace, the ard cut through the soil like a knife through cream. Ards were made to slice through the hard, rocky ground of the Northlands. The soil here, however, was dark, rich, and loamy—perfect for Alaric's purposes.

Alaric walked behind the donkey and ard, straddling the deep furrow the ard cut in the ground with his feet. A cheer went up behind him. He'd initially told Tarr and Eyva to gather a dozen of the crew, but soon nigh thirty of his men had joined the effort.

The last four days had been entirely spent in clearing this patch of forest. Axes had whirred through the air as the men chopped trees and cleared underbrush.

They'd hacked the worst trees apart to use for fire-wood, but dragged the best back to camp. Though they didn't have a ship builder among their number on this voyage, Alaric knew good wood when he saw it. It could be saved until next summer, when hopefully more of his people would arrive from Dalgaard, ready to build homes and perhaps even a new fleet of longships.

Blessedly, the work had kept Alaric busy from dawn

until dusk. By the time he returned to camp each night, he barely had enough energy to eat a simple meal in front of the fire and fall into his pile of furs on the floor of Rúnin's tent.

He shouldn't have had the time or energy to think on his foolishness in kissing Elisead—or his desire to do so again. But his mind and body seemed to be colluding. His thoughts were muddled with the memory of her scent, her lips, her tongue, and his body throbbed with the need to—

Alaric cursed himself once more, willing his blood to cool for the hundredth time in the last four days.

She'd kept to herself, spending most of her time in the tent working on her bride gift—another blasted reminder of Alaric's dangerous interest in her. She was to be married to another, an alliance her father would no doubt kill over if it was endangered. And Alaric had his own mission to think of. If he hadn't gotten control of himself by the river, he might have betrayed all the responsibility Eirik had given him.

But even when he sweated under the midday sun, or when he fell exhausted into his furs at night, or any time he caught a glimpse of auburn hair through the tent's flaps, his responsibility seemed to flee his mind. All that was left was white-hot desire for his flame-haired, honey-eyed forest spirit.

Another wave of cheers snapped Alaric's attention back to his task. He guided the donkey to the right as they drew to the end of their newly formed row. The ard cut an arc into the soil, then began slicing another straight furrow in the ground next to the first.

As Alaric urged the donkey back toward the group of waiting Northlanders, a flash of red caught his attention. As if his thoughts had suddenly materialized, he spotted Elisead, who peered around the broad shoulders of his crewmen.

Alaric hurried to the end of the row, but before he made the next turn, he tossed the ropes to Tarr.

"I think you can take over from here," he said, his gaze seeking Elisead.

When she noticed him, her eyes widened slightly.

He moved to the back of the group of Northlanders and came to her side. "What are you doing here?" he said quietly.

Most of his crew continued to watch Tarr's progress with the ard, but some eyed their leader and his hostage with curiosity.

"I...I needed some fresh air," she said, looking away. "And I heard the noise."

They were only a stone's throw from camp, so the crew's enthusiasm must have been audible. Alaric's men had been more than eager to set their muscles to the job at hand. Their fervor was an indication of just how restless they'd all grown without hard work to do and how keen they were to make their settlement more permanent.

"Have you gotten word from my father?" she asked, as if intuiting the direction of his thoughts.

"Nei, naught."

If Maelcon was aware of what Alaric was up to, he'd likely be stewing behind his fortress walls. Or it was possible he hadn't noticed that the Northmen had decided to plant fields on his land, thus inviting themselves to stay for at least the summer.

As Tarr continued to plow rows in the soil, others began following him, dropping barley into the ruts left in his wake.

"Are we too late?" Alaric asked, glancing down at her.

She seemed startled at first by his question—or perhaps it was surprise at being asked her opinion.

"Nay, I don't believe so," she said after considering for a moment. "Though most fields have been sown and are already sprouting, the summer is early yet."

He nodded. "And what do you think of the spot we selected?"

Again surprise flitted across her delicate features. Unbidden pride swelled in Alaric's chest at the possibility that he was the only man to consult her for her knowledge. Her father was a great fool if he thought his daughter was only good for a marriage alliance.

Elisead scrutinized the little clearing they'd made. Though it was surrounded by tall trees on all sides, the sun was high enough in the sky to give the patch of ground a long swath of sunlight throughout the day— Tarr and Eyva had made sure of that when they'd picked this spot. The ground sloped slightly in the direction of the river to the north, allowing for good drainage.

"I'd say you've chosen well, though I know little of farming," she said, a pretty blush rising on her cheeks.

"But you have been raised on this land, and so you

are my expert in everything about this place," Alaric said softly.

She shook her head and looked at the ground. Gently, so as not to frighten her, he took her chin and lifted it slightly.

"Hasn't anyone told you that you are worth more than a mere bargaining chip in a marriage alliance?"

Her amber eyes widened, and suddenly Alaric felt like he was falling into them.

"Nay," she breathed.

"Not even about your stone carving? Surely others recognize your gift."

She shook her head on a swallow, freeing her chin from his light hold.

"You never showed me how you create such fine designs," he said.

That was because they'd been wisely keeping their distance from each other, a small voice cried in the back of his mind. It was dangerous to learn more about her, because every time he did, his desire for her drove deeper into him, taking root.

Alaric shoved the voice aside, too intoxicated by Elisead's nearness to heed its warning now. He tossed a look over his shoulder, but his crew was still occupied in sowing barley. Without waiting for her to form a response, he took her hand and led her back toward the camp.

When they reached her tent, Alaric lifted back the flaps of wool to allow light to stream inside. They stepped in together and crouched in front of the long stone.

She'd made progress since last he'd seen it. The border was nigh complete, and figures were beginning to take shape in the middle.

Alaric ran a finger along the curling leaves and forest creatures bordering the stone.

"Tell me how you do it."

Elisead reached into the pouch she always wore belted around her waist. She withdrew a lump of charcoal.

"First, I draw out the figures and designs I want." She touched the charcoal to the stone on a patch where the rock's surface was still smooth. With an easy hand, she swirled the outline of an oak leaf.

"Then I tap holes along the outside of my design," she said, returning the charcoal to her pouch. She scooted toward the wooden chest at the foot of her bed and returned with a small chisel and mallet. "It doesn't take much, just a few taps."

This time she didn't demonstrate, but Alaric could see a series of small chiseled divots outlining the last section of border that remained incomplete.

"And then I choose a pebble." Elisead set aside the chisel and mallet, returning her hand to her pouch. He heard the soft clink of several small stones tumbling together, and then she removed one, holding it up for him to see.

It didn't look like aught but a random pebble, yet she seemed to have chosen it purposefully.

"I have several in my collection," she said, seeming to understand the direction of his thoughts. "Each is a different size. They all must be hard enough to wear into whatever stone I'm carving. Most masons use sandstone for their art. Luckily, it is plentiful here, and isn't as useful for fortifying walls."

The more she talked, the more comfortable she seemed to grow. Alaric watched her, enthralled by her knowledge of such a challenging craft.

"You place the pebble between two of the dots you've chiseled," she said, demonstrating with the bit of rock in her hand. "And you run it along, making a path." Her fingers worked the pebble, rolling it back and forth a few inches.

Slowly, Alaric began to notice a groove forming between the two divots. He sat back on his heels, rapt.

"And you can make any design you want like that?"

"Aye—well, rubbing away little pathways in the stone would be the simplest way to do it. But Una taught me the more complicated method. See how the vines seem to be standing out from the stone?"

Alaric looked closer. He hadn't even noticed, but all the designs and patterns seemed to be rising out of the stone rather than being simply tunneled into it.

"I am not so much carving what I want into the rock, but rather removing everything I don't want," she said, still running the pebble along its groove. "It is as if the images are trapped within the stone, and it is my job to free them."

"What is this here?" Alaric pointed to the middle of the stone, where a rough figure was beginning to materialize. Two shapes, one a circle and the other a rectangle, were taking form next to the figure.

Elisead's fingers stilled. "That is me."

"What?"

She dropped the pebble back into her pouch. The light in her eyes from a moment before dimmed slightly. "It will eventually be a woman on horseback. See? Here is the horse's head, and here is her body, sitting sidesaddle. The circle there is a mirror, and the square a comb, which indicates that she's a woman."

Alaric nodded as the shape began to make sense. "And why is this you?"

"For my people, a woman sitting sideways on a horse symbolizes the Virgin Mary."

"She is the White Christ's mother, ja?"

She blinked at him, clearly startled by his knowledge of her God.

"You remember how I told your father I learned the Northumbrian tongue from a woman who was captured by my Jarl?" he asked, giving her a half grin. "The woman, Laurel, grew up in a Christian monastery in Northumbria. She told us about your God, his son the White Christ, and the Christ's mother, Mary."

"A Christian woman living in the Northlands among…"

"Among savages?" He chuckled to show her that her unspoken word didn't offend him. "Ja, Laurel is happy in her new home."

"And has she abandoned her faith in God?"

Now it was his turn to be surprised, for Elisead's question was not spoken with disgust or horror, but rather with curiosity.

He shrugged. "Laurel is happy living in the ways of

the Northlands now, although I think she sees room for her God and ours. Eirik, her husband, certainly does."

"And if they were found out? Must they hide their belief in two different religions?"

Alaric laughed, but then he saw the genuine confusion on her face. "Nei, for Eirik is the Jarl of our village —a chieftain, like your father. He is the one who sent me here."

She blinked up at him, the stone before them forgotten for a moment. "The Picts are said to be of and for the Ancient Ones. But when the priests of Christianity came to us many generations ago, we set the old ways aside and followed God. Sometimes…"

She faltered, biting her lip.

"Whatever you wish to say, you may say it to me, Elisead."

"Sometimes, although I believe in God and am his servant, sometimes…I feel called to the old ways."

"Called how?"

Elisead's eyes scanned the floor as she searched for an answer. "I…I can *feel* the presence of the ancient spirits in the woods, in the river…and in rocks." Her fingers grazed a carved stag leaping nigh off the border of the stone. "'Tis why I am moved to carve. It is almost as if the stone is whispering to me."

Alaric let her words settle around him. She truly was touched, either by a spirit or a god, he knew not which. "And that is a bad thing?"

She drew her hand away from the stag and moved it to the still-emerging figure of the woman on horseback. "I do not know. I am not supposed to stray toward the pagan etchings that whisper to me. Carving is meant only to elevate God. But…but isn't it an elevation of God's creations to celebrate His animals and plants, and to let His stones sing?"

Alaric's lips curved softly. "I fear you're asking the wrong man. But I know my gods would smile on a gift such as yours, not try to control or repress it. And from what Laurel has told me of your God, He sees all. He knows what is in your heart as you carve."

Relief washed over Elisead's beautiful features. Her golden eyes suddenly sparkled with unshed tears.

"Thank you for that," she breathed.

Alaric's gaze dropped to her full, pink lips.

Suddenly the air around them stilled and seemed to thicken with taut desire. Thor's blood, he wanted to kiss her again—*needed* to, for his entire body screamed with demanding lust. Against all his willpower, he leaned forward slowly.

Her eyes slipped to his mouth, and as he had, she tilted toward him.

A mere breath separated them now. How he longed to taste the honey of her lips once again—and so much more. He wanted to worship her body, to make her writhe in pleasure, to hear his name on her tongue as he made her come undone.

Voices suddenly sounded outside the tent. Alaric snapped his head back and reality crashed around him. What in Odin's name was he doing?

"Thank you for the lesson in stone carving," he said stiffly, rising to his feet. She remained seated, her eyes swirling with surprise and longing.

He stepped from the tent just as Tarr, Eyva, and the others filtered back into camp.

"Our first sowing in Pictland is complete," Tarr said merrily, drawing cheers from the others.

A flash of embarrassment washed over Alaric before he quickly concealed it with a practiced smile. He should have been with his crew, not drawing closer to Elisead. His desire could only result in breaking his word and destroying his whole mission.

"Good," he said levelly. "Now on to the next task—making this land our own once and for all."

19

A sennight passed, but still no word arrived from Elisead's father about further negotiations.

Elisead rolled her neck to relieve the stiffness there, but no amount of movement could undo the knots that had formed after a morning spent leaning over the enormous stone in her tent.

She stood, dropping the pebble she'd been using into the pouch on her belt. A little seed of rebellious satisfaction budded in her chest as she surveyed her work.

She'd finished the border, the one area where she was allowed to let her creativity bloom. Vines and leaves curled around woodland creatures, each in motion. It was a testament to the old ways, when the forest was thought to be alive with spirits and gods. The stone itself seemed to dance under the patterns.

The maiden riding sidesaddle in the middle of the stone was more distinct, but Elisead hadn't gotten as far on it as she should have. Nay, instead she'd focused on a new object toward the bottom of the stone.

The long body of the ship was just now surfacing from the surrounding rock. Rectangular sails drifted forward as if emerging from mist. She wouldn't be able to convey the dark red of the sails, but she could add groves to show that they were striped.

Defiance bubbled up once more. Her father would be furious.

The stone was meant to shine a light on Elisead's obedience and purity. As a bride gift, it symbolized the passing of her worth—her virginity, her use in making an alliance, and perhaps even her skill in carving. The last thing Maelcon would want was to hand an unruly woman off to his hoped-for ally. The evidence of her disobedience was now literally carved in stone.

But Una had taught Elisead that the purpose of carving was to honor the *stone*, not men's egos. Una's carvings blended the old ways with the new, paying respect to God for His creations while also letting nature run wild across the stone's surface.

Most of all, Una had instilled in Elisead that to carve was to become one with the stone, which meant that Elisead had to give herself over to its whispered wishes as she worked. And this stone, intended as a bride gift to a future Pictish King, spoke of Northmen now.

Elisead stepped to the tent flaps and pulled them back. A few clouds broke up the sky, leaving the air cooler than it had been in the last several days. But the air was fresh, laced with salt blowing in from the North Sea.

She'd been inside the tent too much in the nigh fortnight she'd been amongst the Northmen, but it seemed to be the only place she was safe from Alaric's searching green eyes.

Safe from her own tugging desire to see him, touch him, and be enfolded in his embrace, more like.

Rebellion once again stirred in her breast as she inhaled the fresh, salty air.

She wanted a Northman.

She could admit it, if only to herself. It was wrong in every way, but she wanted him nonetheless. His gaze, his touch, his kiss had awakened something within her, something that felt wild and free. And something that also felt strangely...*inevitable*, as if the spirits themselves had guided them together.

Elisead bit her lip against the desire to smile. Nay, she could not give in to her own wildness. And it was madness to think that the ancient spirits were somehow driving her toward a Northman. She'd let herself imagine too much.

She turned to reenter the tent, but the dim light and still air within repelled her. She had grown accustomed over the years to moving freely in the woods, despite her father's orders not to. She'd been cooped up too long.

A glance around the Northmen's camp revealed the normal bustle of activity. No one seemed to pay much attention to her. She never ate with them or sat around their fire pit, despite the fact that they switched to the Northumbrian tongue in her presence in a courteous attempt to include her. But she had kept to herself this last fortnight—it was her only defense against the threat of caring for them. Or caring for one of them in particular.

She stepped away from the tent, but still no one looked up. As usual, they busied themselves with sparring, mending, or cooking over the fire pit. Since the first field had been sown, many of the Northmen were occupied in either tending the barley or clearing more land for cultivation.

Involuntarily, her eyes scanned for Alaric. Her cheeks grew warm as she remembered the last time she'd thought he was away from camp and that it was safe for her to wander to the river.

But today she wasn't headed for the river, and so there would be little chance of stumbling upon him naked. Why did that thought cause her belly to sink in disappointment?

She entered the tree line, giving the camp one final glance. Either no one noticed her movement, or no one cared.

Of course, if harm befell her, their hopes for peace with her father would be dashed. It was strange that Alaric never told anyone about the cart accident a scnnight and a half ago. Though he hadn't said more to her about it, she knew he sensed foul play.

But she was only a woman, not deigned to have a say in the maneuverings of men. Did Alaric feel that way? From all she'd seen, Northwomen had a great deal more freedom than Pictish women did. Alaric's sister was a warrior. And Eyva, the other warrior woman in camp, worked just as hard as her husband, Tarr—and got just as much respect from the others.

She ducked under a pine bough as she wandered deeper into the forest. With a mental scold for herself, she brought her attention to the woods around her. She hadn't come out here to worry. She could do that back in the tent.

Elisead inhaled deeply to remind herself of her freedom, at least among these trees, at least for a little while.

Her wanderings took her up one of the many smaller hills that separated the Northmen's camp from her father's fortress. At the top, she tucked her long tunic between her legs and stuffed the material into her belt, giving her greater freedom of movement.

An ancient yew tree spread its arms out, inviting her into its limbs. She began climbing, the feel of the bark beneath her fingertips as soothing as ever.

When she was several dozen paces off the ground, she scooted along an outstretching branch that was as thick as her torso. A salty wind rustled the leaves around her, making them look like a thousand hands flickering merrily.

Another gust of wind separated the leaves enough to give her a view of the river as it wound through the lush green hills. Her eyes traced the river westward and soon enough she spotted the gray stone walls of the fortress. Warriors the size of ants crawled along the wall. Inside, villagers swarmed around the wooden great hall.

What was her father doing at that moment? Was he plotting his next move in the negotiations? Or did he plan on leaving his only child alone with the Northmen forever?

That was a silly girl's thought. Her father was a

pragmatist. He needed her for his much-desired alliance with Causantín mac Fergusa. He wouldn't let harm befall her—unless it was somehow more advantageous for his plans.

Her gaze slid back down along the river. As the slow, clear waters met the more churned, salty depths of the bay, the colors blended and swirled. There, along the shoreline, she could make out spots of off-white wool— the Northmen's tents.

Something tugged deep in her chest at the sight of the Northmen's camp. What were the spirits telling her? Where did her fate lie?

A rock shot past her head, barely missing her temple. It smacked into the oak's trunk just behind her.

She screamed and jerked in fright. Her movement dislodged her from her seat straddling the yew bough and she slipped.

Her hands clawed at the bough, her nails digging painfully into the bark. A heart-pounding moment later, she regained control, clutching desperately to the bough with both her thighs and arms.

If she had slipped just a hair more to the side, she would be hanging upside down from the branch she now clung to—or she'd be on the ground several dozen paces below, dead.

Elisead looked down at the forest floor and swallowed hard.

Feitr stood below the yew tree. He stared up at her, his ice blue eyes flat. He held a sling in his hand.

"What in God's name are you doing?" she snapped.

Though she tried to imbue her voice with authoritative ire, it sounded shrill with fright to her ears.

Feitr shrugged as if he hadn't almost just caused her to fall to her death.

"I needed to get your attention. The wind is high enough that I thought you wouldn't hear me over the rustling leaves."

Elisead's heart at last began to slow, but unease still filled her. "Why do you need my attention?"

"Your father sent me," Feitr said. "He wishes to speak with the Northmen again." A flicker of something crossed his pale eyes, but Elisead was too far up to read it.

"I saw you up here and assumed the Northmen and your father would both like to have you at the meeting. So I got your attention."

Again, his voice was disconcertingly flat. Did he not know what danger he'd put her in? He'd almost hit her with the rock he'd shot. And if she'd fallen, Feitr would be blamed for her death—assuming he didn't just slip away into the woods.

Elisead felt Feitr's cool gaze on her as she carefully made her way down from the tree. The Northman slave had always been strange, but he was no threat, she told herself firmly. He had always obeyed orders without trouble. There was no reason to fear him now.

"What does my father wish to discuss this time?" she said as she planted her feet firmly on the ground. She silently sent up a prayer of thanks to both the old gods and the new for the fact that her neck was unbroken.

Feitr's eyes slid over her, and she quickly untucked her tunic from her belt, hiding her legs.

"Even if I knew, what does it matter? I am a slave and you are a woman, which are almost the same thing. We don't have a say in our fates."

Elisead's mouth fell open in shock. It was the boldest she'd ever heard Feitr speak. His voice held only the faintest barb of bitterness, and yet what he said was all too true.

Feitr stepped forward and took hold of her elbow. She stiffened under his touch, but he didn't seem to notice. He turned toward the Northmen's camp and began making his way through the underbrush, towing Elisead behind.

"The reward for obedience is not found in this life, but in the next," Elisead said. She didn't know why she threw a priest's words at a Northland slave, but the fact that he had linked the two of them to a fate not of their choosing made her uneasy.

"I do not believe in your White Christ," he said over his shoulder. "My gods only see our actions in this lifetime. If a man does not make his own glory, he will be shunned forever."

She shivered at his words. Though she didn't fully understand them, they sent foreboding slithering up her spine.

"And what will you—"

Her words died on her tongue as they suddenly broke through the trees and stepped into the Northmen's camp.

All of a sudden everything was happening at once.

A flash of sun glinted off metal.

Feitr stopped so suddenly that she bounced off his back.

"Take your hand off her."

Alaric's voice was deadly low, his sword tip pressed against Feitr's neck.

20

A laric had been watching Elisead's tent all morning.

'Twas for the best that she didn't emerge, he'd told himself when at last he accompanied a handful of his men to go hunting. Otherwise he'd be hard pressed to leave camp and see to his duties. The temptation would be too strong to stare upon the cascades of auburn hair, her honey eyes, those luscious lips, and each dangerously tempting curve.

When he'd returned from the hunt, one deer richer yet strung tight as his bowstring, he'd gone to her tent to invite her to visit the barley fields with him. The first shoots had sprouted, and the fields already promised to be bountiful.

But the tent had been empty.

Though he trusted without a shadow of a doubt that she was safe among his crew, ever since the cart accident—which was no accident at all—he didn't like the idea of her wandering alone. He'd checked the river where she preferred to bathe, hoping selfishly that he might catch a glimpse of her slim, pale limbs in the cool water.

As he'd made his way back to camp with still no sight of her, worry set in. These were dangerous times, despite the fact that he strove to make her feel safe in his presence. He paced the camp as he considered where to look next, drawing the curious stares of his crew.

He didn't have to wait long.

A rustle in the underbrush along the back side of the camp was his first warning.

Then he caught a flash of white-blond through the trees. By the time he spotted the coppery shimmer of Elisead's hair behind it, his sword was already drawn.

And when he saw Feitr's hand wrapped tightly around Elisead's elbow, the blade moved as if it had a will of its own.

"Take your hand off her."

His voice sounded distant in his ears as he let the blade settle into the hollow at the base of Feitr's throat.

Slowly, Feitr's fingers loosened around Elisead's elbow. She stepped away from the pale-haired North-lander, eyes wide on Alaric.

"It is all right," she said. "He was merely…escorting me back from the woods."

"And he needed to grip you that hard to do so?" Alaric's gaze remained fixed on Feitr. He tried to clear his mind, to think levelly, but he couldn't remove the image of Feitr's fingers digging into Elisead's flesh.

Feitr had been the one to lead the donkey and cart

toward Alaric. He'd been the last one to touch the tampered-with harness.

Feitr had found Elisead in the woods. He'd been alone with her. And he'd laid his hands on her.

And now he stood under Alaric's blade.

A large hand clamped around his where he gripped his sword's hilt.

"Don't do aught rash, Alaric." Rúnin spoke almost inaudibly in their Northland tongue, but by the flicker in Feitr's ice-blue eyes, he'd heard the warning.

"Don't you want to know why I'm here?" Feitr said, his gaze never wavering from Alaric.

Alaric shook off Rúnin's hand but lowered the blade from Feitr's throat.

"Speak, slave."

Feitr didn't seem to mind Alaric's acid tone. "Maelcon requests your presence once more."

Alaric snorted as he re-sheathed his sword. "And he wants proof of his daughter's wellbeing, I imagine. Is that why you so *carefully* guided her back to camp?"

"Ja, he wants to see his daughter," Feitr said, ignoring Alaric's barb. "Or rather, he wants his guest to see her."

At Alaric's sudden stiffening, Feitr smiled softly. "I am not authorized to say more—as you have pointed out, I am only a slave."

Alaric repressed a curse. Feitr was clearly enjoying toying with him. "Very well. We'll depart shortly."

"I'd best not wait on you. I'll tell my master you are on your way." With no other preamble, Feitr gave Alaric his back and made his way into the woods once again.

"Maelcon has a guest?" Rúnin said once Feitr was out of sight.

Alaric shifted his gaze to Elisead, who stood wide-eyed and waiting for someone to explain what had just transpired.

It was rude of Alaric to continue speaking to Rúnin in their Northland language—and cruel to keep Elisead in the dark about his suspicions. But even after Feitr's behavior today, Alaric didn't fully trust his hunch that the Northland slave was behind the attempt to harm Elisead and thereby destroy negotiations between the Northlanders and the Picts.

"Your father wishes to speak again," Alaric said in Northumbrian to Elisead.

"Aye, Feitr said the same to me."

"We will head out as soon as you are ready."

"I am ready now."

Alaric nodded and motioned for her to stay put. He turned to those gathered in the camp and quickly explained that he, Rúnin, and Elisead were once again going to the Pict fortress. His crew seemed buoyed by the hope that another round of negotiations would bring them closer to a permanent settlement.

As Alaric turned back toward Elisead, Rúnin caught his arm.

"Who might Maelcon have as a guest? Are you sure this isn't a trap?"

Alaric met his friend's uneasy gaze. "I'm not sure of aught."

21

Alaric forced his gaze to rest calmly on the gates as a warrior watching them atop the stone wall motioned for them to be opened.

The iron grille protecting the wood was ratcheted up, then the gates began to slowly swing open with a groan.

No horde of warriors poured out. No battle cry went up. No flash of metal was visible to give warning of an attack.

Nevertheless, the hairs on Alaric's nape stirred. He'd longed to bring his entire force of two score Northland warriors with him, but doing so would only shatter the fragile peace that existed between himself and Maelcon mac Lorcan.

Instead, he stood with Elisead between himself and Rúnin, feeling completely exposed.

Who was Maelcon's guest? And why had Feitr gotten

so much enjoyment from taunting Alaric by withholding the information?

At last the gates were opened wide enough for him to see the yard within. But rather than an army of war-ready Picts, Maelcon himself waited on the grassy expanse. His right-hand man, Drostan, stood like an ever-present shadow at his side.

Maelcon motioned the three forward. Doing his best to hide his unease, Alaric forced his mouth into a smile and stepped through the gates.

"I was glad to receive word from your man that you wished to meet again," Alaric said. His gaze skipped around the yard. A few warriors stood at their posts along the wall, but the yard was empty besides their two little groups.

The villagers at last seemed to trust that Alaric and his Northmen wouldn't lay waste to their huts, so the village had been quiet but full when they'd passed it. The villagers' absence from the fortress made it seem all the more quiet.

Maelcon's gaze immediately sought his daughter. At her calm if wide-eyed appearance, Maelcon seemed to relax a hair's breadth, but then he turned back to Alaric.

"I am less than pleased to hear of your latest venture in *my* woods," he said, narrowing his amber eyes, so like Elisead's, on Alaric.

Alaric resisted the urge to clench his fists. So, Feitr had been doing more than just delivering Elisead from her wanderings. He'd been sent to gather information for Maelcon. And apparently the Northman slave had found the barley fields.

"We cannot wait forever for you to come to your senses and agree to my terms," Alaric said, plastering a wolfish smile on his face even as he narrowed his gaze on Maelcon.

"My senses, eh?" Maelcon said, mirroring Alaric's fake smile. "Perhaps my position has changed at last. Or perhaps yours has."

Alaric didn't like the warning couched in Maelcon's words.

The mystery guest. Did Maelcon now think himself above the need to negotiation with Alaric? Was Alaric's hope for a peaceful union of their peoples to be dashed after nigh a fortnight of these games?

Before Alaric could demand an answer from Maelcon, the Pictish chief turned to his daughter.

"You are well?"

"Aye, Father."

"Feitr said he found you in a tree. Alone." Maelcon shot Alaric a scathing glare. "You gave your word to keep her safe."

Alaric had yet to hear Elisead's explanation of where she'd wandered off to and how Feitr had found her. He kept his features smooth.

"Elisead is still within my care, and therefore she is safe. I knew where she was. The only danger she might have faced would have been from your slave's handling of her."

It was a dangerous line to pursue, but Alaric couldn't resist probing Maelcon. Just how involved was Feitr? If he was responsible for a plot against Elisead, was he acting alone or on Maelcon's orders?

Alaric felt Elisead's questioning gaze fall on him, but he didn't turn. The fact that he'd pulled his weapon on Feitr and demanded an explanation proved that he hadn't known where she'd gone. Somehow, though, he trusted that Elisead wouldn't expose his lie.

Maelcon's eyes narrowed even more. "My daughter has naught to fear from me or my people. Feitr is no threat to anyone."

The denial was expected. Nevertheless, Alaric had thrown the first stone. If Maelcon was responsible for the cut harness, he'd now been warned that Alaric was suspicious of him.

"Speaking of being a threat," Alaric said smoothly. "Where is my sister?"

Maelcon motioned for Drostan to open the doors to the great hall behind him. As Drostan pulled open one of the thick wooden doors, Alaric caught a glimpse of the interior.

Feitr stood, white head bowed in obsequiousness just inside the door. He faced the hall—which was filled with armored men.

Alaric went rigid. He'd been wrong. It was a trap.

Just then, Madrena slipped from the hall and Drostan shut the door behind her, blocking Alaric's view of the warriors gathered inside.

Madrena walked forward calmly, head level and gaze fixed on the group standing in the middle of the yard. But instead of greeting Rúnin with a hearty kiss as Alaric would have expected, she went straight to Alaric and took him in a stiff hug.

"There are at least a score of Pict warriors in the

hall, possibly closer to thirty," she whispered in their language into his ear. "I know not why they are here or what they have planned."

Alaric gave her a reassuring squeeze even as the blood hammered in his veins. Both he and Rúnin had been allowed to enter with their swords strapped to their hips. Alaric had a seax tucked into his boot, and Rúnin likely had one as well. But Madrena was unarmed, and Elisead would be completely vulnerable if a battle broke out.

Before he could speak to Madrena, Maelcon cut in.

"Come, I have some news." A smile played under his red-gray beard. "We have a visitor, a most honored guest. I am sure he would like to meet you. And you, Elisead."

Alaric's body hummed with the need to fight, to take action. He would fight to the death if he had to for this mission. But he would not be the one to destroy their peace. Let Maelcon launch the first blow.

Maelcon motioned them forward, and Drostan once again opened one of the wooden double doors leading into the great hall.

Alaric got a more complete view of the hall, which was filled with warriors. They were dressed in the same fashion as Maelcon's men, but the brightly colored woven fabric under their chainmail was a different pattern.

It took all of Alaric's willpower not to pull his sword free of its scabbard. Instead, he stepped forward and walked through the door. The warriors turned silently, watching him with hateful eyes.

A solitary man was on the raised dais at the back of the hall. At Alaric's entrance, he stood from his chair slowly. He was covered in the same chainmail tunic as the others, but a sword with a gem-encrusted hilt rested on his hip.

Alaric was vaguely aware that the others had entered behind him. Drostan closed the door, dropping the hall into a dimness only cut by the torches resting in their sconces along the walls. The fire pit next to the dais was unlit.

He sensed Elisead step next to him, but he didn't dare take his gaze from the man standing on the dais. His dark brown hair was tied away from his face, which was partially obscured by a trimmed beard.

The beard, along with the ornate sword hilt and his position on the dais, gave the man an air of authority, but he appeared to be of an age with Alaric. Judging from his build, the sword on his hip wasn't mere ornament—he held himself like a warrior. Or a leader of warriors.

"Father," Elisead breathed by Alaric's side. "Is that not…"

"Aye, daughter," Maelcon said, his voice dripping with smugness. "It is Domnall mac Causantín."

"Who?" Alaric said, his gaze burning into the man towering over all the others in the hall.

Elisead's voice was barely a whisper. "My betrothed."

22

————

It was too much.

The hall was too crowded. The air suddenly felt hot and cloying. So many sets of eyes bored into her.

The great hall seemed to swirl and bend around her. Elisead couldn't tell if the room was tilting or if she was.

Suddenly she felt Alaric's warm, strong hand on her back, steadying her. Instinctively, she leaned into him, drawing on his solid strength.

Even as the dizziness ebbed, mutters rose around her. Eliscad's gaze landed on Domnall mac Causantín. Her betrothed.

The man's otherwise handsome face darkened as he took in the sight of Elisead leaning against Alaric, his arm wrapped around her protectively.

Domnall took a swift step forward so that he stood on the edge of the dais, towering head and shoulders above everyone in the hall. Just as quickly as it had arrived, Alaric's hand disappeared from her back.

Though there was now an expanse of air between them, Elisead could sense how rigidly he held his body.

"This must be the barbarian Northman Maelcon mac Lorcan has told me so much about," Domnall said, his voice commanding but tight.

"Alaric Hamarsson, captain and second in command to Eirik the Steady, son of Arud, Jarl of Dalgaard," Alaric said smoothly.

Elisead felt her eyes widen slightly at his string of titles. His voice was hard and authoritative, with not a hint of the gentleness he so often showed toward her.

"And you are Domnall mac…what was it again? Mac Castration?"

Several of Domnall's men rumbled in shock at Alaric's overt insult to their leader. Madrena, who stood behind Elisead, snorted loudly.

"I am Domnall mac *Causantín*, heir to the Kingship of Dál Riata and son of Causantín mac Fergusa, King of Fortriu and all the Picts."

Domnall's dark brown eyes burned into Alaric with open disdain, but Alaric seemed not to notice or care.

"Ah, my mistake," he said casually. His eyes glinted with green fire to match Domnall's gaze, though.

"And this," her father said, stepping to her side, "is your bride, Domnall. May I present my daughter, Elisead."

Maelcon took Elisead by the arm and pulled her away from Alaric. Though her father had a smile plastered on his face, the tension in the room was palpable —and his tight grip on her upper arm told of her father's unease.

Maelcon halted at the base of the dais and released Elisead's arm. Slipping into the familiar role of chieftain's obedient daughter, Elisead lowered her head and dipped into a curtsy.

When she straightened, some of the tautness in Domnall's face had eased.

"Your father's tales of your beauty did not do you justice," Domnall said, bending from the dais and capturing Elisead's hand in his. He raised it to his mouth and pressed a kiss against her knuckles. All the while, his eyes roamed over her.

Elisead repressed a shiver. Alaric had looked at her in a similar way, yet for some reason the glint of possession in Domnall's dark brown eyes sent tendrils of unease climbing up her spine.

"Thank you," she managed. Domnall raised his head from her hand but kept it firmly in his grip.

"Come," Domnall said, sweeping his free hand toward the long table and chairs on the dais as if the great hall were his. "We all have much to discuss."

Elisead glimpsed the downward twitch of her father's mouth before Domnall tugged on her hand, drawing her attention back to him.

Without asking, Domnall grabbed Elisead around the waist and simply lifted her up onto the dais by his side. Some of the men in the hall chuckled at their leader's bold display.

As Domnall pulled her toward one of the chairs, she darted a glance over her shoulder. A muscle ticked along Alaric's jaw, his eyes riveted on her—or more precisely, on where Domnall's large hand wrapped around her wrist.

Madrena gave him a nudge toward the steps leading up to the dais. When at last he tore his gaze away from her, he followed Maelcon, Madrena, and Rúnin up the stairs.

Domnall tugged Elisead into a seat next to his at the head of the table. The others settled in the remaining chairs, with Maelcon at the table's foot and Alaric across from Elisead.

"I must apologize again for this unplanned visit," Domnall said to Maelcon. "But my father sent me to check on the progress being made on my fortress in Dál Riata. To travel from his stronghold in Torridon to mine in Dál Riata, I must pass through these lands anyway." Domnall shrugged. "And I was eager to meet the bride I am to claim in a few moons' time."

"No need to apologize," Maelcon said quickly. "You are always welcome here."

"Though it seems I have come at a…delicate time." Domnall shifted in his seat so that he could pin Alaric with his gaze. "Or perhaps it is the perfect time."

"I suppose that depends," Alaric said levelly. "Do you plan on interfering with Maelcon and my peaceful negotiations, or will you allow us to continue unimpeded?"

Domnall stiffened at Alaric's blunt words. His fingers, which were still wrapped around Elisead's wrist, dug in painfully.

Alaric must have noticed her flinch, for his emerald eyes darted to her, then narrowed on Domnall.

Purposefully ignoring Alaric, Domnall turned to Maelcon. "I suppose you hope to yolk the might of these Northland barbarians in the service of your own protection, Maelcon."

At her father's jerking nod, Domnall stroked the dark, trimmed beard on his chin as if considering. "Aye, we've all heard tales of their skill and ruthlessness in battle. In fact, didn't you deal with a band of Northmen not so long ago?"

Domnall was toying with her father, Elisead knew. Of course Domnall was well aware of what had transpired seven years ago—news of the Northmen's vicious attack, and the Picts' narrow victory, had traveled far.

According to rumor, Causantín had publicly praised Maelcon for his triumph over their invaders. But the King never sent aid during those terrible months following the attack when Maelcon lay bedridden from the nigh life-ending wound he'd received in his leg and their people struggled to put their lives back together.

"You were injured in that confrontation, were you not?" Domnall asked idly, as if picking up on Elisead's thoughts. "Most fortunate that you survived."

What was Domnall playing at? In bringing up the battle seven years ago, he was only reaffirming the reasons why her father would wish to form an alliance with the Northmen rather than fall into open hostilities again. But Domnall eyed Alaric with such venom that Elisead couldn't imagine her betrothed wished for negotiations to continue.

"In truth, I don't see the need for an alliance with these savages," Domnall went on, waving dismissively toward Alaric, Madrena, and Rúnin. "With my marriage to your daughter, you won't need the protection of a band of barbarians—you'll have my forces, and my father's, at your disposal."

There was his true motive. In bringing up Maelcon's past encounter with Northmen, Domnall only wished to remind him of his vulnerability—the King of the Picts and his son could grant protection, or they could take it away, depending on whether or not Maelcon did as they wished.

Elisead looked down at Domnall's hand where it wrapped around her wrist. Her fingers had lost sensation, so tight was his grip. His knuckles were white, even though he kept his features even.

Perhaps there was something else afoot behind Domnall's smooth smile and subtly worded threats.

Though he'd been speaking casually to Maelcon, his dark gaze kept tugging back to Alaric.

Alaric stared back boldly, a defiant gleam in his green eyes. Domnall's fingers tightened even more on her.

Was Domnall's barely concealed hostility toward Alaric and the other Northlanders more than mere passing concern for his betrothed's father and his holdings? Elisead silently cursed the fact that she knew so little of the man she was to marry at the end of summer.

But even without prior knowledge of the man's character, it was clear that possessiveness flashed in his brown eyes when he looked at her, and hot hatred bubbled just below his smooth exterior when his gaze landed on Alaric.

What dangerous game was Domnall now silently playing with Alaric? And what would become of Elisead, trapped in the middle?

23

Alaric clenched his fists under the table until they throbbed in agony.

The pain was clarifying, though. It gave him something to focus on rather than the sight of Domnall's fingers digging into Elisead's pale, soft flesh. It gave him something to do with his hands rather than wrap them around Domnall's neck for causing the look of fear in Elisead's shimmering eyes.

Madrena's quick tap on one of his fists under the table was just enough to bring him out of his murderous thoughts.

So, Domnall was against negotiations between the Northmen and the Picts. Alaric yet again reminded himself to ask Elisead what exactly had happened in Maelcon's first encounter with Northlanders. The burned bones along the riverbank not far from his camp were proof enough that the Northlanders had been defeated, but something about Domnall's tone told Alaric there was more to the story.

Alaric flicked his gaze to Maelcon to gauge his reaction to Domnall's subtle warning against their negotiations.

Maelcon shifted in his seat. He tugged his graying beard, a habit Alaric was coming to know as a delaying tactic on Maelcon's part.

"I am much pleased that you agreed to marry my daughter," Maelcon began. "The son of a King, and the future King of Dál Riata, has many choices, yet you chose Elisead."

Annoyance flitted across Domnall's eyes at the flattery, but he said naught.

"Your wedding at harvest time will be celebrated throughout all of Pictland," Maelcon went on carefully. "But that is still two moons away. And as you can see, these Northmen are here now."

Surprise washed through Alaric. Though it raised his ire to be talked about as if he weren't sitting between these two men, he waited for Maelcon to continue. He now knew that Maelcon didn't fully trust Domnall, which meant that Alaric was in a better position to negotiate than he'd initially thought.

"And both Dál Riata and Torridon are many days' journey from this remote corner of Pictland," Maelcon went on. "We thought the hills would keep us sheltered from Northern invaders, but this is the second group to make their way to our gates. If a third band of invaders comes, we would require immediate protection from a large force, which could take more than a sennight to arrive if we had to wait on warriors from Torridon or Dál Riata."

As Maelcon unfolded his respectful but subtly resistant response to Domnall's veiled threats, Domnall's mouth turned down behind his carefully manicured beard.

"And you believe that these Northmen have the necessary numbers to protect you?" Domnall asked, his voice nigh dripping with derision. It was plain to see that Domnall wasn't used to being defied.

"We are a force of warriors two score strong," Alaric said, raising an eyebrow at Domnall.

Alaric barely repressed a genuine grin at the ever-so-slight widening of Domnall's eyes. Clearly he hadn't expected Alaric's crew to be so large. The man's own retinue didn't match Alaric's in size. Even combining Maelcon's forces with Domnall's, they wouldn't stand a chance at overpowering Alaric's fierce warriors, for Alaric was confident that one Northman was worth at least two of any other warrior on the battlefield.

"And as I'm sure Maelcon informed you, we plan on making a settlement in this area," Alaric went on. "Whether we have an alliance or not." Though he preferred not to resort to his own barely-veiled threats, it seemed to be the only way to convey to Domnall that Alaric would not be bested.

"You are quite serious, aren't you?" Domnall's eyes narrowed on Alaric.

"Ja. And I think it is in everyone's best interest for my negotiations with Maelcon to continue —unimpeded."

Domnall played with an imaginary crumb on the wooden table's surface as he considered.

At last, he straightened in his chair. "Then perhaps I should pay a visit to your camp. Maelcon tells me you have been quite busy. Besides," he said, casting a glance over Elisead, "I wish to ensure that my betrothed is being well cared for. Her...*safety* is of utmost importance to me."

Alaric squeezed his fists under the table once more as he saw Domnall's hand tighten around Elisead's wrist yet again. A flicker of satisfaction crossed Domnall's eyes. Alaric had erred in giving away his rage at seeing Domnall touch Elisead. Now Domnall was enjoying tweaking Alaric's anger at Elisead's expense.

Domnall stood suddenly, pulling Elisead with him. "I'll have my men escort us to the camp."

Alaric rose slowly, forcing his hands to unclench. "There is no need for that. You will be safe among my crew."

Domnall snorted. "Forgive me for not trusting you, Northman, but I have only just met you." A few chuckles rose below the dais from Domnall's men.

"It is not a matter of trust," Alaric replied, smiling wolfishly. "It is a matter of what I wish. If I had wanted you dead, you'd be dead already."

Madrena and Rúnin scraped their chairs back and stood, both wearing the same deadly smile as Alaric. It was a bold claim, and yet Alaric didn't doubt his ability to take on Domnall's thirty men with Madrena and Rúnin at his back—especially with the hot rage coursing through his veins at the sight of Domnall's hands on Elisead.

"But if you are afraid of my Northmen warriors, by all means, bring your little retinue." He kept his voice light, but the insult clearly landed true.

Domnall met their grins with a smile of his own, but it looked more like a bare-toothed sneer. "Do you wish to join us, Maelcon, and see the savages in whose hands you have placed your daughter—and my future wife?"

Maelcon rose. "Very well," he said, tugging again on his beard.

Alaric motioned for Domnall to precede him down from the dais and out of the great hall. At last, Domnall released Elisead's wrist. But instead of letting her go, he took her arm and tucked it within his.

"Shall we, my bride?"

Alaric bit his tongue until he tasted blood.

24

"I warned you to be careful."

Madrena's low voice barely cut through the fog of rage swirling in Alaric's mind. His eyes burned on Domnall's back. If his gaze was as sharp as the sword on his hip, Domnall's head would be severed from his neck.

Elisead walked at Domnall's side, her arm still tucked under his. She looked small and vulnerable next to the armored man, who rivaled Alaric in height and size.

"Ja, you did," Alaric said through clenched teeth. "But like most everything a little sister might say to her big brother, it went unheeded."

Madrena snorted. "You're eight minutes older, *twin* brother," she muttered. But then she turned serious once more. "It is obvious to all that you care for the girl. You only bring trouble on yourself, Alaric."

"Don't you think I've realized that?"

The best-case scenario ended with Alaric thwarted

in his desire for Elisead. She would marry Domnall, and he would force himself to forget those honey eyes and cascading auburn locks. Forget her delicate yet callused fingers working stone like clay, shaping it into something new. Forget the sight of the salty wind whipping her tunic around her, making her look like the wild forest spirit she was meant to be.

And Alaric didn't even want to think of the worst-case scenario. Breaking his word to Maelcon, himself, and the gods. Destroying the peaceful negotiations he'd worked so hard for. Falling into all-out war with the Picts. Losing Elisead forever.

Odin's breath, why had he let his attraction for Elisead grow into something more? *Let?* Nei, it hardly felt like he let it happen—her gaze had arrested him, her delicate strength had enthralled him. She was his hostage, and yet now he was the one held in desire's bindings.

Alaric snapped his gaze away from where Elisead and Domnall walked a few paces ahead. There was too much at stake to dwell on his lust for the Pictish woman.

"I'll not put my mission in danger," he said softly to Madrena. Though they spoke in their Northland tongue, Feitr walked with Maelcon and Drostan behind them. Maelcon had claimed that he wanted Feitr along as a servant, but Alaric suspected it was so that the chieftain would have a Northlander's ears in the camp—and another set of eyes to gather information.

The entire group—Domnall and Elisead, Alaric, Madrena and Rúnin, and Maelcon, Drostan, and Feitr, made an odd precession through the village. Villagers peered out through shuttered windows at the curious sight of their chieftain ambling by with the son of a king, a slave, and the Northland warriors they so feared.

As they entered the woods separating the fortress from his camp, Alaric lowered his voice even more.

"An *accident* befell Elisead, though the consequences of her coming to harm seem too great to chalk it up to coincidence."

He quickly explained how the donkey's harness had been cut cleanly and a rock thrown at the animal to spook it.

"Feitr was the last to handle the cart," Alaric said.

Madrena arched a pale eyebrow. "The slave? He slinks around Maelcon's fortress like a whipped dog. You think him capable of such a plot?"

"I know not," Alaric breathed. "He could be acting on his own, though why I'm not sure. He could also be following orders. Or he could be completely blameless."

"The negotiations hinge on both hostages being safe and unharmed," Rúnin said, bending his dark head toward Alaric and Madrena. "If someone is trying to hurt Elisead, they could just as easily set their sights on Madrena."

"Has aught happened?" Alaric asked.

Madrena frowned. "From the first, Maelcon has asked me many questions about our plans. He seems keen to gather information, though I expect you have done the same with Elisead. That is the way of things when it comes to hostages—both sides try to learn about the other. It seemed only natural."

"Ja," Alaric said, his agitation growing. "But have

any accidents befallen you? Or have you simply sensed something…off?"

Madrena hesitated, glancing between Alaric and Rúnin.

"What?" Rúnin said, his body suddenly taut.

"A few nights ago, I awoke to the sound of footsteps outside my chamber. Someone tried to open the door, but of course I had already repositioned the bed in front of it, as I have done every night."

Relief bathed Alaric briefly. "You acted as any Northland warrior would in the midst of the enemy."

His mind returned to Elisead's surprise at the freedom Northwomen had and the fact that women could become warriors if they chose. "These Picts underestimate you, likely because you are a woman. But whoever wishes these negotiations to disintegrate into war won't misjudge you again."

Madrena nodded, her face set in the hard lines of a warrior. "I'll be more alert for any signs of a threat."

"That is not enough," Rúnin bit out. "'Tis too dangerous for you to remain in that viper's den. Some plot is afoot, and I'll not lose you to it."

"I no more want to lose my sister to some Pictish schemer than you want to lose your mate, Rúnin," Alaric hissed. "But there are greater stakes here. The fates and lives of everyone in Dalgaard could hang in the balance. Eirik is counting on this settlement for the future of our people."

Madrena held up a hand. "You two can stop bickering about it, because it is *my* choice. And I choose to stay in the fortress." She locked her pale gray eyes on Alaric. "I still believe these negotiations can work."

"Ja, we just need to keep Domnall's rutting nose out of it," Alaric said, shooting the man another glare.

"And ferret out whoever is plotting against our settlement," Rúnin added.

"And keep Elisead's tunic in place when she is in your presence," Madrena whispered only loud enough for Alaric.

He would have upbraided her for the impertinent remark if it weren't so cursedly close to the truth. His desire for Elisead was becoming a dangerous liability.

Alaric's crew of Northlanders stood tense and at the ready when their party broke through the tree line and stepped into the camp. Though his men's preparedness eased some of his worries, Alaric still felt wound as tight inside as the Northmen looked.

"All is well," Alaric said loudly to the Northlanders. "This man is Elisead's betrothed. He and Chief Maelcon wished to see how we are faring."

The Northmen slowly resumed what they had been doing before the party's arrival. Some muttered under their breath and exchanged glances, though.

Domnall strolled through the camp as if he were inspecting a child's game of Hnefatafl. His stride was arrogant, yet Alaric didn't miss the man's sharp gaze as he silently counted the tents and assessed the band of Northmen not so subtly staring him down.

Alaric made the barest of efforts to guide Maelcon, with Drostan and Feitr shadowing him, around the camp.

"Our ships are there." Alaric pointed toward the bay's shore. "And we have begun cultivating fields over there—but you already knew that."

Maelcon eyed Alaric for a long moment, but he apparently decided that it wasn't worth addressing Alaric's barb about Feitr spying for him. He moved toward the bay where the longships were dragged up along the sandy shoreline.

The chieftain's gaze settled on the carved and painted dragon prows butting onto the sand.

"There will be more ships arriving next summer, as soon as the seas are calm enough."

Though Alaric could have turned the words into a threat, he kept his voice even and low instead. If Maelcon truly didn't trust Domnall, as Alaric suspected, this could be the opening he'd been waiting for to push the chieftain toward an agreement.

Maelcon grunted, then ran a hand along the tightly fitted wooden slats comprising the hull. "Such a shallow draft," he said, almost to himself.

"Ja. We could have gone farther up the river had we wished to. Right to your fortress."

"Aye, I know what these ships are capable of." Maelcon's gaze drifted toward the water for a long moment, his amber eyes lost in memory.

Now was the time for Alaric to make his move.

"Imagine what an entire fleet could accomplish."

"What they could destroy."

"Or what they could defend against. What they could build."

Maelcon's eyes fixed on Alaric. Though the chieftain

kept his face hard, he was clearly swayed by Alaric's words.

"I've told you already, my people will settle here with or without your blessing. The fields we are cultivating should be proof enough of that. But we can both benefit from an alliance."

"And what of my alliance with Domnall? Surely he is correct that with him as a son-in-law, I have no need of Northmen's alliances."

Alaric turned slightly from the bay and let his gaze drift over his crew. Some sparred nearby, their blades flashing in the midday sun. Others stood talking, their eyes on Domnall as he strolled past the fire pit. He held Elisead's arm in place under his by pulling her close to his side, even though she was clearly trying to put distance between them.

"I'll let you be the judge of that."

Maelcon's eyes followed Alaric's, and out of the corner of his vision he saw Maelcon's mouth turn down in distaste.

Just as Alaric moved to guide Maelcon back into the camp, a ruffle of motion behind him snagged his eye.

Feitr stood knee-deep in the bay's lapping waters, his hands skimming over one of the longships. A look of longing stole over his features, followed by a flash of pure hatred in his pale eyes directed at Maelcon's back.

When Feitr's gaze flicked to Alaric, the slave instantly dropped his hands from the longship and lowered his head, resuming the meek countenance he bore in Maelcon's presence.

What in Thor's name had Alaric just witnessed?

Many slaves did not like their masters. Did the look in Feitr's icy eyes rule out the possibility that he was doing Maelcon's bidding in cutting the harness? Or did it indicate that Feitr's hatred of Maelcon ran deep enough that he would cause the man's daughter harm?

Naught about Feitr made sense. A knot pulled tight in the pit of Alaric's stomach as he led Maelcon back toward the others. Drostan and Feitr followed silently, and Alaric couldn't stop the hairs on the nape of his neck from rising.

25

Elisead jumped at the fire's loud pop. She was pulled tighter than a hunter's bowstring.

She kept thinking that the tension in the Northmen's camp could not continue—surely a breaking point would be reached and either there would be overt aggression or a diffusion of energy.

Yet as the evening wore on, the pent hostility simmering between Domnall, Maelcon, Alaric, and the other Northlanders rose to nigh boiling.

It didn't help that Domnall wouldn't take his hands off her, despite her efforts to slip out of his grasp. But whenever she tried to move away or reclaim her arm, his grip would only tighten.

Domnall's possessive hold on her had clearly not gone unnoticed by either Alaric or her father. Both eyed Domnall, Alaric with barely veiled antagonism and her father with resigned distaste.

For his part, Domnall's arrogant aloofness was

wearing thin, and he now wore a scowl behind his well-tended beard.

Talk around the fire pit had inevitably swung back to negotiations. With each of Maelcon's carefully worded dodges, Domnall grew more sour.

Alaric was strangely quiet as Maelcon deflected Domnall's increasingly insistent urgings not to ally with Northmen.

Just when Elisead feared she would jump out of her skin if the fire crackled one more time, Domnall stood, drawing her to her feet by her elbow.

"I can see that you would rather work your jaw endlessly than make a decision now, Maelcon," he said. Though Elisead would never dare say so, it seemed that her father had already made a decision—it simply wasn't the one Domnall desired.

Maelcon stood slowly. "Aye, perhaps the light of day will shed clarity on this situation," he said. The sun had set but the trees were still filled with the blue glow of twilight.

Suddenly Alaric's warm, large hand closed around her free arm.

"I'll bring Elisead to the fortress tomorrow at first light, then," Alaric said smoothly.

"I see no reason why she cannot return with me now," Domnall replied, twisting his body slightly so that Elisead was pulled into his side.

Alaric instantly let go of her arm, else she be yanked between the two men.

"You would use your bride as a bit of rope in a tug-of-war?" Alaric said. Though his voice was still level, his eyes flashed green fire in the low light.

"Alaric." Madrena's tone held a warning, even as she and Rúnin rose from the fire and stood at his side.

"What say you, Maelcon?" Alaric said, turning to her father. "The terms of our negotiation involved the exchange of hostages. I have entrusted my sister's safety to you, as you have your daughter's. Do you wish to return the hostages and end our negotiations?"

Her father tugged on his beard. "Nay," he said at last, his voice more assured than it had been all day. "Domnall, we will continue this in the morning. Until then, release my daughter into Alaric's care."

"Very well," Domnall said at last, loosening his grip. Elisead immediately stepped away from him and toward Alaric. Domnall's dark eyes narrowed on her as she did. "But at least show me where my betrothed sleeps at night. I would be assured of her innocence in this den of savages."

Blessedly, most of the other Northmen had already moved away from the fire pit. Otherwise, Elisead feared she'd find herself in the middle of an insulted and armed band of warriors.

Alaric actually seemed to relax a hair's breadth, perhaps because Domnall no longer pawed at her. And his departure was imminent, if only for the night.

"This was to be my tent," Alaric said, striding toward the largest of the structures. "When Elisead arrived, she was given the best I have to offer."

Domnall snorted in derision, but then eyed the tent. "And where do you sleep, then?"

"Here," Alaric said, pointing at the closest tent to hers.

When they reached her tent, Alaric drew back the flap. It was strange to have Elisead's little safe haven inspected by Domnall. Her stomach sank as she realized that as Domnall's wife, this would be the norm. She waited outside the flap, praying for this ordeal to end quickly.

Domnall strode inside and turned in a circle, taking in the modest but comfortable accommodations. His dark eyes lingered on the raised mattress piled with furs.

Why did she get the feeling that he was trying to impugn her virtue? Was it just to get a rise out of Alaric, to rub his face in the fact that she was to become Domnall's? Or was there more to his insistence on inspecting her sleeping quarters?

"What is that?" Domnall pointed to the partially carved stone taking up much of the floor space in the tent.

Maelcon slipped past Elisead to stand at Domnall's side.

"Ah, you were not meant to see that until you were wed," her father said in an overly jovial voice.

"What is it?" Domnall repeated.

"It is your bride gift. My daughter is quite the skilled carver. She's been working on this stone for several months in preparation for the wedding. It will be quite the honor, if not a surprise, when she presents it to you come summer's end, will it not?"

Now Elisead saw what her father was about. He hoped to smooth things over with Domnall even if he decided it was in his people's best interest to continue talks with the Northmen.

Domnall's eyebrows rose slightly as he surveyed the stone.

"Here is a depiction of the Virgin Mary," Maelcon said quickly. "She represents my daughter's purity as she comes to you. And there you can see the beginnings of an army of men. They represent the strength of the future King of Dál Riata."

Domnall continued to eye the stone in the low light coming through the tent flap.

"And what is this?" He crouched suddenly at the base of the stone, his hand shooting out to trace the longship Elisead had begun carving.

Her stomach plummeted to the floor. "That is… It is incomplete."

Her father, eager to keep Domnall placated, leaned over his shoulder and peered at Elisead's latest addition.

"I'm sure it is just…" But the words died in Maelcon's mouth as he continued to look upon the long, low ship, its rectangle sails so distinctive.

"Slave, bring me a torch," Domnall snapped at Feitr, who stood outside the tent. Feitr leapt to do his bidding.

"'Tis naught," Elisead said, but her voice sounded distant and strained in her ears. She felt Alaric's searching gaze on her, but he remained silent as he stood holding the tent's flap back.

Feitr hurried back bearing a thick stick whose end was aflame. The flickering fire cast leaping shadows through the tent as Feitr held the burning stick up at the doorway.

The shadows threw the Northman longship in starker relief, revealing Elisead's careful work to bring the ship forth from the stone. Domnall's face darkened, his fingers tracing the longship. Stabbing fear tore through her. She clutched her hands tightly so as not to ring them in panic.

"What is a Northman's ship doing on my bride gift?" Domnall's voice was low, yet the danger in his words only seemed heightened by his tone.

"I was just…" Elisead's voice failed as she scrambled to explain herself. *I felt called to carve it. I am drawn to the Northmen in some inexplicable way. I sense my future lies with them.*

What could she possibly say that would not end in disaster?

"Elisead." Her father rounded on her, his eyes wide. "What have you done?"

Domnall rose slowly behind her father.

"You soiled my gift with a symbol of *them*?" He pointed toward Alaric, who stood rigid and focused on Domnall.

"I did not mean—"

"What else have you soiled, *Northman*?"

Elisead gasped, but before she could defend her innocence, Alaric moved like lightning. Suddenly he was inside the tent and a mere hand span away from Domnall.

"You will leave. Now."

Everything seemed to freeze for a long moment. With Alaric dropping the tent flap, the tent's interior fell into the obscured blue light of late evening. The torch's warm glow filtered through the wool siding, but it felt as if Elisead, her father, Alaric, and Domnall were trapped in their own world. Feitr, Drostan, Madrena, and Rúnin might as well have been across the sea, though they only stood on the other side of the tent's flaps.

Then everything sped up—horrifyingly so. Domnall's fist drove through the air right at Alaric's face. Maelcon stumbled backward from the two men, bumping into Elisead. Alaric's hand flew up, blocking Domnall's punch. The tent flaps were ripped back. Madrena, Rúnin, and Drostan plowed inside, their shouts colliding.

Elisead tumbled backward, landing on the bed Alaric had intended to sleep in himself. Her head spun in terror. Alaric and Domnall were locked together, Domnall's fist in Alaric's hand, neither man yielding.

"You have touched her, haven't you, Northman?"

"Keep questioning her honor and mine, Pict. My sword has gone unbloodied for too long."

"Enough!" Maelcon bellowed, regaining his footing.

But Domnall wasn't done. He sneered into Alaric's face. "I knew when word arrived warning me that you took Elisead as a hostage that my bride would be sullied by—"

"What?" Alaric's eyes blazed. "Who sent word?"

"I said enough!" Maelcon wrenched himself between the two men, prying their hands apart.

"I will not lower myself with a used woman," Domnall spat, eyeing Elisead on the bed.

"What are you saying?" Maelcon said, eyes widening.

"You had a chance to become the father-in-law of the King of Dál Riata. Instead you chose to ally your-selves with these filthy barbarians and whore out your daughter to appease them." Domnall smoothed back his disheveled hair, trying to regain control of himself. But his words only enflamed Maelcon.

"It is *you* who have dishonored my daughter," he snapped.

"Careful, Maelcon," Domnall warned. "You do not wish to have me—or my father—as an enemy."

Maelcon stiffened, his hands clenching at his sides. "As I already said, perhaps we should wait for the light of day to discuss all of this further. You have traveled far and are likely wearied—"

"My men and I will leave at first light," Domnall bit out. "Clearly you do not wish to continue your alliance with me. Consider our union dissolved." He cast one last look at Elisead, but then turned away. As he maneu-vered past Alaric, he tilted his head and muttered some-thing, but Elisead couldn't make out the words.

"We will discuss this later," her father hissed at her before shuffling after Domnall.

The four men who were returning to the fortress—Domnall, Maelcon, Drostan, and Feitr—gathered into an uneasy clump just outside the tent. Next to them, Madrena and Rúnin spoke sharp and low in their rolling language. At last their voices dropped off. Madrena fell in with the tense group of men and without a word, they moved off into the woods. Feitr's torch grew dim as they drew farther away.

Rúnin stepped into the tent at last, taking in the

sight of Elisead tumbled on the bed and Alaric standing taut, still staring at the place where Domnall had been.

At last, the nightmarish spell holding them all seemed to break.

"Are you well?" Alaric asked, coming to Elisead's side. She sat up, but she didn't trust her legs to stand.

"Aye, I am fine." At least physically. But her mind swirled in horror at all that had transpired since first laying eyes on Domnall earlier that day.

Alaric stood before her for a long moment, seeming to be struggling to say something.

But her head was beginning to grow heavy and fogged as she waited. Too much had happened. Domnall's arrival. The nigh strangling tension between Domnall, Maelcon, and Alaric. The discovery of the longship she'd carved. The dissolution of her engagement. It all threatened to wash her away on a wave of overpowering anguish.

Just as Alaric opened his mouth to speak, she held up a trembling hand. "I think I will turn in for the night. I…I cannot…"

Alaric jerked his head curtly and stepped back. "I understand. As your father said, things will be clearer in the light of day. Rest now."

Rúnin stepped out of the tent, and Alaric followed. But just before he slipped through the flaps, he paused. "You are safe here, Elisead."

She nodded wearily, but he continued to stare at her. His eyes glowed a dark green in the low light.

At last, he let the tent flaps drop. Elisead fell back on

the bed, completely spent. Tears slipped through her lashes as she squeezed her eyes shut.

Alaric's strong hand steadying her. His green eyes cutting into her. Domnall's sneering insults. Her father's anger at her for the carving. She didn't know what she was crying for, only that she felt lost, unmoored on a storm-swept sea.

She clapped a hand over her mouth to stifle the sobs. Tears racked her until she was swallowed by the dark oblivion of sleep.

26

This isn't over.

　　Domnall's hissed words, meant only for Alaric's ears, tumbled endlessly through his mind.

Domnall was a fool, but worse, he was a fool with power. What did his threat mean? Would he seek vengeance against Maelcon for not cutting off negotiations with the Northmen? Or would he take it out on Elisead?

Alaric could admit that the thought of Domnall ending his betrothal with Elisead gave him a vicious satisfaction. But he didn't trust that Domnall was done with Elisead, Maelcon, or himself just yet.

When at last the tension had drained from the camp and his men turned in for the night, Alaric hadn't bothered seeking his bed on Rúnin's floor. Nei, he would not be sleeping this night. Instead, he'd taken up position outside Elisead's tent.

Her muffled sobs had clawed through his chest and torn straight to his heart. Over and over again, he cursed Domnall for his cruel treatment of her. The man had roughened her with his hands, but worse, he'd sullied her with claims against her innocence.

Alaric stifled a curse directed at himself. Though he'd nigh seen red at Domnall's insults, hot shame branded him.

He *had* touched Elisead, even though he'd staked his honor on not doing so. Memories of their kiss heated his blood and sent his manhood aching. The truth, the one he didn't want to admit, was that Domnall had been right—at least partially.

Elisead had done naught wrong. But Alaric had broken his word and threatened his mission with that kiss. He'd dishonored himself and Elisead by letting even a shadow of doubt fall upon her.

Now Maelcon's alliance with Domnall was crumbling, but that only renewed Alaric's determination to settle the terms of their negotiation and move forward in peace with the Pictish chieftain.

A seed of an idea was beginning to sprout. Domnall had discarded Elisead and cast shame upon her, leaving Maelcon vulnerable and Elisead dishonored. But there was a way to shore up Alaric's alliance with Maelcon and bring Elisead under his protection fully. Dare he consider it?

Elisead's scream brought his head snapping up.

He bolted to his feet on instinct. His sword was partially drawn and glowing blue in the moonlight before his mind caught up to his body. Of course she was safe—he'd been couching outside her tent all night to ensure it.

Rúnin's dark head shot out of his tent. Alaric quickly re-sheathed his sword and held up a hand to halt Rúnin.

"All is well," he said softly. "She likely just had a nightmare, but I will check on her."

Rúnin nodded and withdrew back into his tent with a barely audible grunt of relief.

Alaric ducked his head into Elisead's darkened tent. He paused to let his eyes adjust, but another cry of fear rose from the shadowed bed.

Careful to avoid the enormous stone on the ground, he moved to where Elisead lay. In the low light, her pale skin glowed like the moon itself. She tossed her head against the downy mattress, her brows drawn together. Muttered words, spiked with fear, drifted from her lips.

"Elisead," he whispered. Gently, he took her shoulders in hand and gave her a little shake. "Elisead, wake up."

She cried out, her hands clawing at him in panic. He gave her another shake, and blessedly this time her eyes popped open.

"It is Alaric," he said quickly. "You were having a nightmare."

"Alaric?" Her breaths were coming fast, her voice still laced with fear.

"Ja," he replied, lowering himself so that he sat on the edge of the wooden frame that lifted the mattress off the ground.

She heaved a sigh of relief, but he could still feel her trembles where he held her shoulders.

"It was the bones again and…and Domnall was taking me away, and——"

"Shhh," he soothed. "'Tis over now." He ran his hands up and down her arms. His touch seemed to calm her, but still she clutched the front of his tunic.

"Alaric…" she faltered, "don't…don't go. Stay and comfort me for another moment."

Though a warning bell rang distantly in the back of his mind, he was beyond helping himself. Her scent, of the woods and her sweet skin, rose up and enveloped him. Her eyes were depthless pools in the darkness, but he knew she gazed up at him pleadingly.

As if under the spell of the forest spirit that lived within her, he lowered himself onto the mattress by her side. His arms slid around her, pulling her into his chest.

She was greedy for his touch, for she pressed the full length of herself against him, nuzzling her head onto his shoulder and holding him close by his tunic.

His blood suddenly flashed hot. It hammered through his veins and roared in his ears. Against all he knew to be right, his manhood surged at the feel of her soft body melting into his hard one.

But was this not right? It felt like the most right thing he'd ever done, as if his whole life had been leading up to this moment when he could hold Elisead in his embrace.

She gave a soft sigh as if she felt it too. Her warm breath fanned against his collarbone where his tunic opened at his neck. Even the touch of her breath sent a shudder through him.

"Alaric...?" Though her body was limply draped over his, her voice was hesitant and anxious.

"Ja?"

"What Domnall said...about the two of us..."

Anger sliced through the fog of lust clouding his thoughts. "That whoreson had no right to impugn your honor."

"But...but it wasn't just him. I saw the look in my father's eyes when he beheld the Northman's longship on the stone. He suspects it too."

Alaric let out a slow exhale through his teeth. "Ja, so do Madrena and Rúnin."

"They all assume that something has passed between us, that something..." She shook her head against his shoulder.

"Ja," he said again, longing mingling with resignation. "But naught can happen."

His words hung for a long moment in the darkness of the tent. He cursed himself for his own hypocrisy, for even as he spoke them, he tightened his arms around her, unwilling to let her go.

"I made a promise to your father, and to my people. Even though you are no longer engaged to Domnall, I cannot dishonor myself by breaking my word, nor can I turn my back on my mission. I cannot—"

"I know," she breathed.

With every shred of willpower he possessed, Alaric forced himself to loosen his hold on Elisead and sit up.

"You should try to get back to sleep," he said, his voice huskier than he'd intended.

She nodded, but he saw the subtle motion of her throat bob as she swallowed. Her eyes shimmered in the low light with unspoken emotion.

Alaric tore his gaze away, lest his willpower fail him against his surging desire to claim her mouth—claim her in every way, right here on this bed. Make her his, for all eternity.

He jerked to his feet and strode quickly to the tent's door, not letting himself look back at her where she lay splayed on his bed. With a sharp inhale, he dragged in the cool, salty night air. But the darkness couldn't hide the truth.

By every god in all the realms, he wanted her —*needed* her.

He paced one length of the tent, then turned and paced the other so that he circled her like a prowling animal. But he was not the predator—nei, his desire for her hunted him as if *he* was its powerless prey.

At last he crouched at the tent's far end so that he faced the forest. He dragged his fingers through his hair. He was only a man. What chance did he stand against a longing so strong?

His swirling thoughts once again returned to the idea that had begun to sprout just before he'd heard Elisead's cry. Could he still control his own fate and make Elisead his at the same time?

A twig snapped far off in the woods beyond where Alaric knelt, ripping his attention from his own tortured thoughts.

His whole being went taut. A soft wind whispered across his skin, stirring the dark trees and making the forest look alive.

Alaric sniffed the air, but the breeze was coming off the bay behind him. Besides the rustling of the leaves and pine boughs, all was quiet. Those in the camp had long ago turned in, with the fire reduced to a low smolder.

Another twig snapped. That was not a coincidence. Either an animal stalked the woods just beyond the camp, or someone lurked there.

Alaric pursed his lips and whistled softly. It was a particular bird call that Rúnin had taught him. Breath stilled and eyes alert on the forest, he waited for Rúnin's response to drift from the tent next to Elisead's.

But before Rúnin's returned whistle, the woods exploded in movement and noise.

"Attack!" Alaric bellowed, hoping his men would make sense of his warning shouted in the Northland tongue.

Just as his sword slid free of its scabbard, a swarm of armored warriors poured forth from the trees. They had drawn so close, unnoticed under the cover of night, that they would have swallowed the camp unimpeded had Alaric not sounded an alarm.

The camp sprang to life just as three warriors fell on Alaric, swinging their swords all at once at his head.

Alaric's mind went quiet as his instincts took over. He blocked a blow meant to separate his head from his neck even as he twisted away from a second blade. The third sliced his shoulder, and he felt warmth flow down his left arm.

But instead of dulling his reflexes and slowing his mind, the feel of his own hot blood being spilled sent pure, white energy through Alaric.

A battle cry ripped from his throat as he spun, slicing his first attacker across the stomach. The man's chainmail prevented the blow from being lethal, but he fell back nevertheless.

Alaric's blade continued through the air, tilting downward toward his second attacker. This time, his sword found the gap where the man's helmet met his chainmail. Blood sprayed across Alaric's face as the man toppled before him, nigh decapitated.

Just as Alaric met the third attacker, the first one regained his footing and charged. But suddenly Rúnin was at his side, bellowing his own battle cry. Like a deadly serpent, Rúnin dodged the attack and spun, ramming his sword into the back of the man's neck. Alaric didn't have time to thank his friend, however, for he was engaged in delivering a deadly blow of his own.

Shrieks of victory and death filled the camp. Distantly, Alaric hoped that none of his crew had been set upon without hearing his warning. If any of them fell under a Pictish blade, he prayed it would be with a weapon in hand so as to be welcomed into Valhalla.

More warriors poured from the night-darkened woods. Time slowed as Alaric and Rúnin met them side by side in a deadly dance. Blood pounded in Alaric's veins and flowed over his skin. He lost himself in the motion of blocks and blows, his body melding with his sword.

But then a terrified scream ripped through the fog of battle.

Elisead.

27

Blood-chilling screams tore Elisead from sleep's embrace.

For a moment, she feared she was still caught in her own nightmares, and this time, Alaric wasn't there to soothe her. But the sounds were too real, too near, to be of the dream world.

She bolted upright as the noises of death and clanging metal barraged her.

Panic froze her. The camp was under attack. And the battle raged mere feet from her.

Her head spun and sickness welled in her throat. Nay, she could not get washed away in the overwhelming fear and cacophony now. She had to keep her wits about her.

With her heart pounding an erratic beat, she slipped from the mattress and crawled on her hands and knees toward the closed tent flaps. Partway there, though, she hesitated. What good would it do to leave the tent only to crawl into the middle of the battle?

A savage scream sent her jumping. She had to clap a hand over her mouth to prevent from crying out, though she distantly doubted one more scream would matter now.

Was she safe inside the tent? Was she safe anywhere? Her whole body began to shake.

"Stop it," she whispered to herself. "Hold yourself together."

Crawl under the wooden platform that holds the mattress off the ground, a little voice said. A trickle of strength began to flow within her. She could do this. She would survive.

She pawed her way back toward the bed, forcing her limbs to move even as someone fell into the tent, tugging the woolen siding for a moment.

But just as she began wedging herself under the wooden bed frame, the whole tent reverberated again. Weak moonlight suddenly fell upon her. Someone had yanked back the flaps at the front of the tent.

Elisead jammed herself under the bed, but she wasn't fast enough. A hard hand caught her ankle and pulled, dragging her across the floor.

Unadulterated terror seized her. A high scream ripped from her throat as she clawed desperately at the ground, but her attacker was too strong.

"You whore."

Impossibly, her horror hitched higher at the voice. *Domnall.*

"You think I would let your defilement with the Northman go unpunished?"

Domnall dragged her toward the tent flap. As she twisted on the ground, she slammed into the stone that was to be her bride gift to Domnall. Her shoulder went numb, but where she'd made contact with her head, she felt a sudden liquid warmth. Her vision darkened for a long moment and the world spun.

Elisead blinked fiercely, desperate to regain her sight. The darkness lessened slightly, and the sudden breeze made her realize she was outside.

At last, Domnall released her ankle. He loomed over her, a black shadow against the night sky. Then she saw the dull glint of a blade. Domnall drew his sword over his head, the slivered moon sliding along its sharp edge.

Time ground to a halt. Elisead inhaled, but distantly she knew she wouldn't have time to scream again before Domnall's blade cleaved her. The salty air burned her throat. She would die a heartbeat from now.

The sword began its torturously slow descent. Though she longed to escape at least for one breath to the safety of darkness behind her eyelids, she could not look away. The blade arced toward her, its path unstoppable.

But then suddenly it *did* stop. Domnall's blade froze in midair, clanging so hard against another sword that both vibrated even as they locked together.

Elisead's gaze traveled up the length of the sword to the golden warrior who held it. *Alaric.*

Though she knew it was him, he looked utterly savage. Blood splattered his face and clothes. His eyes danced wildly, filled with unfettered bloodlust. He crouched next to her, his sword jutting across her to protect her body from Domnall's blade.

Domnall's dark eyes flashed in the moonlight. He pushed down on his blade with all his might.

Alaric bared his teeth but held fast under Domnall's weight. As if he had transformed from a mere warrior into a pagan god, Alaric began not just resisting Domnall's attack, but pushing back. He rose onto one knee as he drove Domnall's sword upward and away from Elisead an inch at a time.

Now it was Domnall's turn to bare his teeth. He grunted in exertion and rage as Alaric continued to gain ground. With a sudden burst of energy, Alaric shoved to his feet, flinging Domnall's blade back.

Elisead scrambled backward on the ground, her eyes fixed on the two men as they prepared to launch themselves at each other.

But then more shouts sounded from the woods beyond where the Northmen were still locked in combat with Domnall's men.

Including a woman's battle cry.

More warriors were suddenly streaming from the forest. Her father's men! And Elisead spotted Madrena by her flowing ice-blonde hair. The warrior woman wielded a sword like the others, hacking her way through Domnall's men.

Alaric and Domnall froze, both taking in the sight of Maelcon's forces coming to the aid of the Northmen.

"You'll die this night," Alaric vowed, raising his sword at Domnall once more.

"Halt!"

Maelcon charged through the camp on his enormous steed bred for battle. He reined in hard as he reached the two men.

Alaric froze in mid-attack, but he didn't lower his weapon. Domnall darted his gaze between Alaric and Maelcon.

"Why do you stop me from killing this whoreson?" Alaric snapped, his eyes still burning on Domnall.

"Because he and his men are already defeated," Maelcon panted from atop the warhorse. "And I want him to deliver a message."

Alaric considered Maelcon's words for a moment, still holding Domnall motionless under the point of his blade. At last, he raised his fingers to his lips and brought forth a piercing whistle.

Behind her, the shouting and clanging of metal suddenly halted.

"Drop your sword," Alaric bit out to Domnall.

Domnall actually dared to hesitate. "So you can kill me dishonorably in front of my men?" he sneered.

"Nay, you fool," Maelcon snapped. "So that you can run to your father and tell him he has a new enemy."

Alaric whistled again, and suddenly the Northmen were herding Domnall's remaining men in a circle. Seeing them, Maelcon's warriors joined the effort. They rounded up Domnall's bleeding and diminished force into a tight ball.

"Do I have to tell you again?" Alaric narrowed his eyes on Domnall, still looking more like a wild and fearsome animal than a man.

Finally, Domnall's arrogant sneer faltered. His eyes

flickered to where the remains of his men huddled under both the Northmen's and Maelcon's warriors' blades. Slowly, he lowered his sword, dropping the tip into the churned dirt at his feet.

Her father straightened in his saddle, raising his voice for all to hear. "You'll return to Torridon and tell your father, King Causantín mac Fergusa, that the marriage alliance between himself and my people is severed. You'll also tell him that you were defeated, and that you and his army will give my lands a wide berth from now on."

One last spark of defiance lit Domnall's dark eyes. "Nay, for I am to go to Dál Riata, not Torridon."

"Very well," Maelcon snapped. "Go to Dál Riata instead, and wait until your father summons you for an explanation when your wedding doesn't occur come harvest time."

Domnall gritted his teeth, but at last he nodded his understanding. "Someone get me my horse."

Elisead's searching gaze landed on a large, well-bred steed near her tent where Domnall must have dismounted to attack her. Drostan, who stood at her father's horse's side, retrieved the animal and handed the reins to Domnall.

Just as Domnall mounted and reined his steed toward the dark woods, Alaric's voice cut through the silence.

"And tell your King that more Northmen are coming—so many that he will never be able to beat us all back. And we are here to stay."

Domnall's gaze seared into Alaric, but he said

naught. With one hand, Domnall waved for his men to fall in behind him as he spurred his horse into motion. The group, now little more than half the size it had originally been, limped away into the forest headed southwest.

"Follow them—from a distance—to make sure they leave my lands," Maelcon said quietly to Drostan. The warrior nodded and gathered a few others for the task.

Elisead turned her gaze on Alaric, who still stood with his blade gripped in his hand. As his eyes fell on her where she sprawled on the ground, the wildfire finally seemed to bank within him.

He re-sheathed his sword in one fluid motion and was suddenly crouching over her.

"Are you hurt?"

Alaric's sudden rush toward her drew her father's eye as well. "Elisead!" he blurted, swinging down awkwardly from his horse.

Elisead sat upright, touching her head where her blood flowed. "I will be fine," she said, even as the camp swirled slightly.

"You'll return to the fort with me," her father said, crouching as well as he could given his old leg injury.

Alaric stiffened, but before he could interject, Maelcon went on.

"You'll *all* return to the fort," he said loudly. "This camp isn't safe, at least not while Domnall is still nearby."

"He never stood a chance of overpowering us," Alaric said flatly.

"Aye, well, even still, I'll not have my daughter

sleeping on top of a battle field tonight," Maelcon said. "And you and your men are welcome within my walls."

Elisead could hardly believe her ears. Did that mean that her father and Alaric were finally coming to terms?

"Very well," Alaric said with a nod. Murmurs rose among his men, but none defied their leader.

Alaric reached for Elisead, scooping her up as if she weighed next to naught. But when she slipped her arms around his shoulders, he flinched and grunted.

Suddenly Madrena was at her brother's side. "Are you well?"

"Ja," he said. "We can see to our injured once we reach the fortress."

Within the warm safety of Alaric's arms, Elisead dared to let her eyes scan the camp. Bodies littered the ground, broken and bloodied. Moonlight glinted dully off Domnall's fallen warriors' chainmail. In fact, almost all the bodies were armored. How had the Northmen survived such an attack nigh unscathed?

Alaric's crew filtered to their tents quietly, reemerging with a few items and weapons in their arms. At last, the Northmen, followed by her father's warriors, began making their way toward the fortress farther up the river. The two groups fell into an eerie silence as they drew away.

Elisead buried her face in Alaric's neck. Even though the night had been filled with terror and death, she knew she was safe in his embrace.

28

"His only hope was to catch us by surprise, but I took that from him a moment before he attacked. Even if I hadn't sounded the alarm, he was outnumbered."

Alaric sat in a heavy wooden chair in the small chamber that Maelcon used for private meetings. Maelcon sat across from him, his bad leg jutting out to the side.

Though Alaric had noticed the chieftain's slight limp the first time he'd laid eyes on him, the old wound seemed to bother Maelcon more than usual after a night on horseback.

Maelcon grunted. "I knew Domnall was arrogant, but I didn't realize how great a fool he was."

"And how did he and his nigh thirty men slip out of your fortress unnoticed?"

Maelcon stiffened. "He didn't go unnoticed, or have

you forgotten that we came to your aid only a few moments behind him?"

Alaric crossed his arms, ignoring the pinch in his shoulder. He'd stitched it closed in the wee hours of the morning in the great hall. The wound wasn't serious, thank Odin. Nor had there been many severe injuries. They'd only lost three warriors in Domnall's surprise attack and taken about a dozen of the bastard's men in return.

Pushing aside the mild pain, Alaric remained silent, pinning Maelcon with a hard look.

Maelcon exhaled through his nose slowly. "I fear…I fear he had help. From inside the fortress."

That was what Alaric had suspected, but to hear it from the proud chieftain sent ice into his belly.

"I have already questioned the guards stationed on the wall and at the gate," Maelcon went on. "Domnall told a few of them that he and his men weren't going to wait until first light to leave." Maelcon shook his head. "Blessedly, one of my guards thought such behavior was strange and alerted me, but Domnall was already on his way to you by then."

Alaric rubbed the stubble along his jaw, considering Maelcon. He'd suspected the man to be behind the attempt to harm Elisead and set upon Madrena in the night. And if Maelcon hadn't sullied his own hands, then Alaric had guessed the chieftain might have given the order to someone like Feitr.

But based on Maelcon's souring toward Domnall, who could have just as easily destroyed their negotiations, and his obvious protectiveness of his daughter,

Alaric was willing to take a chance and trust him. At least partially.

"I believe you have more to worry about than some gullible guards. What did Domnall mean when he said last eve that he'd received word of my presence here?"

Maelcon shook his head. "When Domnall arrived yesterday morn, he said he was merely passing through. He was eager to see Elisead, but I chalked that up to a groom anxious to confirm his bride's beauty. I know not what he meant about being sent for."

"More foul play," Alaric muttered. He would reveal no more to Maelcon for the time being. At least the chieftain was finally starting to be more forthcoming with Alaric. "And do you think Domnall will come back?"

Maelcon tugged on his beard, his bushy eyebrows drawing together. "I know not."

Alaric arched an eyebrow at him. "Tell me the truth, Maelcon. You fear he will return, which is why you invited my Northmen into your fortress. You hope that your walls, combined with my force, will be enough to ward off Domnall and his father's army if it comes to that."

Again, Maelcon exhaled long and slow. "I doubt they will bother. We are a small and remote band, hardly worth the King of Pict's attention. Causantín might be swayed if Domnall makes a big enough fuss over the broken engagement, but the King is already granting his son reign over Dál Riata. Causantín has larger things to worry about—the Northumbrians are a constant nuisance, and as you said, more Northmen arrive every summer."

"Then if your Pict King is so uninterested in you, why did you seek to make a marriage alliance with his son? And why have you resisted my offer of alliance?"

Alaric tried not to let his annoyance color his voice, but he'd lost patience for Maelcon's games and delays. True, the chieftain had aided his men last night and had at last invited them into the fortress. But the man still seemed to cling to a misplaced hope that Alaric wasn't serious about staying.

Maelcon shifted in his chair, repositioning his stiff leg. "Before Causantín, there was no King of the Picts. Aye, we had Kings of various territories, and chieftains of smaller areas and groups of people beneath them. But Causantín brought all of Pictland under his reign. Of course, he's kept us largely safe from Northumbrian encroachment. And he brought together the smaller Kings through alliance and trade. But a few remote corners have remained harder to secure."

"And this is one such corner," Alaric said. "So your desire for protection from enemies and Northlanders alike was only part of your reasoning."

"Aye. I have long resisted living under a distant King's thumb—or any man's thumb for that matter."

That explained why Maelcon bucked at Alaric's arrival and declaration that he and his people would be staying. "You hoped to leverage some degree of power —or at least independence—by marrying your daughter to Causantín's son."

Maelcon nodded. "But it seems that independence

in this new world is vanishing, just like the lesser Kings of Pictland were swallowed by Causantín."

"The same is happening elsewhere. The Northlands have long been ruled by Jarls, but now Kings are claiming control over both the Jarls and all their lands. Power is being consolidated. Only the bold—and the strong—will have a chance of breaking away."

Maelcon eyed Alaric across the small space separating their chairs. "And which are you—bold or strong?"

Alaric lifted his lips in a grim smile. "I am both. I promised you your daughter would have my protection while she was my hostage, and I have kept that promise. I also told you that with our peoples united, you would have the might of my Northland warriors at your back —last night I proved that as well."

And yet, Maelcon hesitated.

"But if you are still unsure of my seriousness," Alaric said carefully. "I have another suggestion for how to knit our interests together and assure our mutual benefit in the alliance I propose."

Maelcon leaned forward, guarded interest on his face. Alaric had claimed to be bold, and now was the time to prove it. His heart hammered in his chest as he opened his mouth to form the words.

Suddenly the door to the small chamber burst open. "Forgive me, Chief," Drostan said quickly, taking in the sight of Alaric seated across from Maelcon. "I thought you were alone."

Maelcon waved his warrior in. "What is it?"

"We followed Domnall and his men as far as the

mountains. They continued southwest toward Dál Riata."

"Good," Maelcon said, his face hardening.

"I'll send some of my men back to the camp today," Alaric said. "They can dispose of the bodies and secure our supplies—if we are to stay here in the fortress, that is."

Maelcon nodded to Alaric, meeting his eyes. Though satisfaction swelled within Alaric at his victory, it was short lived, for he still needed to tell Maelcon his next plan.

With another wave from Maelcon, Drostan silently departed, closing the door behind him.

"Now, what is your proposal to sweeten this alliance?"

Alaric felt like an untested lad entering his first battle. But he was a Northman—he didn't cower or flee from conflict, he faced it. He rose from his chair, planting his feet wide and crossing his arms over his chest.

"I would wed Elisead."

29

Elisead had been lingering in her chamber long enough. It had been a trying night, aye, but she could tell from the bustle from the great hall echoing down the corridor outside her chamber that others had found a way to face the day.

She'd barely slept, but if she was honest with herself, it wasn't because the shadows threatened or nightmares loomed. Nay, it was because the memory of Alaric's arms cradling her sent her limbs tingling. His scent, of sweat and battle but also of his skin, lingered around her.

Her chamber had felt strangely empty compared to the tent she'd been sleeping in for over a fortnight. She hadn't realized it, but she'd become used to the knowledge that Alaric slept only a few feet away from her in the nearest tent.

Madrena had vacated Elisead's chamber quickly upon their arrival back at the fortress. She'd slept with

Rúnin and the others on the floor of the great hall. Madrena's open and fierce affection toward Rúnin made Elisead blush. For some reason, the North-woman's unapologetic desire for her mate sent Elisead's thoughts into dangerous territory—not the territory of a virgin daughter of a Pictish chieftain.

As her father had hustled her to her chamber last night, she'd caught a glimpse of Alaric with the others in the great hall. He was carefully peeling off his bloodied tunic to inspect his injured shoulder.

He'd looked every inch the fearsome Northern warrior. His body was all hard lines and ridges. She would have thrown herself into his muscular arms, dirt, blood, and all if she had been the free forest spirit he called her.

Instead, she'd walked dutifully by her father's side toward her chamber, allowing him to close the door tightly behind her. Yet in the darkness of her room, her thoughts were her own—and they had run wild.

But now it was time to face the light of day. Elisead had washed as best she could in her small basin and dressed carefully. She'd plaited her hair with fumbling fingers. Her fate awaited her beyond her chamber door. It was a fate that no longer involved Domnall, thank God. But what it *did* include, she was unsure.

Elisead pushed herself out of her chamber and forced her feet to carry her toward the great hall. Her steps faltered as she heard the bang of a wooden door ahead.

"Out!"

She hurried forward at the sound of her father's

angry shout. Just ahead in the corridor, she saw Alaric stride out of her father's private chamber and into the great hall. Maelcon was on his heels, his face red with anger. She dashed ahead but came to a skidding halt when she reached the great hall.

"When you calm yourself, you'll see that—"

"My daughter? Marry a Northman? You insult us both, yet you have the audacity to tell me to calm down!"

A strangled gasp cut through the air. Elisead realized belatedly that the noise had come from her throat. Both Alaric and her father turned toward her, Alaric's eyes penetrating while Maelcon's were clouded with rage.

"You…you wish to marry me?"

All at once, her vision filled with an imagined future as Alaric's wife. Her whole body nigh hummed as if the spirits themselves desired such a fate.

Before Alaric could answer, Maelcon interjected.

"It is out of the question."

"When you are done blustering, you'll see the mutual benefit. We already share an interest in her well-being. She would be the tie between our people, ensuring that both parties seek what is best for all," Alaric snapped back at him.

Elisead's belly twisted painfully. The vision of the future and the humming in her body vanished as one. Bitterness surged in the back of her throat. Aye, Alaric wanted to marry her—for the "mutual benefit" he and her father would reap.

"In my lands," Alaric went on, shifting his gaze back to Elisead, "a woman gets a say in her own fate. Perhaps you should consult your daughter before you decide for her."

Maelcon opened his mouth to protest, but Alaric held up a hand, shooting him a glare fierce enough to stay his protests for a moment.

"I…" Elisead shook her head a little, trying to clear her thoughts and unknot her twisting innards. "I do not know."

Suddenly it was all too much. She spun on her heels and bolted for the doors leading from the great hall to the yard. She needed air, else she would faint like a silly, weak girl.

Just as she pushed one of the double doors open, a warm, callused hand came down gently on top of hers.

"Let me explain myself to you, Elisead," Alaric said softly.

"Nay, I need…I need to think. I need air."

"Where will you go?"

"Anywhere!" she blurted. But she forced herself to take a calming breath. "To the woods."

Alaric looked down at her, his golden head bowed toward her. His strong, handsome features darkened slightly. "It isn't safe. I'll accompany you."

How was she supposed to think clearly with Alaric's large, muscular frame looming over her, his scent, washed clean of the battle last night, clinging to her?

She felt fragile in Alaric's presence, but it was different than when she became overwhelmed by too many competing sensations. Aye, she felt suddenly more aware of every breath of air against her skin, every shade of green in his searching eyes.

But this time she did not wish to shift her gaze away, curl in a ball, and wait for the storm of sensations to pass.

"Let me explain," he repeated softly.

She didn't believe for a moment that she'd be able to clear her mind with Alaric speaking to her of the practical reasons and political advantages for their marriage. But she also saw the set of his jaw. He would not be swayed.

"Very well."

Maelcon made a noise behind them as if to object, but neither paid him any heed. Elisead strode into the yard and called for the gates to be opened. She and Alaric walked out into the midday sun, her heart hitching strangely.

"Tell me, Northman," she said when they'd passed the village and entered the woods. "Why should I marry you?"

HE WATCHED as Elisead and Alaric made their way past the gates and through the village. Though he longed to curse aloud, he resisted the urge. He'd waited so long and worked too hard to give up his composure now.

As he so often did, he'd gone unnoticed in the great hall. Lingering in the shadows had afforded him the opportunity to witness Maelcon's outburst and Alaric's persistence in seeking a marriage with Elisead.

It only made sense that the man would want to

marry the chieftain's daughter. Alaric's desire for Elisead had always been obvious.

Indeed, he himself had long lusted after the girl. Though he'd detested the thought of her marrying Domnall, the arrogant fool, he'd forced himself to accept his fate to always wait, watch from the outside, and never taste the sweeter spoils in life.

But the chieftain had gone too far this time.

He'd always thought he'd had no true power, but when he realized that if he could thwart Alaric and Maelcon's negotiations, *his* hand would be the one guiding fate.

His first move, to cut the donkey's harness and set Elisead in harm's way, had been ill conceived and foolish. While having the girl take a tumble and perhaps even break a bone would have surely halted negotiations and flared tensions between Maelcon and Alaric, his true aim wasn't to harm Elisead, for he had other plans for her.

The attempt to stab Alaric's sister in the middle of the night was a much wiser maneuver. She was expendable, and given Alaric's protectiveness, it would have surely led to an all-out war.

But the bitch had blocked the door, and ever since then, she'd been alert and watchful. He hadn't been able to get her alone, and he wasn't ready to make a move out in the open yet.

Secretly sending word to Domnall should have been enough. Yet even Domnall couldn't set things to right. It had been a mistake to hope the spoiled bastard could help. It would have required sacrificing Elisead to the preening future King, yet he could have accepted it if it had meant Alaric would be thwarted in his plans. While Domnall's egotistical possessiveness would have served his purposes, the arrogant fool was too rash to be controlled.

And now Domnall was long gone. Time was running out. Maelcon was foolish enough to advance negotiations with Alaric, and the Northman's every action proved that he meant to stay. If Maelcon permitted Alaric to wed Elisead, no amount of under-handed scheming would stop this nightmare.

It was time to act. It wasn't his way to work in the open, though. He had one last hope of avoiding disaster. But if a marriage went forward, all would be lost— unless he stopped it.

He knew what he was capable of if it came to that— he was born to be a killer, a warrior. Could he also be a leader?

He slipped away from the fortress walls, uneasy at being so visible. One more chance. And then he'd be forced to expose his plan at last.

30

Tell me, Northman, why should I marry you?

Alaric didn't answer for a long time, though he chewed on Elisead's words relentlessly.

He waited as they wove their way deeper into the forest. With a little nod, he fell back, letting her take the lead. She'd begun walking in the direction of the camp, but then she seemed to reconsider. Turning west, she guided him silently through the trees.

Soon they were surrounded by hills that grew in size as they continued. Elisead skirted to the right around a rocky rise and led him along a babbling creek. The air was cooler under the denser cover of trees here. Though the ground was uneven, a blanket of moss coated everything.

He'd never ventured this far into the forest in this direction, even on his hunting trips with a few of his men. Yet Elisead seemed to know every rock, every bend in the creek. She placed her feet with the familiar ease of one who knew the land like it was an extension of her own body.

At last, she slowed in front of a large, jagged rock outcropping that rose sharply from the creek bed. Moss, ferns, and saplings clung to the top of the outcropping, despite its sheer sides. But its face was bare, exposed in the dim light trickling through the canopy of boughs overhead.

As Alaric drew to her side, he noticed shapes and patterns adorning the rock's surface.

He traced a finger along the soaring wings of an eagle carved into the rock. Though his hand met stone, the animal looked alive, caught in motion and frozen forever.

"You did this."

"Aye," she said, watching his fingertips caress the stone. "Long ago."

Alaric smiled softly at the designs. There were animals of all kinds. He recognized bears, wolves, more birds, deer, and even little squirrels. And the patterns— swirling lines, triangles, waves, and vines—were rudimentary versions of the ones he'd seen on the bride gift she'd been carving.

"You were quiet as a child," he said, keeping his eyes on the stone. "You came here to escape the noise and activity of the fortress and village. You were small for your age and didn't fit in with other children, but here, you lost yourself in the wilderness."

Her amber eyes widened, and he couldn't help feeling a swell of satisfaction at the apparent accuracy of his guesses.

"But I can't parse it—did you always make etchings in stones, even before you were trained to do so? Or did carving become the funnel through which you poured the forest spirit that has lived within you since the beginning?"

She swallowed, and his gaze shifted to her slim, pale throat where it bobbed delicately. Another surge of satisfaction went through him, but this time it was tinged with a darker lust. He reveled in the effect he had on her, for it meant that he was not the only one who was held tight in desire's bindings.

"I...I never carved before Una taught me. But I drew with bits of charcoal. Here." She placed her hand next to his on the cool stone. "It all washed away long ago. But the same images and patterns came to me then as now. It is as if..."

He waited while she struggled for the words.

"It is as if the stone speaks to me. Or rather, the stone speaks *through* me—it speaks the forest's voice, and I bring it forth."

Elisead turned to him, searching his face with those wide, honey-colored eyes. "But what does this have to do with you asking my father if he'll let you marry me?"

"That was a mistake."

At her sharp intake of breath, he realized he'd erred.

"Nei, 'twas not a mistake that I told him I wish to wed you. Only, I shouldn't have asked him the way I did —I shouldn't have asked him at all. As I told him, where I come from, a woman gets to have a say in who she marries. I should have...I should have asked *you*."

She shook her head in wonderment. A few auburn

strands escaped her plait and fell around her face. "From all you have told me and all I have seen of your people, your land is a strange place indeed."

"Perhaps in time you will not find it so strange. Perhaps I could…show you more of our ways."

He stepped closer, forcing her to tilt her head back to maintain eye contact. Though they didn't touch, only a hair's breadth separated their bodies. If he inhaled deeply, his chest would brush against the swells of her breasts.

She shook her head again, but this time she seemed to be trying to clear her thoughts. "You still haven't answered my question. Why would I ever consider wedding you?"

A smile tugged at the corners of his mouth. She was as stubborn as her father. "You tell me."

Her brows drew together. "You seek an alliance. You wish to prove your seriousness about settling to my father, and you hope that by marrying me, you'll secure his commitment to keeping the peace between our peoples."

"Ja, that is what I told him."

The crease between her brows deepened slightly. "Was that not the truth?"

"Nei, it wasn't."

He lifted his hand slowly from the stone and extended it toward her. With gentle fingertips, he brushed a red lock that had come free of her braid. He tucked it behind her ear, letting his fingers linger there for a long moment.

She sucked in a breath but never exhaled it. Her

eyelids fluttered for a moment as he traced her ear with the pad of his finger.

"I cannot deny that a marriage alliance is advantageous to my mission. But that is not the reason why I wish to wed you. The truth is, I want you."

The silence that stretched was only broken by the soft bubbling of the creek behind them, but Alaric doubted he would have noticed if someone had blown a horn directly in his ear. He felt as if he were tumbling into those bottomless amber eyes.

"Where I am from, we do not deny pleasure when it is to be had, for life is too short and painful otherwise."

"And that is what you want? Bodily pleasure?" Her eyes flared with the boldness of her words, but he sensed a deeper question in their depths.

"I want much more than that with you, Elisead. Neither of us can deny the pull we feel any longer. It is a pull toward pleasure, but also something far greater."

Her breaths grew short and shallow as he spoke, but still he needed to say more to her.

"*I want you,*" he repeated, his voice low and ragged. "I have since the moment I saw you running like a wild forest spirit through these woods. I have wanted you even when it jeopardized my honor, my mission, and my people. I want you to be mine forever."

His declaration seemed to stun her. She stared up at him, wide-eyed, her berry-pink lips parted slightly.

But her surprise couldn't match his own. Ja, he knew he'd been drawn to her. What man wouldn't be stirred by her vivid hair and eyes, her small but curved frame that was meant to be held, and the wildness within her that would never be tamed?

He'd wanted to claim her body, to taste her sweetness and unleash the spirit behind her delicate exterior. But as the words had tumbled forth from his tongue, he realized that possessing her body would never be enough.

The blinding rage he'd felt at Domnall's treatment of her—and his own protectiveness—should have alerted him, yet only now was the deeper truth of his words hitting him. He wanted to bind himself to her for all eternity. The suddenly clarity was like a bolt of lightning from Thor's own hammer.

"And now it is your turn to tell me the truth," he said, his fingers curling around the back of her head and twining in her braid. "Tell me you want me, too."

With his palm pressed alongside her throat and his fingers in her hair, he could feel her pulse pounding wildly. Delicate trembles stole over her.

"I…I know not."

"Do not lie to me, Elisead, for I can see it in your eyes and feel it in your body." His words came out harsher than he'd intended, but the thought of her denial tightened an aching knot in his chest.

"I…I *cannot* want you," she breathed, her eyes clouding.

He felt his face darken. "What does that mean?"

"You are a Northman. Your people have murdered mine."

"None of my men have—"

"Nay, not your men, but your kind. Seven years ago."

Unshed tears shimmered in her eyes. Alaric had to grit his teeth against the stab of pain those tears triggered in him.

"I cannot change the past, nor can you. Only the future lies within our power to shape."

She nodded, biting her lower lip.

His fingers reflexively tightened on her nape. "And you *do* want me, even though I am a Northman. Admit it."

Something cracked in her resolve. "Aye, I want you, too."

Pleasure surged through him. "Then let us change the fate of our peoples—together."

She shook her head, but his hand in her hair held fast.

"Have I not proven the fact that I will never let harm befall you?" he asked. "Have I not proven that our interests in peace and prosperity for this land and its people are the same?"

Reluctantly, she answered. "Aye, you have."

"Then why do you still hesitate?"

Her gaze slid from him to the rock. She bit her lower lip again as her eyes scanned the grooves she'd made years ago, clearly struggling to form words.

Alaric's mind spun back to the night before, when Domnall had seen the stone she'd been carving for him —and the modification she'd made to it.

"What about the longship you carved on your bride gift? Why did you add it?"

"I know not."

He waited, his hand still buried in her hair and his body so close to hers that he feared he might lose his wits. But his silence demanded an answer.

At last, she sighed in defeat. "There is no sound explanation for it. I simply…felt the need to add it."

"Because you wished me and my men to leave? Because you never wanted to see or be reminded of me again?" he asked incredulously.

"Nay," she said on another sigh of exasperation.

"Then because you feared me so much? Because you thought we would destroy your people and leave only smoldering ruins before sailing to the Northlands once more?"

"Nay!"

"Then why?"

"Because I felt… I *knew* our futures were forever entwined," she bit out, frustration pinching her brows.

"And how did you know?"

"The stone…demanded it. I could not turn away from its call."

"But you would turn away from me, even in the face of what your spirit knows. Why?"

"Because…?"

"Why?" he demanded.

"Because I am afraid!" she blurted out. "I'm so afraid of the way you look at me, and the future. I'm afraid of what will happen to my people and yours, what will become of my father now that he has shunned Domnall and King Causantín."

The tears welling in her eyes spilled over at last,

making trails down her creamy cheeks. "And I am most afraid of the way I feel. You are a Northman, my people's enemy, and yet I want you like I've never wanted aught before. I crave your touch, your very nearness. I need—"

Alaric could take no more. He dragged Elisead against his chest and bent his head. His hungry lips fell on hers.

31

A torrent of sensation washed over Elisead at the contact of their lips. But it was naught compared to the storm that raged within.

It was as if a dam had broken in her heart. Hearing of Alaric's desire for her had pushed her close to shattering, yet she'd held back. Like a coward, she'd hidden from the truth. Yet Alaric had stalked her even as she'd tried to flee, vanquishing all her foolish reasons for denying the powerful longing she had for him.

And then she'd truly broken. Her words had spilled forth, baring her to the very soul before him.

Alaric was a warrior. She'd never seen him cower from a challenge. But she was not so brave as he. She was afraid. Yet instead of turning in disgust at her fear, he'd claimed her with his embrace.

His lips scalded her to her core as he kissed her. Their mouths fused together hotly. Their first kiss, which still curled her toes to think of, seemed tame compared to the unbridled need they silently communicated with their bodies.

She could fight it no longer. Elisead gave herself over to the crashing waves of desire rocking her. She wanted him—needed him. Only Alaric. Forever.

She tilted her head back, giving him access to her mouth more fully. He instantly took what she offered. His tongue caressed hers, barely restrained in its demands.

The hand that was in her hair tightened reflexively. His other arm snaked around her, holding her flush against his body. The memory of Alaric rising from the river was burned into her mind, but to feel each rock-hard plane and chiseled ridge, as she had last night when she'd lain in his arms, was entirely different.

Her own body, so small and soft by comparison, melted into him, yielding like honey. But unlike the night before, there was naught gentle or hesitant about him now.

The heat—by all the gods, old and new, the heat of him. And the heat that was building within her—surely she would burn alive from the sensations coursing from her scalp to her lips, and shooting from where her breasts crushed against his chest to pool deep in her belly and between her legs.

Yet she was greedy for more. His touch was like the sweetest mead. Her head spun, drunk on Alaric's scent, his lips, his hands.

Then she was actually spinning. Alaric turned, taking her effortlessly with him. He put his back to the creek and walked her toward the large stone she'd once sought for refuge and solace. With his hands cushioning her, she came flush with the stone. It was cool even through her tunic.

His hands encircled her waist, holding her in place. As he continued to claim her mouth, one hand slid low down her hip, then around to her bottom. Even though there was hardly a wisp of air between them, somehow he managed to pull her hips even more completely against his.

She could feel the rigid length of him straining against his trousers and knew what it meant. He lusted for her, hard and hot.

His other hand brushed along her ribcage until it reached the underside of one of her breasts. Suddenly she felt achy and needy there. As his hand closed around her breast, she gasped against his mouth. She never knew just how sensitive she was—and how much sensation could shoot from just one point of contact with Alaric's warm hand.

His thumb began to move slowly over the peak of her breast, and the new bolt of sensation made all the others pale. His touch was both the source and the relief of this exquisite torture. She needed more.

Suddenly his hands were behind her knees and she was boosted in the air. He lifted her, wrapping her legs around his hips and pinning her against the stone. Her long tunic hitched up her legs, exposing them to the forest air. His hardness settled between her legs, against that place which ached and burned with an urgency she'd never experienced before.

To her back was the stone, and pressing against her

was Alaric's solid strength. All she could do, all she wanted to do, was yield, take his hardness into herself, and make herself whole by binding them together.

"Take me," she panted against his mouth.

He pulled back but kept her suspended between himself and the stone. "What?"

"Bind us together for all eternity," she breathed.

A growl of pure pleasure rumbled in his chest. She felt the reverberations in her breasts, which sent a shiver through her.

"Nei, not like this," he said, though it appeared to pain him.

She blinked at him through the fog of lust clouding her vision. "How, then? I have never…"

A string of rolling words in his Northland tongue erupted from him. He took a deep breath, visibly struggling to regain control. All the while, she could feel the hard length of him pulsing against her through his trousers, his hands nigh clawing at her.

"I only meant that for your first time, I do not want to behave like a beast," he said at last, pinning her with those searing green eyes. "You deserve the finest feather mattress, the softest furs. You should have the sweetest mead poured over you and licked off. You should be worshipped like the god-made spirit you are."

She felt a blush creep up her neck and into her cheeks. She knew the basics of what went on between a man and a woman, but the images he painted with his words sent hot yearning shooting through her whole body.

What would it feel like to be laid bare before Alaric

on a downy mattress? To have the furs tickle her exposed skin? To feel his tongue lapping at every inch of her?

Could a person die of longing? Could she burn from the inside out with the desire that raged within her?

"I cannot wait," she choked out. "I need to be one with you, now and forever."

"Say you'll marry me. Say you will be mine for all time in the eyes of my gods and yours." His voice was low and edged with demanding. This was the golden Northman warrior she'd seen on the shores of the bay what felt like ages ago. This was the man to whom she already belonged, heart and soul.

"Aye. I will wed you."

Suddenly Alaric released her legs and she came down onto wobbling feet. He yanked his scabbard and belt free, tossing them aside on the forest floor. Then in one deft move, he pulled his tunic over his head and spread it out over the moss.

As he pulled her down onto his tunic, her fingertips brushed over his arms. Every inch of him was warm golden skin, yet he was as hard as the stone that had just been at her back. Her gaze flitted to his shoulder, where stitches held together the skin along a wound as long as her forefinger.

"Are you sure you can—"

He growled, easing her backward onto the ground. The moss was soft beneath her, and his tunic kept the dampness that was ever-present this deep into the woods away from her back.

"No scratch will stop me from claiming you," he

breathed, his lips fluttering against hers. His hands found the hem of her tunic and slipped under.

As he drew his hands up the outsides of her legs, he let them pause for a moment behind her knees. His calluses tickled her there, and she squirmed against him.

In response, he ground his hips into hers, making her fully aware once more of his arousal. His lips found her throat, and he trailed kisses down it even as his hands continued upward again.

Even though he held his weight above her, she felt as though her chest was being crushed under the building anticipation. Her breaths came ragged and her legs trembled even before he reached their juncture.

And when he did, his touch was barely a brushing contact. She sucked in a gasp, her head falling back onto his tunic. His fingers fluttered past her most sensitive part once again. Unbidden, her knees fell open, beckoning him in.

She was already slick with desire. In opening her legs, the cool forest air caressed and teased her, even lighter than Alaric's touch. But she burned, and somehow she knew that the only relief she would ever find lay with Alaric.

At last he touched her completely, his finger sliding down her slickness. She shuddered uncontrollably and a moan rose in her throat. He kissed the hollow in her neck, then nipped her ear.

His free hand came up to her breast and cupped her, sending a lightning-hot bolt of sensation from her nipple to where his finger stroked.

"I must do this right," he panted against her neck.

She didn't comprehend what he meant, for sensation was building and building upon itself within her. But then he lifted himself from her and cool air replaced his heated touches.

"What—"

Before she could speak her confusion, he yanked her belt off and tossed it aside with his. Then he was scooting her clothing, tunic and underdress together, up her body.

Suddenly she was exposed, laid bare before him on the forest floor. She shivered, but not from the cool air that lapped at her flushed skin. It was from the look in Alaric's eyes as he gazed upon her.

Those emerald depths, normally so lively, were filled with a raw hunger that made her breath catch. He gazed at her as if he would devour her. His eyes traveled up her legs and across her waist to her breasts, which pebbled in the fresh air.

She sank her teeth into her lower lip, suddenly unsure of the sharpness in his eyes. She more than admired his form—in fact, it was hard not to stare at him as he crouched over her now, his chest bare and beckoning.

But then he caught her chin in one large hand, gently dislodging her lip from her teeth's grasp.

"Freyja's breath," he whispered.

She shook her head in confusion.

"One of my gods," he said, his gaze still darting over her. "The goddess of all beauty and pleasure."

Her uncertainty dissipated in a flood of heated gratitude. He took her lips in a kiss once more, his hands seeking her breasts. She arched into him, eager for more of the delicious pleasure he had awoken within her.

"Remember this," he breathed against her lips. "Remember how wild and free you are, my little spirit. I want you to feel like this always."

His words emboldened her even more. She wrapped her arms around his shoulders, careful of his stitches, and drew him down more fully on top of her. She spread her legs to accommodate him, loving the hardness barely contained by his trousers pushing against her.

Sensation was once again piling on top of itself. Elisead's head spun dizzily as Alaric's tongue caressed hers, his hands skimming over her breasts and her stomach. With each ragged breath, his touches grew more frantic. She suddenly realized that her fingers had turned into claws on his back as she urged him on.

One of his hands disappeared as he worked the ties on his trousers. He carelessly yanked them down and kicked them and his boots off, never taking his mouth from hers.

And then she felt his manhood, hot, hard, and yet velvety smooth as it brushed past her leg.

This was the moment she'd wanted. He positioned himself at her entrance but stilled, looking down at her.

"Aye?" It was the first time she'd heard him use the word in her tongue, even though he spoke the language well. He waited, jaw ticking and weight suspended over her on his elbows.

"Aye," she breathed, holding his emerald gaze.

A look of possessive satisfaction flashed in his lust-filled eyes. Then he drove into her, slowly but steadily.

She arched to accept him, but even with her body damp and begging for him, pain shot through her.

A moan, somewhere between pleasure and pain, escaped her lips. Alaric froze, buried deep within her. Though she could feel his arms quivering under her fingertips with the effort to remain motionless, he waited.

At last, her body began to adjust to the sensation of him filling her. The breath came easier in her lungs, even though her whole being hummed as waves of sensation continued to crash within her.

With aching slowness, Alaric began to move, drawing away and easing back in. After several rocking thrusts, she started to meet his motion. The softness of her body melted against his hardness, and the pain faded, leaving only building ecstasy.

His shifted his weight onto one elbow and slipped his hand between them. His thumb found a spot of pure pleasure just above where their bodies joined. Lightning heat flashed through her, causing her breath to hitch.

There was no more room for sane thought. She yielded to instinct, letting the wild spirit within guide her. Sensation washed away everything but the ever-building pleasure until she thought she would forget how to draw breath into her lungs.

And then suddenly her whole body shattered into a thousand shards of light and heat. Distantly, she registered that she called out his name as she spiraled through paradise.

With one hard thrust, Alaric's voice joined her own. He tensed above her as the same ecstasy that had claimed her conquered him, too.

"You are mine," he panted, slumping over her. "And I am yours. Forever."

32

She was his.

No matter how many times Elisead remembered his words, they sent a shivering thrill through her.

To be claimed by this powerful, unbending Northman warrior was something that would have been completely outlandish to her a mere fortnight ago. And now she could imagine no other fate for herself than the one entwined with Alaric's.

But even more shocking had been his statement that he was hers, too. The golden-headed man walking silently at her side was hers. He was her protector, her champion, but also her companion, to walk with by her side for all their days.

And from what she had learned of the Northland ways, they were *partners* in their joining. She'd sensed from the first that Alaric saw her differently than all the men she'd known before him. He listened to her, asked her advice, and took pride in her carving skills, even encouraged her. She felt more alive—more herself—than ever before. It was as if in his presence she was as free as she felt running through the woods, hearing the whispers of the spirits.

He glanced at her, his green eyes dancing with the secret they'd just shared. Reaching out, he plucked a leaf from her hair.

"You truly look like a forest goddess, little spirit," he said, shining a smile on her. But then his face darkened slightly. "I fear that your father will know what we have done the moment we set foot in the fortress."

When the haze of passion had at last cleared and they'd untangled their bodies, that same worry had stolen over her. She'd dressed slowly, carefully smoothing her tunic of wrinkles and dirt. And as they'd walked back toward the fortress, even her elation at their union was blunted slightly by her uncertainty.

"Aye, mayhap," she said, looking at the leaf he spun in his fingers.

"Do not worry, sweet Elisead," he said lowly. He tossed the leaf aside and took her hand in his. As they continued on through the trees, she drew on some of his strength.

"I will tell him that we are to be married at once," she said. "He will come around. It is in his best interest as well as yours."

Alaric stopped again, turning toward her and taking her by the shoulders.

"Let me be clear, so that you never have cause to doubt me. By Odin's last breath, I would marry you even if it meant betraying my mission and destroying my honor. That is…a difficult thing for me to accept, for honor is all a man truly has, and this voyage is not just for my own glory, but for the wellbeing of all my people."

He clenched his jaw, his eyes clouding with some unreadable emotion for a long moment. But then he exhaled slowly through his teeth, and his gaze focused on her once more.

"By some blessing of the gods, though, marrying you allows me to keep my word and secure my mission. I do not know what I have done to deserve such luck. But understand me well—I would burn the whole world to make you mine, Elisead."

She fought back the raw emotion that rose in her throat at his words. "Nay, I will not doubt you again," she breathed.

"Thank you," he said, a smile tingeing his lips faintly. "And just to be sure, I'll make it my new mission when we are wed to woo you properly."

She blinked, feeling her own smile mirror his. "What do you mean?"

He tucked her arm under his and set off at a lazy pace once more. "In the Northlands, a woman gets to have a say in whom she will wed."

"Aye, you've said that before."

"Well, it means that a man vying for a woman's commitment must work to win her over. Courtship is quite the sport in the Northlands."

Elisead widened her eyes on him. "Sport? You must be exaggerating."

"Nei, I speak the truth," he replied with a chuckle.

"And a deadly sport at that. If an insult is given by either the man or the woman, or either of their families, a blood feud can settle upon all involved for generations."

She shook her head slowly. "I don't think I'll ever understand your ways."

"Ah, mayhap not, but now we have naught but time." She felt the warmth of his smile on her and she couldn't help but reciprocate.

But then a question that had perplexed her suddenly rose to her lips.

"Are Madrena and Rúnin married?"

Alaric snorted. "Nei."

"Why not?"

He shrugged. "Most Northlanders believe in marriage, of course. Madrena has always been…different. She likes to do things her own way. She and Rúnin have an understanding about what they are to each other. They might as well be married, for they are solely devoted to each other, but their arrangement as it is works for them."

"But *you* wish to be married, do you not?"

"Ja," he said, a soft smile lifting his lips. "More than anything, I wish for our peoples, as well as our gods, to witness us pledge ourselves to each other."

His smile widened into a mischievous grin. "Mayhap because we are to be married first, this courtship will go smoother than most," he went on. "For I will already have both you and your father's blessings on the union, so I can avoid the pitfalls many Northmen face. I could even write verses praising your beauty!"

"Is that not normal in your land?"

He chuckled again, a low and silky sound that sent tendrils of awareness through her.

"Ja, many a man has composed verses expounding on his woman's comeliness. But it must be done in secret, for any such open declarations are taken as an insult to her honor."

"Why?"

"Because any man who can craft verse upon verse about a woman's…charms…implies that he's already sampled them."

Alaric actually winked at her. She felt a hot blush creep up her neck.

"But since we will be wed, there is no dishonor in praising my wife's beauty."

"*Wife*," she said, the blush heating her cheeks. "I very much like that."

Throwing back his golden head, he laughed. She longed to freeze this moment in time, for never had she felt so happy before.

"Your father will acquiesce," he said, his laughter fading but merriment still sparkling in his vivid green eyes. "Do not worry, little spirit. We simply need to—"

Suddenly the mirth drained from his face. His whole body went rigid next to her.

"What? What is it?" she asked, abrupt panic rising within her.

She followed his gaze to the swath of forest ahead.

Smoke trickled through the trees, winding around boughs and smearing the blue sky overhead.

Before she knew what was happening, Alaric had

ripped his sword free of the scabbard on his hip and grasped her by the wrist. He bolted toward the smoke.

She stumbled after him, barely keeping up with his long strides. As the stench of burning filled her nostrils, a terrible dread nigh choked her.

33

The scent had alerted him.

If he hadn't been so focused on Elisead's beautiful smile and her honey eyes, he would have seen the smoke sooner. As it was, even his lust-clouded mind had been penetrated by the smell of burning.

He skidded to a halt where the tree line ended suddenly. With his blade poised for an attack, he released Elisead's wrist but pushed her behind him.

"The fields," she panted in disbelief.

"Ja." He'd recognized the barley fields by the abrupt edge to the otherwise thick forest. It had been painstaking and laborious work to clear away so many trees and such abundant underbrush, but he and his crew had carefully made this bare patch in the woods.

But the sight that met him was a nightmare version of the barley fields. When last he'd seen them only a day ago, the soil was still in its carefully plowed rows. Green shoots had stood almost knee-high, promising a good harvest in a few moons' time.

Now the fields lay smoldering and destroyed. Some of the barley had been burned, while other areas of the field that were likely too green to catch fire had been ripped apart. The soil at his boots was churned, with broken barley stalks strewn and smoking everywhere.

"Who would do this?" Elisead whispered behind him. She peered around his shoulder, a look of stricken horror on her face.

Alaric scanned the field for movement, but the only shift was the lazily rising smoke. "I know not."

But then his mind flew to the camp he and his crew had made only a stone's throw away. He grasped Elisead's wrist again, but this time he moved on careful, silent feet as he slipped toward the camp. He kept his sword raised in case the perpetrator still lingered, but the woods were quiet and still, revealing naught.

He edged his way into camp, shielding Elisead with his body. All the tents still stood, their wool sidings unmarred. He stepped around the tent Elisead had been using to get a clear view of the entire camp.

Chainmail-clad bodies still lay broken and bloodied on the ground. Flies hung in the air, and several ravens took flight as Alaric approached.

"Do not look, Elisead," he bit out. He'd meant to give his crew the order to return to the camp and dispose of the remnants of last night's battle with Domnall's men, but he'd instead brought his proposal of marrying Elisead to Maelcon, then gone out into the woods with Elisead.

He felt Elisead tense within his grasp and knew she hadn't heeded his command. She made a sound that was half-gasp, half-scream.

Alaric pushed down the rage—for himself at forgetting to give the order, but also at whoever had burned the fields—into the pit of his stomach. He spun, gripping Elisead by the shoulder and forcing her to turn with him so that her back was to the carnage.

"Just breathe," he said, willing his voice to be soft. "Focus on my eyes."

She blinked up at him, gulping several breaths. "I…I know it was like this last night when I stood here," she said, her voice cracking. "But it was so dark then, and I didn't see…"

"Shhh," he soothed. "Do not overwhelm yourself."

She nodded, holding his gaze more steadily now. But just as she was pulling in a deep breath, he heard the sound of footsteps in the forest to the northwest. Many footsteps.

He shoved Elisead behind him, sword flashing in the late afternoon sunlight. Time stretched as Alaric's nerves were pulled taut, trying to gauge how many people moved in the woods beyond the camp.

The first figure he saw bore a wild head of red hair and a bushy beard. Tension suddenly drained from him in a flood.

"Olaf!" Alaric barked.

The movement in the underbrush stilled for a moment, but then a dozen of Alaric's crew strode out.

"Where have you been?" the ruddy giant demanded with no preamble.

Alaric slowly re-sheathed his sword and pulled Elisead protectively to his side. "We had some sorting to do," he said.

"Madrena and Rúnin sent us out to check on the camp," Tarr said, coming to Olaf's side. "We could see smoke from the fortress walls. We searched the fortress for you, but when Maelcon said you and his daughter were out here, we feared the worst."

"We are fine, and the camp is untouched," Alaric said, "But the barley fields have been destroyed."

The dozen warriors before him tensed as one.

"That was the source of the smoke you saw," Alaric went on.

"Who?" Tarr breathed through clenched teeth.

"I know not. I came here to check on the camp, but it has been left untouched for some reason."

"Perhaps whoever destroyed the field heard us approaching?" Elisead offered softly at his side.

"Mayhap. Or they knew that the smoke would draw others from the fortress and they didn't have time to reach the camp," Alaric said. "Whatever the reason, we will discover who did this."

Alaric strode back toward the burned field, his men falling in behind him. The sight of the destruction once again sent a hot knot of rage into his belly.

He slowly began to pace the perimeter of the field, looking for a clue as to who had torn and burned it. Elisead remained close at his side, her eyes wide as she glanced into the surrounding trees.

"Boot prints," Alaric said over his shoulder to the

others, who had fanned out and were examining the field.

"How many?" Olaf called back.

Alaric knelt and examined the tracks. They were of average size for a man, with no distinguishing features. But they were all evenly spaced and similar in length and shape.

"They could all belong to just one man," Alaric responded, "But they could be *any* man's tracks."

"Alaric!"

He jerked to his feet at Elisead's frightened voice. She pointed toward the far end of the field, where he and his men had piled the larger rocks they'd uncovered as they'd cleared the field.

Even from several dozen paces away, Alaric could see that something marred one of the stone's faces. Dread tightened his throat.

He strode toward the pile of rocks. The others must have sensed his sudden focus, for they followed him to the far end of the field.

There upon the largest stone were scratched two runes in charcoal.

"Ashes and man," he said. "The same as before, next to the burned bones."

He dimly registered Elisead's shocked gasp beside him.

The rumble of his men's unease reverberated behind him.

"Who made the carving where the burned bones lie?" Tarr asked, his voice as grim as Alaric's.

"I did."

Suddenly every set of eyes was on Elisead. She shrank into Alaric's side under the narrowed stares of his men.

"You'd best remove the suspicion from your eyes," Alaric warned them. "Now."

"If she carved those other runes—" Olaf began.

"Elisead has been with me all day," Alaric snapped. "There is no way she did this. The boot tracks clearly belong to a man. And I suspect this act was done out of spite, to warn us to leave these lands."

"Domnall?" Tarr said, his brows lowered.

Alaric considered the possibility for a long moment. Domnall had made no effort to hide his hatred of Alaric and the other Northlanders. Had he somehow doubled back and made one last effort to thwart relations between the Northmen and Picts?

Before he could sort out the tangle of his thoughts, however, Elisead spoke up.

"Nay, I don't think so."

Once more, all eyes were on her.

"Why is that?" Alaric asked, trying to keep the edge from his voice so as not to frighten her.

She caught her lower lip with her teeth for a moment. "He knew of the attack by Northmen invaders seven years ago, and also that my father and his men beat them back."

She shot a cautious glance around the group of Northlanders as if to make sure they weren't angered by her words, but when they remained silent, she went on.

"But he never saw the place where…where we burned the Northmen's bodies…or the runes…"

"Elisead," Alaric said, holding her with his gaze. "I think it is time you told us exactly what happened seven years ago."

34

Elisead swallowed hard, but it did little to alleviate the unease nigh choking her.

Though she knew she was not in danger from the dozen warriors staring her down, they were still a frightful sight, each one of them fierce and unyielding in his own right.

And how would they react to the story of how her father and his men had killed and burned their fellow Northlanders, leaving their charred bones as a warning to others?

Elisead gave herself a little shake. There was no time to be overwhelmed by her fears.

"Seven years ago, Northmen sailed into the bay and up the river to the fortress. There was only one longship, but it teemed with warriors. They poured from their ship and onto our shores so quickly that..."

Alaric's warm hand came around her protectively.

He remained silent, but she drew strength from his arm holding her to his side.

"The fortress's gates were open, for it was a beautiful summer day and the villagers moved freely in and out. We had no warning. The gates had to be closed to save the fortress and all those within, but...but many villagers were trapped outside."

She squeezed her eyes shut for a moment, trying to push away the memories of their screams.

"Many innocents were slaughtered. The Northmen took them as easy prey. They ransacked the village, killing all those in their path then hunting for valuables. But we are a simple people. We hold no great wealth or treasures, other than the land itself. The Northmen weren't satisfied with the loot they managed to plunder from the huts. They burned them, then turned their insatiable appetites on the fortress."

She could feel Alaric tense next to her, but still he did not interrupt.

"They laid siege to the fortress all day, but the walls and gates held true. Nevertheless, my father knew that they could not simply wait for the Northmen to give up—he saw the hunger in their eyes for the spoils within the fortress. When at last the Northmen moved away from the walls for the night, my father and his men hatched a plan. The Northmen made their camp beyond the village. Soon we could see a bonfire from the walls, and the sounds of their merriment over their day's kills reached our ears."

Alaric frowned, but Elisead knew it wasn't directed at her.

"My father ordered the gate opened only wide enough for one man at a time to slip out," she went on. "It was dangerous, for if the Northmen had noticed their movement, they could have set upon the men outside the fortress's walls and perhaps even forced the gates open. But they were lost in their revelry. At last, my father's entire force of warriors was outside the gates. It was a terrible moment when we closed the gates and lowered the grille behind them, for they were trapped outside the safety of the walls with the Northmen."

Several of the men before her shifted. A few crossed burly arms over their chests. They seemed to all know what would happen next.

"My father and his men set upon the raucous Northmen. They managed to catch them by surprise."

"Like Domnall's men caught us by surprise last night?" the giant called Olaf said, raising a bushy red brow at her. "You Picts seem to have a penchant for sneak attacks."

"Silence, Olaf!" Alaric snapped, causing Elisead to jump in fright.

Alaric pinned the ruddy giant with narrowed eyes even as he soothed Elisead with a hand on her back. "We are not the same as those other Northmen," he said to his men, though the words sank into Elisead's swirling mind as well. "They acted with dishonor by killing women, children, and unarmed men. The gods saw that, and their foolish celebration as well."

Elisead's thoughts flew back to the first time she'd laid eyes on him. She had feared for her life in that moment. And now she was to wed this man. She wouldn't have believed it a fortnight ago, but these Northmen were good and honorable—they were naught like the invaders seven years ago.

A few rumbles of agreement with Alaric's admonishment rose from the men towering over Elisead. Alaric went on, his voice calmer now. "What would you have the Picts do? Roll over and expose their bellies to their invaders? These Picts are our allies now, our neighbors. And one day soon they will be our family."

His penetrating gaze shot to her for the briefest moment before returning to pin Olaf once more.

"Very well," the man said. His mouth turned down in a frown behind his red beard, but he nodded his head in deference to Alaric. "I spoke out of turn. I simply grow weary of waiting. I am tired of all the underhandedness. It is our people's way to *act*."

"Ja, I wish to act too," Alaric said grimly. "But we cannot take action until we determine who has burned our field and attempts to thwart our settling here."

The men's voices were even louder in their support of their leader this time. When they quieted, Alaric tilted his head toward Elisead, urging her to continue.

"As you say, Olaf," Elisead said with a nod to the giant. "My father and his men attacked under cover of night and in secret. They outnumbered the Northmen nigh two to one, but that only shows how greatly they feared the Northmen who fought so unmercifully. My father's men managed to overpower them, though not without great cost. We who remained in the fortress watched from the walls. The battle wasn't over and victory secured until the first rays of morning sun touched us. The light revealed a field of blood and bodies."

Elisead swallowed, forcing down the bile that rose in her throat.

"My father ordered the bodies moved to the mouth of the river, where the Northmen had entered and set their sights on the fortress. His warriors were so exhausted, and many injured, from the long battle that we in the fortress—mostly women, children, and the elderly—were tasked with...with dragging the bodies downriver."

The men's eyes widened on her, and Alaric's fingers sank reflexively into her back.

"I was only twelve summers old at the time, but every last shred of strength was needed. I did as I was ordered." She shuddered. No amount of time would ever erase the memory of the stench of death, the weight of the corpse she had struggled to drag behind her, or the blood that wouldn't seem to come out from under her fingernails for a sennight afterward.

"We left the bodies along the sandy bend in the river, as you saw. We...burned them."

This time, she did choke on her words. The memory of the smell of burning flesh made her want to gag even seven years later.

"We knew we were condemning them to Hell, but my father gave the order. His leg had been severely wounded and he'd lost a great deal of blood. I am not sure if the battle lust still gripped him, but we did as he commanded." A sob tore from her throat, which she barely managed to muffle behind her hand.

Alaric's brows drew together. "You fear that in burning them they have been sent to your netherworld of suffering?"

"Aye," she said, blinking up at him. "We didn't bury them. Even though they were pagans, we still should have behaved like Christians. Instead we burned them just to be sure they would suffer for all eternity." It still frightened her that her people had resorted to such savagery. She held no sympathy for the Northmen who'd so mercilessly murdered innocent villagers, but it was God's place to judge them, not her people's.

His face softened slightly. "Elisead, in the Northlands, we burn our dead to free their spirits for the afterlife. You did not desecrate them, at least not according to the Northland ways."

"But…" She shook her head in confusion. "But we are Christians. We should not have behaved like pagans."

"Whichever gods, yours or mine, were watching the events of that night, they know where warriors who fight dishonorably go for the rest of eternity," he said softly. "Do not rebuke yourself so harshly for your father's actions. The Northmen were sent to the gods in their way. And only the gods can decide their fate now."

She nodded, feeling a breath of relief for the first time when it came to those dark memories.

"And you were the one to etch those Northland runes into the rock near where the bodies were burned," Alaric prompted.

"Aye," Elisead said, giving herself another little

shake to keep going. "Una was staying with us in the fortress. She'd already begun to teach me her ways."

"But how did you know to use those two runes?" Tarr said, his dark blue eyes pinning Elisead.

"We found Feitr," Elisead replied. "He had been wounded in the battle, but had survived—barely. He must have crawled from the battlefield into the woods, but he didn't get far. He was found by one of my father's men as we were gathering bodies. He was…so young. Only a few years older than I, and I was just a child."

Grim realization flitted across Alaric's features. "He was likely on his first raid. How did you get him to explain the runes?"

"Pointing and hand signals, mostly. He was dragged before the burning pile of his fellow warriors and made to watch them roast. After many demands, which I'm sure he barely understood, he eventually drew the two symbols in the sand. My father ordered me to leave a marking on the rocks nearby, one that would last forever. It was meant to be a warning, a way to ward off other Northmen from threatening our lands and people."

She looked up at Alaric, feeling her lower lip tremble. "Please, you must understand. My father's concern has always been for his people. Please know that he is not an evil man, though some of his actions have brought suffering and destruction to others."

"Ja, I understand, Elisead," Alaric said softly. Even still, a muscle in his jaw twitched.

"My father took Feitr as a slave. Though he wanted us all to know how dangerous Northmen were, he thought it would reassure us to see one kept at the fortress as a slave. It was supposed to remind us of our victory, that we had conquered the Northmen in the end. But we all feared that one day, more would arrive."

Her voice dropped off and she dared a glance up at the warriors before her. Yet to her surprise, they were all listening impassively. None glared at her now. Mayhap they were simply content to know of the dark history that had overshadowed their efforts to settle here. At least now they knew what they faced when dealing with her father and her people.

"But you said Domnall never knew of all this?" Alaric asked, drawing her attention once more. She glanced at the charcoal rune markings etched onto the rock before her.

"Nay. Word eventually reached Torridon that my father had beaten back a band of Northmen, but Domnall would have never seen the runes or learned of their significance."

"Then who did?" Tarr interjected.

She bit her lip. "There are too many. My father. Most of his men who fought that night. And Feitr, or course."

Alaric's hand tightened around her back. "*Feitr.*"

35

"Where are you going?"

Elisead struggled to keep up with Alaric's long stride. He ought to have slowed for her, but the rage pounding in his veins was too strong.

"Back to the fortress."

He'd ordered Olaf, Tarr, and the others to clear the camp of the bodies and carnage from last night. But he had more pressing matters to see to.

"Alaric!" Elisead dragged him to a halt by his arm. "If you truly wish to be my partner in life, you'll explain yourself. Why do you believe Feitr was the one to destroy the field? And how will we tell my father that we plan to wed?"

Alaric cursed himself under his breath. Of course Elisead was right. He longed to burst into the fortress, extract Feitr's reasons for the many attempts to thwart his negotiations, and demand that Maelcon bless his union with Elisead.

But he wasn't charging into battle. He had to think like a leader, not just a warrior. And he had to think like a man worthy of being Elisead's partner.

He dragged a hand through his hair and let out the breath he hadn't realized he'd been holding.

"Forgive me," he said, softening his voice. He brushed a lock of hair, which shone like copper in the late afternoon sun, back from her worried features.

Their breathless lovemaking just a few hours ago felt distant now. So much was still tangled in knots. But he sent up a prayer to Odin that by tonight, all would be sorted and settled.

"Your father needs to know that someone within the fortress—likely Feitr—has been working against us."

Her brows drew together. "Feitr is harmless. He has never once rebelled against my father—or anyone." But a shadow crossed her face as she spoke.

"What is it? Tell me what troubles you."

"It is just…when he found me the other day and brought me back to camp…"

Alaric's jaw ached as he clenched it. The memory of Feitr's hand wrapped around Elisead's arm still burned in his mind.

"He fired a rock at me," she said. "He claimed he was only trying to get my attention, but I nearly fell from my perch in a tree."

Something clicked into place in Alaric's mind.

"And someone threw a rock at the donkey's hindquarters to spook it—someone who knew the donkey's harness had been cut cleanly to make it snap."

Elisead's eyes widened. "Threw…or used his slingshot. So you *did* believe it was foul play that led to the cart accident."

"Ja. I am sorry to have kept it from you, but I feared frightening you. It already seemed like far too much that you had been traded in a hostage negotiation and were forced to live in a Northman's camp. But I suspected from the first that someone wasn't pleased with the fact that we were negotiating with your father. Your well-being was the only thread holding our negotiations together."

"But why would Feitr want to destroy your talks with my father? What does he stand to gain?" she asked, staring up at him with confusion clouding her amber eyes.

"I know not," he said. "Which is why I am all too eager to get back to the fortress. Others may be in danger—including my sister. And it is all the more reason why I'll vow to marry you before your father. We must band together if we are to survive this nefarious schemer."

She took hold of his hand and nodded for him to continue on through the woods toward the fortress. Pride swelled within his chest. She trusted him to protect her. And he would—with his last breath.

The gates were open as they approached the fortress. Madrena and Rúnin stood in the yard. Madrena charged toward them as they crossed through the gates, with Rúnin striding more calmly behind her.

"Where are the others?" she snapped, worry drawing her brows together.

"They are at the camp," Alaric said quickly. "We met them there."

"And where have you two been?" Suddenly Madrena's pale gray eyes were sharp on them. Realization flitted across her features, to be replaced with a frown.

"We needed to discuss something...important," Alaric replied. But his sister knew him just as well as he knew her.

"Alaric, tell me you haven't thrown away all our hard work this past fortnight," Madrena said. "Tell me you haven't—"

"We are to be married," he interjected.

At Madrena's wide-eyed stare, he went on. "I have already broached the subject with Maelcon. Both Elisead and I want this. And it will only aid our mission."

Madrena shook her head, clearly confused. "We can discuss that later. What of the smoke we saw coming from the forest? And why are the others still in the camp?"

"They are disposing of the bodies from last night's skirmish. But the smoke wasn't coming from the camp. It was the barley fields."

Rúnin cursed, his already dark features clouding over.

"I need to speak to Maelcon. You should both join us," Alaric said over his shoulder as he guided Elisead past Rúnin and Madrena toward the great hall. "Mayhap then we will all have our answers."

They found Maelcon pacing the length of the great

hall. The hall was empty. Maelcon's men and the residents of the fortress were likely giving their chieftain a wide berth, for it was obvious from the moment Alaric stepped foot in the hall that Maelcon was furious.

The older man's graying head snapped up as Alaric and the others approached. Relief briefly crossed his furrowed features at the sight of Elisead, but it was quickly replaced with hot hatred directed at Alaric.

Before Maelcon could unleash his rage at him, though, Alaric held up a hand.

"We need to speak."

36

Though the chamber was barely large enough for all five of them, Maelcon paced the short length between his chair and the door. He limped slightly, his old wound clearly exacerbated by the tumultuous events of the last two days.

"And you are sure it is someone from within my fortress?"

Alaric repressed the impatient reply that almost erupted from him. He shouldn't fault Maelcon for not wanting to believe that someone living within his walls was working against him.

Maelcon had resisted listening to aught Alaric had to say, still fuming over the fact that Alaric would propose to marry his daughter. But when Alaric had explained the cart accident that wasn't an accident at all—which Rúnin confirmed—Maelcon had sunk into his chair, stricken at the news that Elisead had been in danger.

Now he paced frenetically, clearly too incensed at all

Alaric had said to sit still. Alaric, too, wished to pace, to punch something, to drive his blade into whoever threatened his mission—and Elisead.

Instead, he clenched the arms of his wooden chair until his knuckles whitened.

"It has to be one of your people," he replied levelly. "Though I have had some…defiance among my men, none would attempt to thwart our mission. There is no benefit to them in doing so."

"But what is the benefit to Feitr, whom you've clearly decided did this?" Maelcon asked, spinning on his heels to make yet another pass across the small room.

"That is something I have not yet determined," Alaric said darkly. "But I will ask him…firmly. Where is he now?"

"I sent him to the village where he was needed to help repair the thatch on one of the villagers' huts," Maelcon replied.

Madrena stood suddenly. "We should go get him. Now."

"Nei, Madrena," Alaric said, standing also. "I do not wish to spook him. And I will be assured that we are all safe and prepared before confronting him. For all we know, others within the fortress may be working with him to stop an alliance between the Picts and the Northlanders."

Madrena glared at him, but Rúnin drew her back down into her seat with a gentle hand. "Alaric is right. A dozen of our warriors are still at the camp. Our force is divided, and we still don't truly know who our enemy is.

We cannot simply rush into a battle with so little knowledge and preparation," Rúnin said lowly.

A laden look passed between Madrena and Rúnin. Such a brash charge into danger had almost cost Madrena her life last autumn, Alaric knew. If it hadn't been for Rúnin pulling her back from the brink, Madrena would likely be dead right now.

"We will wait, then," Alaric said. "In the meantime, alert those of our crew who are within the fortress."

"And I'll talk to my men as well," Maelcon said.

"Nei, for we don't know who might be working with Feitr." Alaric's voice brokered no argument. At last, Maelcon nodded.

"There is something else, Maelcon," Alaric said. "Something Elisead and I wish to discuss with you in private."

Without further prompting, Madrena and Rúnin rose and let themselves out of Maelcon's chamber soundlessly.

Maelcon's eyes narrowed on Alaric, but before he could speak, Elisead stood at Alaric's side and took his hand.

"Alaric and I are going to wed, Father," she said, her voice firm. "You know it is in everyone's best interest. It is time to let your resistance to this matter go."

Maelcon fumbled for words, all the while tugging on his beard.

"Our people will be more secure with an alliance," Elisead charged forward, not giving Maelcon a chance to come up with a response. "We needn't fear retribution from the likes of Domnall or the King with a force of

Northmen warriors at our backs. And the Northmen won't go away. More of them will come. You must decide which side you want them on—do you want them to be your allies, or your enemies? How much can these walls truly withstand when——"

"Enough!" he snapped, his eyes flaring at his daughter.

Alaric had to resist the urge to gaze upon her with awe. She was a more persuasive negotiator than he'd realized. With an inward smile, he filed away the knowledge that his future wife, who appeared so demure, was a more than worthy adversary.

"When did you add the Northmen's longship to your bride gift?"

Elisead blinked in confusion at Maelcon's sudden shift in topic.

"Mayhap a sennight ago. Why?" she replied, her delicate brow furrowed.

Maelcon nodded in resignation. "And you knew even then that you would marry Alaric."

Elisead's eyes widened on her father. "Nay, I didn't. I hadn't even considered it until——"

Maelcon held up a hand, silencing her. "But you sensed it, did you not? That is why you added the ship."

Alaric stared down at Elisead, who was clearly struggling to answer. Though he'd wanted her from the first, he'd never allowed himself to hope that he could somehow bind himself to the woman at his side until the thought had taken root last night. Was it possible that Elisead had wanted him all along as well?

At last, Elisead let out a long breath. "I…I sensed

something, aye. The stone guided me to carve the ship, and I...felt something telling me that my fate was entwined with the Northmen—with one Northman in particular."

Even as Alaric's heart leapt into his throat, Maelcon sank into the nearest chair.

"I should have learned long ago that trying to control your carving is like trying to control the weather. You are a force of nature, my daughter."

Elisead's eyes suddenly shone bright with emotion, but before she could respond, Maelcon waved a hand and spoke in a voice that was suddenly weary.

"Aye."

"Aye what?" Elisead breathed.

"Aye, you two will marry."

Before Alaric knew what was happening, Elisead launched herself into his arms. He grunted as she bumped his stitched shoulder, but he wouldn't let a little pain dull this moment.

Married. He'd never considered the prospect before. He'd always kept his mind on the next battle, the next challenge, the next voyage. But now no matter what the gods had in store for him, he would have Elisead at his side.

"Save that until a priest can be brought," Maelcon said sourly as he eyed his daughter in Alaric's arms.

Elisead disentangled herself and faced her father once more, a blush pinkening her cheeks. Alaric could only pray that Maelcon wasn't astute enough at reading his daughter's embarrassment to guess that they had already done far more than hug.

"How long will that take?" he asked, feeling his own lust stirring at the memory of what they'd shared in the woods earlier.

"A sennight, or perhaps more," Maelcon said.

"We'll have a Northland ceremony as well as a Christian one," Alaric declared. Maelcon's face darkened, but Alaric wouldn't be deterred. This marriage represented the union of their peoples. His crew would certainly be pleased to have a grand celebration as if they were back at home.

But it wasn't time to celebrate yet. Alaric once again grew sober at what lay ahead.

"No matter what happens with Feitr, I will keep Elisead safe," he said. "I swear it on my life."

HIS TIME HAD RUN OUT.

He slipped away from the wooden door. Maelcon, the old fool, had folded at last. Alaric would wed Elisead, and then there would be no undoing their alliance.

Unless he acted now.

Maelcon and the others paid so little attention to him. They all thought he was busying himself, just as he always did, seeing to his tasks without so much as a peep. Yet no one had noticed him lingering in the shadows outside the chief's private chamber.

Walking on silent feet, he crept along the great hall's walls toward the large double doors. He'd have to bide his time for a few hours until night fell, but then he'd strike.

Burning the fields had been desperate. He should have known that it wouldn't deter Alaric, the stubborn bastard. But he'd had to try everything before resorting to what now lay ahead.

He didn't relish his task, but it was better than the alternative—an alliance between Northlanders and Picts. It soured his stomach. The thought of his people lowering themselves in such a union was more than repulsive. It was an insult, one that he could not allow to be carried out.

If it meant taking lives, so be it. He was born a warrior. But perhaps he was fated to be a leader, for he was the only one who could steer his people into the right once more.

He sidled through the great hall's doors and slipped into the yard. There were only a few hours until night-fall. The darkness would give him the cover he needed to slip back into the great hall and strike.

Though his body hummed with the need to act, he forced himself to crouch in the shadows next to the stables. He had waited this long and worked meticulously to bring about his goal. Soon enough, his plan would be set into motion—and then he would be unstoppable.

37

A t last darkness fell over the fortress.

The men who'd visited the camp had returned at dusk, sweaty and exhausted from disposing of the bodies of both Domnall's men and the three of their own rank they'd lost.

Though Alaric longed to give his fallen men the proper Northland funeral ceremony they deserved, there was no time for that. At least they had died fighting an enemy. He had to trust that the Valkyries had seen their bravery and had whisked them away to Valhalla for the endless feasting and battle that all warriors hoped to attain in the afterlife.

His crew had all been briefed with the most urgent information—there was a threat within the walls of the fortress. Someone—or several people—didn't want to see the Northmen settle. But he'd also told them that he was going to wed Elisead, thus sealing their alliance with the Picts forever.

Though his men were clearly uneasy at having no direct enemy to strike, no clear path of action, they nevertheless complied with Alaric's order to wait and remain calm. Alaric would be the one to handle Feitr. He wouldn't let anyone take the satisfaction of pinning the schemer under his blade and having the truth out of him once and for all. The last thing Alaric needed was the entire force of his crew lashing out and either spooking their enemies or taking the chance for retribution from Alaric.

He longed to charge into the village and drag Feitr in by the neck. But the darkness descending on them would force him back soon enough. For now, Alaric needed to see to Elisead's safety.

"On the morrow, this will all be over," he said softly to her as he guided her toward her chamber down the corridor built on the back side of the great hall.

It had been a tense few hours as they'd waited for nightfall. He wished he and Elisead had been able to savor the joy of their impending wedding. Instead, he'd been busy plotting his confrontation with Feitr. She'd stood by his side quietly as he paced and planned, first with Madrena and Rúnin, and then with the rest of his men.

"Aye, I know," Elisead said, though her voice was tight with fatigue and worry.

He opened the door to her chamber and stood aside to let her in.

"And when it is, we'll properly celebrate our betrothal."

"What is involved in a Northland wedding?" she

asked, turning to look up at him with those depthless amber eyes.

He closed the chamber door behind him, never taking his gaze from her. She was so beautiful, just like a wild forest spirit. And she had the heart and strength to match. What had he done to earn the gods' greatest imaginable gift?

The chamber was dim except for the low fire that burned in the metal brazier. Even the summer nights could be cool here, as in the Northlands. How Alaric longed to stay with Elisead and keep both of them warm until the sun rose.

"There is a ceremony officiated by a *goði*—a priest. It is held out in the open, so that the gods are free to see the union of the two people and their families."

He stepped closer to her, but instead of backing up, she held her ground. It meant that they were almost touching, her head tilted back to hold his gaze.

"And then?"

"Then there is much feasting and merriment—the finest honeyed mead flows freely, music is played, and at the end of the evening, the newly married couple is sent off to...seal their union."

Unbidden, his manhood stirred in his trousers. Memories of the afternoon spent entwining himself with Elisead burned hot in his veins.

"Oh." Was it his imagination, or was her voice unusually breathy and uneven all of a sudden? Was it possible that her thoughts ran along the same heated lines as his? "That is not so different from our own ceremonies."

"And do your people celebrate a honey moon?"

She blinked up at him and shook her head slowly. "Nay. What is that?"

"It is a time when the new couple gets to know each other more…intimately. They have a full moon cycle to retreat into their own pleasure. They drink as much honeyed mead as they please and indulge in the physical intimacies of marriage. If their mead runs out before the moon cycle is up, it is considered a bad omen. But most couples reemerge more fully bonded—and quite satisfied."

A beautiful blush rose to Elisead's cheeks as he spoke. She was still shy at such sensual talk.

But Alaric knew based on this afternoon—and her reaction to even the slightest passing touch from him— that a deep, untapped well of passion resided within her. His heart hammered and his manhood surged to life at the thought of awakening her lust and freeing the wild spirit that lived behind her shy exterior.

"Mayhap…mayhap that is a tradition that we should observe. To honor your customs."

At her words, he almost dragged her into his embrace and crushed her against him to claim her mouth fully. But he resisted. He wanted her to come to him this time, to begin testing the depth and breadth of her desire.

Her warm breath fanned over the hollow in his neck where his tunic parted slightly. They were so close, and yet only her breath caressed him.

"Ja, indeed."

Tentatively, she raised her hand and brought her

fingertips to his face. At the first brushing contact of her fingers against his jaw, he barely managed not to jerk at the flood of sensation. He clenched his teeth, but then her fingers ran along the bristle on his face to where a muscle jumped in his jaw.

Her fingertips traveled down his neck for a moment, then she moved them to his lips. The calluses on the pads of her fingers from carving taunted him, raising the blood to the surface of his skin and increasing the torrent of sensation.

At last, she deigned to end his torture. She rose on the tips of her toes and wrapped her arms around his neck to steady herself. Then she brought her lips to his in a feather-soft kiss.

He inhaled sharply. Even the lightest of touches from her rocked him to the core. He could take no more. He needed to be in control, lest he come undone completely at her gentle kiss.

Lacing his fingers through the auburn waves of hair cascading down her back, he tilted her head and deepened their kiss. She opened her mouth to him immediately, her tongue beckoning him in.

A groan rose in his throat as his blood hammered hotly in his veins. Her whole length was now pressed against him. His manhood strained against his linen trousers. Unable to resist, he ground his hips into hers, a silent promise of the pleasure they would soon share in his motion.

Suddenly a sharp knock sounded at the door. Alaric jerked his head up from Elisead's, struggling for breath.

"What is it?" he barked, far harsher than he'd intended to.

"Feitr has been spotted approaching the gates from the village." It was Madrena's level voice, though he knew his sister well enough to guess that she'd intended to interrupt them. Of course she couldn't resist an opportunity to give a barb to her older brother.

Alaric cursed softly. "Stay within your chamber," he said to Elisead. "All will be well, I promise. But I won't risk your safety if things get out of hand."

She gazed up at him with those wide honey eyes, her lips parted and reddened from their kiss. "Aye," she breathed.

He turned to the door, but her hand on his arm made him pause.

"Be careful. I...I care for your wellbeing as well."

Warmth that was different than the hot lust from a moment before flooded his chest. He gave the hand that was on his arm a squeeze. Her show of emotion left him speechless. All he could do was wordlessly tell her with his gaze how much she moved him.

After a long moment, he forced himself toward the door once more. With one last look at her standing in the middle of the chamber, her eyes shining on him, he stepped out and closed the door behind him.

38

"I want her guarded," Alaric said to Madrena and Rúnin, who stood waiting for him outside the chamber.

Madrena and Rúnin exchanged a glance. "We will remain here," Madrena said, squeezing Alaric's shoulder.

"Nei, I want you at my back when I confront Feitr," he said. He strode past them and into the great hall, where a few of his men leaned against the walls or sat at the tables that had not yet been brought out for the evening meal.

"Olaf," Alaric called. The burly man jumped to attention and came to stand before Alaric.

"You have questioned me publicly on this voyage," Alaric said with ice in his voice.

Olaf stood steady under the criticism, though he bowed his head slightly. "Ja, I have, Captain. And in doing so I shamed myself. I hope that does not tarnish my honor in your eyes," the red giant said.

"I would entrust you with an important task, but I must know if I can have absolute confidence in you."

Olaf's face hardened into eager determination behind his ruddy beard. "Task me with aught. I am more than ready to restore my honor. Let me prove myself to you."

"I want you to guard Elisead's chamber," he replied in a low voice. "Naught will threaten her this night."

"Ja," Olaf said, straightening to his full height. "I vow my life on it."

Alaric pounded the giant on the shoulder. Pride for this man, and for all in his crew, swelled within him. Perhaps he was finally learning how to lead.

Olaf strode toward the narrow hallway at the back of the great hall that led to the private chambers, his head held high with the honor bestowed upon him by his captain.

Just then Maelcon strode into the hall, his face a mask of worry.

One of Maelcon's guards slipped through the hall's doors at the same moment.

"You asked me to tell you when Feitr returned from the village, Chief," the man said. "He has just crossed through the gates."

"Thank you," Maelcon said, pulling on his beard anxiously. "You may return to your post now."

"Northlanders," Alaric said to his crew. "Do not act rashly. I'll handle Feitr." He turned to Maelcon. "Tell your men the same, but instruct them to keep their eyes open for anyone who might make a move to come to Feitr's aid. We still do not know if any others are working with him."

Maelcon nodded and strode to the back of the hall, where a few of his men stood waiting for his orders.

"You two," Alaric said, pivoting to Madrena and Rúnin. "With me."

The three of them strode out of the hall and into the yard. Alaric fingered the sword on his hip. He likely wouldn't have to use it—at least not at first. But he longed to draw it, if only to feel its reassuring weight in his hand. For he went into battle now, even if it was just him against Feitr.

The yard was quiet, though Alaric knew Maelcon's men lined the walls where they stood on watch. It was a strangely calm night, with nary a breeze from the sea to stir the air.

A flash of white snagged Alaric's eye. Feitr's ice-blond hair shone silver in the rising moon. He was walking right toward them, his body loose and his strides relaxed.

"Feitr," Alaric said, forcing his voice to remain even.

He'd already planned out where he wanted to confront the Northland slave. If Feitr somehow had more of Maelcon's men in his service, Alaric would not be set upon in the yard. Nei, he wanted to be in control of their venue, so that no one could attack him from behind.

Feitr faltered in his steps halfway across the yard. "What is it?" he said, eyeing Alaric, Madrena, and Rúnin. "What do you want?"

"A word about Maelcon's war steed. You tend to him, do you not? I wish to see the saddle you use."

Feitr stared at Alaric for a long moment, his hard features cast in shadow with the rising moon behind him. "Ja, this way," he said at last, turning toward the small stables to his left.

Alaric fell in behind him, gritting his teeth against the desire to attack. He had to be patient for just a few more moments.

They slipped inside the stables, which were darkened, but the slatted wood panel walls permitted a few beams of moonlight to slip within.

As the door closed behind Rúnin, Alaric's hand darted out like lightning. He grabbed Feitr by the back of the neck and spun him around. With two swift strides, he slammed Feitr into the back wall of the small stables.

Feitr's pale blue eyes bulged as Alaric's hand closed around his neck, pinning him to the wall.

"I have a few questions for you," Alaric said, his voice deadly calm. "And I would appreciate the truth."

Feitr sputtered and fought against the hand around his throat, but Alaric's strength and size was superior to his.

"Confess to plotting against me and my men, Maelcon, and Elisead, and you will get a swift death. But I want to know why."

"Why…?" Feitr croaked. Alaric eased his hand a hair's breadth to allow Feitr to speak.

"Why I plotted against you?" he said at last, his voice a disbelieving rasp.

"Ja, you have been working to destroy our negotiations. I want to know why. What do you gain?"

Feitr shook his head the small amount he could given Alaric's hand pinning him. "I have not…"

Despite his attempt to control himself, Alaric squeezed his hand in rage and lifted Feitr clear off his feet by the neck. "You mean to claim that it was not you who cut the donkey's harness and then handed over a cart that you knew would break away, putting Elisead's life in danger?"

"Nei!"

"And it wasn't you who fired a rock at the donkey to spook him?" Alaric reached down with his free hand and yanked out the slingshot tucked in Feitr's belt. He held it up in front of the man's face.

"Nei, it wasn't!"

Alaric narrowed his gaze on Feitr, who continued to struggle in his hold. "And it wasn't you who tried to break into Madrena's chamber in the night so as to end negotiations between the Northmen and the Picts?"

"Nei, I swear," Feitr panted.

Alaric looked down at Feitr's feet, which dangled and thrashed several inches off the ground. They were caked with mud. Alaric saw red as he returned his gaze to the slave's bulging blue eyes.

"You have mud on your boots. I'm guessing you're going to claim that you also weren't the one who destroyed our barley fields this afternoon, though that would be a lie, just like everything else you've said."

With his free hand, Alaric yanked the seax from his boot and brought it to Feitr's heart.

"I am innocent!" the man gurgled. "I swear on all of our gods! I swear it on Odin's breath and Thor's hammer. I swear on Freyja and will beg Hel to drag me to her realm if I am lying!"

Alaric froze, the dagger's blade hovering over Feitr's chest. He did not take such vows lightly, even if they were spoken by a lying schemer. He lowered Feitr so that his feet touched the ground once more, but kept his grip firm enough that he had no chance of escape.

"The mud on my boots is from working in the village. Maelcon sent me there to help some of the villagers repair their thatching. I have been working there all day in the dirt and mud. Ask anyone in the village!"

"And the rest of it?" Alaric asked coldly. "How do you explain yourself?"

Feitr's pale eyes flew around the small stables in thought. "I am only a slave. Maelcon doesn't let me keep even the smallest knife to eat with. How could I have possibly cut the donkey's harness?"

Alaric remained silent, so Feitr went on. "And I am not allowed on the wall. Only soldiers are permitted up there, for the safety and protection of the fortress. How could I have fired a rock at the donkey, as you say I did, without being on the wall?"

"But you did fire a rock at Elisead when she was up in a tree. She told me."

"Ja, to get her attention and to bring her down."

"To make her fall?" Alaric's hand reflexively tightened for a moment on Feitr's neck.

"Nei," he rasped. "Why would I want to harm the

chieftain's daughter? What could possibly come to me, besides a terrible and slow death?"

"That is exactly what you'll get in a moment if you don't start making more sense," Alaric snapped, though he withdrew the tip of the seax from Feitr's chest.

Something wasn't fitting right. Feitr's fear was real, but Alaric couldn't tell if his claims to innocence were as well.

"I care naught for the girl," Feitr said. "I have barely interacted with her in all these seven years I've lived here as a slave. I would never try to harm her, for she is my master's daughter."

"And how do you explain the fact that you told me to leave this land—leave while I still could? Was that not a threat, a warning to end negotiations? And when I didn't heed you, you decided to end my talks with Maelcon yourself."

It all pointed toward Feitr. Yet for some reason Alaric was growing increasingly uneasy. Some warrior's instinct screamed at him in the back of his head. But was it telling him not to trust Feitr? Or was the danger actually coming from a different direction?

Feitr shook his head again adamantly. "My words were no threat. They were a plea."

"Explain yourself," Alaric bit out.

"Alaric, what are you doing?" Madrena hissed behind him.

He waved for silence with the seax. The stables fell quiet except for the occasional snort or shift of animal flesh from the small handful of stalls on either side of him.

"I...I wished to go home," Feitr breathed at last. "When I saw you arrive at the fortress, I thought I was saved from this life of slavery at last. But then when you told the Chief that you wished to stay, I feared I would never see my village in the Northlands again. I hoped to convince you to go, to sail home—and take me with you."

Alaric heard Rúnin exhale slowly behind him.

"But your bitterness, your obvious hatred of Maelcon—I saw it in your eyes when you stood next to my longships." Even as he spoke, Alaric's certainty dissolved as he tried to collect the last threads of evidence against Feitr. "You wished to lash out at him, did you not? If not at him directly, then at his daughter?"

Feitr's face soured. "What slave loves his master? Ja, I hate Maelcon, for he slaughtered my people and made me watch them burn. He enslaved me." He shook his head again "This land... This land will never be home. They worship the White Christ here, and they spit on many of our ways. And here I am a slave, even though I was fated to be a warrior. But for some reason, *you* wish to stay."

Alaric could barely comprehend what he was hearing. "Ja, we will stay," he said, his voice distant in his ears as his mind raced to comprehend all that Feitr had said. "We will make it our home."

"I knew that to be true by the second time you came to the fortress. You would not be warned off, even in the face of Maelcon and Drostan's resistance."

"What did you say?" Alaric snapped, his thoughts suddenly quieting.

Feitr's eyes widened in confusion. "I knew you'd stay, even though Drostan urged Maelcon not to make an alliance with you."

Alaric's mind flew back to all the times he could remember seeing Drostan, Maelcon's ever-present shadow. The man was clearly a warrior, but Alaric had never really *looked* at him closely.

Drostan had been at Maelcon's side on the wall when Alaric had first arrived—and when Maelcon had ordered an attack on Alaric's crew. He'd been there in the yard when the donkey and cart had been led out of the stables. And he would have been within the fortress when someone had tried to enter Madrena's chamber in the night.

The man had stood by silently during several rounds of negotiations, never giving a hint of his thoughts.

"Feitr," Alaric said suddenly. "Did Maelcon ever teach you how to write in his language?"

Feitr's face contorted. "Nei, of course not. I am a slave, not some scholar or holy man."

"What is it, Alaric?" Madrena demanded urgently. "What are you thinking?"

"The missive sent to Domnall. Maelcon claimed to know naught about it. The man hasn't always been forthcoming with me, but his face is easy enough to read. I believe he was telling the truth that he had no knowledge of a message informing Domnall of our presence and urging him to come to the fortress."

"Then who did?" Rúnin asked.

"Drostan," Alaric breathed. "It all points to Drostan."

He released Feitr's neck suddenly. The man fell forward onto the straw-covered ground, coughing and rubbing his throat.

"Take him," he barked at Madrena and Rúnin. "Bring him into the great hall and watch him."

"Where are you going?" Madrena called after him as he burst out of the stables.

"To find Drostan."

39

Several heads snapped up as Alaric barged into the great hall. He vaguely registered his men's questioning looks, but he didn't slow.

Alaric darted toward the back of the hall, where Maelcon's men had gathered to warily eye the Northmen who occupied their hall. But as Alaric's gaze scanned the group, his stomach twisted forebodingly.

Neither Maelcon nor Drostan stood among the others.

"Where is your Chief and his right-hand man?" Alaric barked to the group of Pict warriors.

Their eyes widened, some in offence, others in thinly veiled fright. But Alaric didn't have time to soothe their worries.

"The Chief wanted to retrieve his sword from his chamber. Drostan should be here, but...no one has seen him for several hours," one man brave enough to speak up said.

The dread knotting his innards turned to stabbing ice.

Without waiting to explain, he dashed toward the opening at the back of the great hall where the corridor leading to the private chambers ran.

Maelcon's meeting chamber was the first door along the hallway. The door stood ajar and the room was empty. Alaric made his way farther down the corridor.

The dim pathway curved slightly to the right, for the chambers and the corridor itself had clearly been added on to the great hall after it had stood for some time. The wood was younger in this part of the structure. And whoever had added these chambers had been forced to bend them with the curvature of the circular stone wall ringing in the fortress, as there was little room between the wall and the great hall here at the back. Alaric hurried his steps, suddenly feeling trapped in some dark, twisting maze.

As he continued to curve right, a pair of booted feet suddenly appeared ahead. Someone was sprawled on the ground.

Alaric sprinted the last few steps to Elisead's chamber.

Nei.

Olaf lay prone on the floor—in front of Elisead's open chamber door.

Alaric plowed into the chamber, yet it was just as empty and quiet as Maelcon's meeting room. His eyes darted to every corner of the small space, but Elisead was gone.

He fell to his knees in the corridor at Olaf's side.

The red-headed giant was pale, his eyelids drooping in unconsciousness.

Then Alaric saw the blood. He hadn't noticed it at first, for it pooled underneath Olaf's large frame on the stone-covered floor. He turned Olaf slightly and saw a vicious wound in his back.

Hot rage mixed with fear, nigh choking him.

Suddenly, Olaf stirred and groaned. Even a cowardly attack at his back wouldn't take down this fierce Northland warrior.

"Olaf," Alaric said, giving his shoulder a shake while trying to be mindful of his injury.

Again, the man groaned. His eyelids lifted partway, and even that small motion seemed to be a struggle.

"Olaf, what happened?" It took all of Alaric's willpower not to shake the man until he spoke, for doing so would get him naught.

"I…" Olaf's red beard trembled as he tried to move his mouth. "I failed you."

"Nei, for you took a blade in the back for me," Alaric said, his throat threatening to close. "What can you tell me? Who attacked you? Where is Elisead?"

Olaf shook his head weakly, his eyes losing focus for a moment. "Maelcon…"

"What?" Alaric's head spun with panic. "Maelcon did this?"

"Nei, Maelcon…" Olaf gritted his teeth, his pain obvious. "Maelcon's chamber."

Alaric jerked to his feet. He knew Olaf wasn't referring to Maelcon's meeting room, for he'd already found it empty. Maelcon's personal chamber lay just a little farther down the corridor from Elisead's.

Before he knew what he was doing, he'd bolted from Olaf's side and plunged deeper into the corridor.

"I'll send for help," he shouted over his shoulder to Olaf. "Just hold on!"

But the truth was, he refused to lose any time in finding Elisead. If she were safe in her father's chamber, he would dash back into the great hall and call for the help Olaf needed. But if seeking help for Olaf left Elisead in danger a second longer…

A voice in the back of his head warned him to be cautious. The hairs on his arms rose as alarm bells rang in his mind, but he shoved down his instincts as Maelcon's door came into view.

The door was ajar. There was not even enough time to draw his sword. Instead, he barreled into the chamber, throwing back the door with his shoulder.

Elisead stood in the middle of the room, her eyes wide with terror.

Behind her stood Drostan, half his face covered in blue paint and one arm wrapped around Elisead's waist.

And a dagger pressed to her throat.

At Elisead's feet, Maelcon lay face up in a pool of blood. His throat had been slit and his eyes were wide and unseeing in death.

"I wouldn't do that if you value her life," Drostan said quietly from behind Elisead.

Alaric hadn't even realized it, but his hand had flown to his sword. He'd half-drawn it by the time Drostan's warning registered.

He froze, the hilt of his sword burning in his hand, the blade begging to be freed completely.

But then Elisead inhaled sharply, and a trickle of blood snaked down her neck at the point where Drostan's dagger pressed slightly harder.

The room felt like it was spinning wildly around him, with only Elisead's beautiful, terrified eyes anchoring him.

Slowly, he pried his hand off his hilt and let the sword fall back into its scabbard.

40

U nease had filled Elisead the moment Alaric had
stepped from her chamber, but there was naught
she could do now. That didn't stop her from pacing restlessly, though.

She had no idea how much time had passed, but it
seemed to stretch as her instincts warned her—of what,
she could not tell. Some indefinable presence whispered
to her that something was wrong.

Suddenly there was a heavy thump outside her
chamber door. She jumped nigh out of her skin and had
to clap a hand over her mouth to stifle her cry of
surprise. With trembling fingers, she reached for the
handle. But before she grasped it, the door flew open.

Drostan's large frame filled the doorway. Elisead
exhaled sharply, relief flooding her to see her father's
most trusted man.

"Drostan, what—"

But then she noticed that he wore the blue paint her

people used as they entered battle. Alaric had warned of a dangerous confrontation, but not a battle that warranted war paint. Her gaze trailed from his dyed features to what he held in his hand. A bloodied dagger dripped in his grip.

There hadn't been time to scream.

He lunged at her. With one arm, he bound her in his grasp and lifted her clear off her feet even as she struggled against him. But then he pressed the dagger to her throat, stilling her.

"What are you doing?" she panted, trying to twist away from the blade at her neck.

"We are going to see your father," he said calmly.

He carried her through the door and toward her father's chamber. As they entered the corridor, she caught a glimpse of Alaric's stubborn but loyal warrior Olaf slumped and bleeding on the floor.

Elisead sucked in a breath and prepared to scream as loud as she could. But the dagger pressed again, ever so slightly harder. Her mind swirled as she considered what to do. The rain of blows she'd landed with her heels on Drostan's shins hadn't slowed him in the least. The dagger at her neck prevented her from screaming. Would someone come down this corridor anytime soon? There was no reason to—no reason that anyone would save her.

Drostan strode to her father's chamber and kicked the door open.

Her father spun around from where he stood looking down at his old ornamented sword in the open chest at the foot of his bed. His amber eyes, so like Elisead's, flashed over them, widening in shock.

"Drostan, what in God's name are you doing? I trusted—"

That was as far as he got.

Drostan suddenly flung her against the wall. She slammed into it and slid to the floor, her vision blurring for a moment. There was a scuffle, then a heavy thump as the sword Maelcon had set aside after his injury seven years ago hit the ground.

Her father's scream, which turned into a gurgle, snapped her out of her daze.

He lay on the ground a pace away, a deep red line drawn across his throat. Blood flowed freely as he blinked in stunned disbelief.

Her own scream ripped from her throat, but there was no one in the corridor beyond her father's chamber to hear it. Before she could scramble to her father's side, Drostan dragged her to her feet and pressed the dagger against her neck once more.

"Why?" she cried, still fighting against his strength even though it was useless.

Drostan held her upright, facing the door. It was as if he was waiting for someone.

New dread nigh stole her breath away.

Alaric.

Her heart was rending in two, half for her father, who lay struggling for breath at her feet, and half for Alaric, who would unknowingly walk into Drostan's trap at any moment.

Her father continued to fight even as the pool of

blood slowly expanded around his head. Time stretched horrifically as if she were trapped in a nightmare. Every gurgling inhale Maelcon tried to take lasted a lifetime.

His wide eyes looked up at her, then shifted to Drostan. Another sob ripped from her throat. Dagger be damned. She struggled with all her strength against Drostan's unmoving arm pinning her.

"Let me go to him!" she screamed. "Let me give him a last moment of comfort."

"Nay," Drostan said flatly.

"Why?" She was hysterical now, but she didn't care.

"Because I will not allow you to engage in needless sentiment," Drostan said behind her. "I am doing what is best for our people, just as Maelcon taught me. There is no need to make this more than what it is."

"And what is it?" she grated out, her gaze still locked on her father. The light behind his amber eyes was at last starting to fade. Part of her wished to fall to the ground and beg any god who would listen to bring him back, to undo the long slice across his throat delivered by Drostan. But another part of her knew it was a mercy that he was slipping away now.

"It is a change in leadership for our people, a passing of the mantle."

Helplessness washed over her, making her feel sick. "You are crazed," she breathed.

"Nay, *Maelcon* was crazed for thinking it wise to make an alliance with those barbarian Northmen."

Her father shuddered one last time, and then his eyes, still fixed on her, dimmed.

"Nay!" she screamed. But her ability to fight against

Drostan suddenly drained away. Hot tears blinded her and spilled in an unrelenting torrent down her cheeks.

She didn't know how long she was forced to stand there, dagger at her throat and her father's body at her feet. And then all of a sudden the door flew open and Alaric was there.

Though hope surged through her at the sight of him, it evaporated as the dagger dug into her flesh. She felt a trickle of her own warm blood running down the column of her neck.

And then Alaric's hand was moving away from his sword. She wanted to scream at him to kill Drostan, never mind her life. Saving her wasn't as important as stopping the monster who'd been right in their midst all along.

But the blade kept her silent. All she could do was watch as yet another nightmare unfolded before her.

"Close the door." Drostan's voice was even and low. He must truly be mad to be able to remain so calm after murdering a man in cold blood, a man who'd trusted him completely.

Alaric complied without taking his eyes off Elisead.

"Why, Drostan?" Alaric said, his whole body humming with tension. His empty fists were clenched at his sides, his eyes burning with green fire. Even from several paces away, Elisead could see the muscles in his jaw flexing.

Drostan actually snorted, the first indication that he didn't have ice water for blood.

"I don't need to explain myself to a filthy Northman."

"You wear the paint of your people," Alaric said carefully. "Maelcon said it is how you got the name Pict, for you don the blue dye when you enter battle."

Was Alaric stalling? A flicker of hope sparked deep in her hollow chest. Did he have a plan? Might this nightmare somehow end at last?

"But you are not entering battle," Alaric went on. "You have killed your Chief like a coward, not a warrior. And now you threaten a woman, as only weaklings and dishonorable men do. Both my gods and yours see—"

All of a sudden Drostan lunged forward, shifting the dagger from Elisead's neck. Both she and Drostan collided with Alaric.

Alaric blinked down at her, a sudden gust of air leaving him. Drostan stepped back, dragging Elisead with him.

What she saw made sickness rise in the back of her throat.

Drostan's dagger protruded from Alaric's middle, buried to the hilt.

"Nay!" she screamed again, her chest burning and her voice raw.

Alaric raised trembling hands to the dagger and gripped the hilt. With a nauseating jerk, he tried to pull it free, but it remained lodged in place. He coughed, and blood began seeping across his tunic where the blade was buried.

"Keep it," Drostan said, tilting his head toward the dagger stuck low in Alaric's chest.

With a vicious shove, Drostan sent Alaric tumbling

to the floor alongside Elisead's father. He landed in the pool of blood spreading from Maelcon's body.

A blessed numbness stole over Elisead as she stared down at her love dying at her feet next to her father. It was as if her mind knew that she would shatter, never to be whole again, if she could understand the full weight of what was happening. Dimly, she sent up a prayer of thanks for the small mercy of detachment.

Drostan hauled her toward the back of the chamber, where a door was hidden in the paneling. Her father had never been forced to use the secret opening that provided the only other exit or entrance into the great hall besides the large double doors at the front, but when he'd added this wing of private chambers, he'd insisted that it would come in handy one day. A distant bitterness at that thought scuttled across her increasingly numb mind.

Her determination to fight had been stripped from her, along with the ability to feel the pain that would surely sweep her away forever if she allowed herself to comprehend what was happening.

Alaric's eyes followed her across the room as he struggled and failed to sit up.

"I love you." His voice was a raw whisper, but his eyes blazed with the same green fire that had burned her to her very soul.

"I love you, too."

Before she could say more, Drostan slammed the hidden door closed behind them, cutting her off from Alaric forever.

Her father's most trusted warrior dragged her to the left

through the narrow gap between the wall's cold stones and the back of the great hall. He slinked along the wall until the great hall's wooden siding ended. Ahead stood the stables.

Drostan straightened and pulled her to his side.

"Make a move and I'll strangle you," he hissed. Casually, he walked into the open space that separated the great hall and the stables, pulling her by the hand. The yard was quiet and dark before them. Moonbeams cast deep shadows in the corners. Naught moved.

Elisead knew there were several guards stationed along the wall, but they were looking outward for a sign of attack, not inward for treachery among their ranks.

Drostan's hand tightened painfully on her wrist, a warning to remain silent. He'd already killed three men this night—Olaf, Maelcon, and Alaric—and she knew with a removed calmness that he wouldn't hesitate to kill her either.

He pulled her inside the stables and quickly saddled two horses—her father's war steed and a young mare that Elisead occasionally rode. She preferred to travel under the power of her own two feet, but the animal had been a gift from her father, so she'd kept it.

Drostan guided the two horses by their reins with one hand and hauled her after him with the other. He led them back the way they'd come, through the narrow passage between the back of the great hall and the wall.

At last Elisead's slow mind comprehended what he was doing.

"You think to slip out of the postern gate."

He yanked hard on her wrist to silence her, but it

seemed to confirm her guess. Sure enough, he halted in front of the narrow door that had been hacked out of the thick stone wall. The postern gate was rarely used, for behind it, the hillside upon which the fortress was built fell away in a jagged, rocky escarpment.

Putting his shoulder to the door, Drostan pushed. To Elisead's surprise, the door opened smoothly, without even a squeak from the old hinges. He must have planned this escape, she realized dimly, and oiled the hinges ahead of time. How long had he been plotting against her father and Alaric?

She balked at going through the door, for she feared tumbling down the steep slope on the other side with naught but the moon to light her footing. But her slight resistant only seemed to anger Drostan. He bent and hoisted her over his shoulder, then walked through the gate, pulling the horses behind.

Elisead squeezed her eyes shut. If Drostan slipped, or if the horses spooked, she would plummet onto the sharp rocks far below. But amazingly, Drostan began to sidle his way down the cliff. The horses, though picking their footing carefully, followed after his swift tug on their reins.

At long last, they reached the bottom of the escarpment. The river cut a path along the back side of the fortress, leaving a narrow, sandy bank at the bottom of the cliff.

Drostan nigh threw Elisead onto the mare, then mounted her father's warhorse, still holding both of their reins. The soft sand below the horses' hooves muffled the noise as Drostan spurred the animals into motion.

Elisead glanced up at the fortress walls towering atop the cliff. No one had raised the alarm. No one knew that her father and Alaric had been killed, and that she'd been taken.

A sob escaped her lips, but the night swallowed the sound.

41

Maelcon's blood had cooled.

It seeped into Alaric's tunic, mingling with his own blood, which was still warm where it oozed around the dagger buried in his chest.

He blinked up at the ceiling. Blessedly, there was no pain. But a blankness had stolen over his mind, chilling him and leaving his thoughts muddled and distant.

Strange. He had always imagined the gods would claim his life in some raid or great battle. Not because his bloodlust ran so hot—nei, but because it seemed like a good way to go, and he'd never spent a great deal of time dwelling on his future.

But in more recent days, he'd had several odd moments where he'd seen a longer life with Elisead flash in his mind, almost as if he was glimpsing the future.

And now he lay on the cold stone floor. With Elisead ripped from him, he was left alone to die in a foreign land.

He'd been told by some men who'd narrowly evaded death that a strange calm came over them in the last moments. But although he felt numb, he was not calm. His mind kept flitting back to Elisead's frightened eyes. She was strong, ja, but he had no idea what Drostan would do to her. The numbness started to burn away, to be replaced with white-hot rage.

Suddenly he heard footsteps in the corridor. He tried to call out, but his voice was a thin croak.

"Olaf!" It was his sister's voice, sharp with fear. Relief washed over Alaric as he heard the old giant's grunt of pain. Olaf was still alive, at least.

Madrena called for help, and soon more boots echoed in the corridor. And then the chamber door opened.

"Oh gods, nei!" Madrena cried. "Do not take my brother!"

"Alaric!"

Both Madrena and Rúnin were at his side at once. Their faces filled his field of vision, the panic and fear in their eyes unmistakable.

"So much…blood," his sister breathed, looking down at him.

"Maelcon's," Alaric rasped.

Madrena's eyes darted to where Maelcon's body lay. Then her nigh-colorless eyes refocused on Alaric. With trembling fingers, she reached out and touched the dagger protruding from his chest.

"Tried to get it out, but couldn't." He attempted a smile, but from the look of horror on both Madrena and

Rúnin's face, he feared it was more of a grimace. "Help me."

Madrena and Rúnin exchanged a look. "It will only bring about the end more swiftly, Alaric," Rúnin said softly.

"Nei," Alaric said, feeling another surge of anger. His rage was actually clearing his thoughts, making room for him to act. "If it had hit aught important, I would be dead already." Even his voice was growing stronger.

"Alaric, this is madness," Madrena said, but she was eyeing him with less resignation now.

He gripped the hilt of the dagger and pulled. That made the pain flare to life in his body for the first time. He grunted. The dagger budged a fraction of an inch. He tried again, but his hand was slick with blood. Rúnin took hold of the dagger's hilt and braced himself. In one swift yank, the blade came free.

Alaric bellowed as pain flooded into the spot where the dagger had been. Madrena jammed the heel of her hand against the wound to stanch the blood.

"Look at this," Rúnin said, holding up the dagger. The blade, which had blessedly only been slightly longer than Alaric's forefinger, was bent back on itself at the tip. "It must have struck your ribs."

Madrena's eyes widened. "But how did it miss his lung? Or his innards? Did the blade simply...avoid all his vitals?"

Rúnin shook his head slowly. "I have seen men survive many wounds, but naught quite like that. The gods must be smiling on you, Alaric."

He didn't feel particularly blessed as another wave of pain washed over him where Madrena's hand pressed into the rib bone that had saved his life.

But then the gravity of everything that had happened that night suddenly slammed into Alaric's chest, nigh stealing his breath.

Drostan was the schemer who'd tried to thwart his negotiations with the Picts. Maelcon was dead. And Drostan had Elisead.

Alaric was not going to die. Not before he destroyed Drostan and freed Elisead.

He jerked to his feet with a sudden burst of energy, but fresh pain claimed him at the movement.

"What are you doing?" Madrena snapped, coming to her feet at his side. He leaned against her, unable to steady himself.

"Drostan killed Maelcon and took Elisead. I'm going after them."

"The only place you're going is to Hel's realm if you don't see to that wound," Madrena retorted. "You are not a god, Alaric. Though they may have deigned that you would survive that dagger, you need to be in a healer's hands now."

"Nei," he said, righting himself and rounding on Madrena. "And do not try to stand in my way."

"You don't even know where Drostan is taking her!"

That gave him pause. Though the fog was clearing from his mind, pain now replaced it, clouding his thoughts.

"Drostan was likely the one who sent a missive to Domnall telling him to pay a visit to the fortress," he muttered. "He tried to end negotiations between Maelcon and me, but when that didn't work, he hoped that Domnall could put a stop to them—either with the threat of breaking their alliance or with Domnall's retinue of warriors."

"But Domnall and the remains of his army were driven from here," Rúnin inserted. Madrena shot him a dark look but remained silent.

"Drostan wishes the Northmen vanquished from this land."

Alaric's head snapped up at the sound of Feitr's voice in the doorway.

"He hates all Northmen. He tried to convince Maelcon to let him beat me to death when they found me in the woods seven years ago, but Maelcon said I would serve as a better example if I were kept as a slave instead."

Feitr's pale eyes fell on Maelcon's body. Hatred, followed quickly by resignation, flickered in his gaze.

"Your master is dead," Alaric gritted out, pressing his hand into the wound in his chest. "Which means that by the laws of the Northlands, you are free."

Feitr nodded slowly, though pain still lingered in the icy depths of his eyes.

"I will find a way for you to get home, Feitr, but you must tell me—why does Drostan hate Northmen so much? And where would he take Elisead? What would he do to her?"

Feitr met Alaric's eyes at last. "His family was in the village when we first arrived. They were slaughtered. I only learned later, when I overheard him trying to convince Maelcon to drive you out of his lands."

"And Elisead?" Alaric snapped.

"Elisead is Maelcon's only offspring. In my time here, I have learned that the Picts allow women to be the heirs of their leaders. Generations ago, they used to pass down rulership through women. Now it is rare, but still done."

Alaric's heart twisted as realization dawned even before Feitr was done speaking.

"Elisead will become the chieftainess of these people now. Drostan likely wishes to marry her so that he can claim this fortress and the lands for himself."

"And he thinks he can simply return to the fortress purporting to have married Elisead? Does he imagine that we will simply hand it over to him?" Madrena said, her voice tight with outrage.

"Nei," Alaric answered. "When he returns to drive us away and claim the fortress, he'll bring an army with him." His mind swirled as the pieces fell together at last. "Domnall's army."

Before he knew where he was going, Alaric had bolted from Maelcon's chamber and was sprinting down the corridor toward the great hall. He didn't slow even as lighting pain jolted through him with each footfall. He drove the heel of his hand into the wound, willing himself onward.

He plowed through the great hall and out into the yard. His gaze flew to the stables. The door had been left carelessly ajar.

Inside, the stables were unusually quiet.

"Alaric!" Madrena shouted as she burst into the stables after him. Rúnin appeared behind him, his hand wrapped around Feitr's arm.

"Two horses are missing. How in the nine realms did he slip out of these walls with the gates closed?" Alaric demanded.

"He must have used the old postern gate," Feitr said.

Even before he'd finished speaking, Alaric threw a saddle on the only horse he could find. It was a ragged looking mare whose best days were long behind her. Even still, she was longer of leg that the Northland ponies Alaric was used to.

"Are there no better animals I can use?"

"Nei," Feitr said. "The Chief only kept three horses, plus a few donkeys. No one ever travels far enough from the safety of the fortress to make it worth caring for such expensive animals as horses. There are mules in the village for pulling a plow, but naught else."

"Then this old nag will have to do."

"Alaric!" Madrena's voice was no longer merely incredulous. Now it held an edge of desperation to it. "What are you going to do?"

"I'm going to find Drostan and bring Elisead back before they reach Domnall's men," he said, swinging into the saddle. If it had been any other time, he would have laughed at how ridiculous his own words sounded. But desperation meant he'd have to follow even the most ill-conceived of plans.

"By yourself? I'll not let you go out there alone, especially not injured." She moved aside for him as he urged the old mare into the yard.

"Unless you plan to run alongside me or ride a donkey, then ja, I'm going alone. A second rider on this old horse will only slow me down. Open the gates!" Alaric barked to the men on the wall.

He spared a glance down at his sister as he reined the horse toward the gates. Her eyes shone with fierce love and worry as she gazed up at him. "You are in charge until I return," he said. "I expect everything to be in order when I get back."

Madrena bent and ripped a long strip of wool from the bottom of her overdress. "Laurel, forgive me," she muttered under her breath as she tore the fine material Laurel had so painstakingly woven for Madrena back in Dalgaard.

She handed the strip of material up to Alaric. "At least bind the wound."

He quickly wrapped the cloth around his ribcage several times and tied it snug. He met his sister's gaze once more, but there were no words needed between them. They were both Northland warriors. Neither one of them would ever turn away from a threat to those they loved.

Just then, Rúnin grabbed Alaric's arm. "Take this." He handed Alaric the bent dagger, still dark and wet with his own blood.

Alaric hefted the blade in his hand, then tucked it into his belt.

"I'd best give this back to Drostan."

42

_____

S he couldn't stop shivering.

The night was surprisingly mild, with no wind to rustle through the trees, yet Elisead shook atop her mare, for the quaking chills rose from her very heart.

Only a few moonbeams managed to filter through the thick foliage overhead and gild the forest floor, but both her horse and Drostan's were surefooted. Or mayhap the reason they moved so smoothly was because Drostan had confidence in where he was leading them?

As the terror that had been coursing through her veins ebbed, it was replaced with this shivering. The numbness of shock and fear left naught but pain in its wake, raw and choking. Though she longed for the sanctuary of detachment to return, its absence cleared her mind enough to think.

Drostan didn't mean to kill her, as he had Alaric and Maelcon. If he did, he would have done so already. He could have cut her throat at the fortress, or stabbed her and left her body in these woods. Nay, he must have some other plan.

And if he didn't intend to kill her, at least not yet, it meant that she could learn what his plans were—and perhaps even hamper them.

"I need to stop," she said. Her voice, raw from crying, came out a ragged croak.

Drostan spared her a quick glance, but returned his gaze to the forest ahead without answering.

"Please," she tried again. "We have been riding for hours. I need to relieve myself."

She could see in the weak moonlight that Drostan frowned, but still he did not respond.

The horses moved at a swift walk. Judging their speed and her distance off the ground, she had a fairly good chance of coming away unharmed if she threw herself from her mare's back.

She flung her leg over the animal's neck and leapt toward the ground. As her feet came in contact with the forest floor, one of her ankles rolled out from under her. She tumbled, trying to protect her head as she twisted away from the horse's hooves.

Drostan cursed loudly. Elisead's roll finally petered out and she came up onto her knees. Even before she could rise to her feet, though, Drostan's hands wrapped around her arms. He yanked her to her feet so hard her teeth snapped together.

"Fool girl!" he shouted in her face, shaking her by the shoulders.

"I am not trying to flee!" she screeched as her head

whipped on her neck. "I only need to stop for a moment."

Drostan stilled at last, glaring down at her. The blue war paint cutting across one side of his face made him look half-man, half-monster—which he was.

She shrank back, suddenly unsure of her initial assumption that he wouldn't hurt her. What did she really know of Drostan, after all? She'd never paid him much mind, so like a shadow was he at her father's side. He was ever the loyal warrior and her father's most trusted man.

Yet here she was alone in the woods with him, her father and Alaric's blood on his hands. God knew what plan spun in his twisted mind.

She needed to know what he was hatching and why.

But first, she had to lull him into thinking she was no threat at all.

"Please," she said again, her voice trembling almost without the need for her conscious effort. "I just need to relieve myself."

Drostan cursed again, but released her with a shove toward a large clump of underbrush.

"Be quick about it."

She hobbled behind the underbrush, her ankle protesting with each step. When she was done, she slowly made her way back to Drostan's side.

"I only wish I understood where you are taking me and why." She looked up at him pleadingly.

He grabbed her by the arm and pulled her back toward the horses a few paces away. She didn't resist, though her ankle throbbed at his hurried pace.

Drostan lifted her back into the mare's saddle and silently remounted his horse.

Elisead saw her window of opportunity closing. Desperation clawed at her, but she forced her voice to remain docile and submissive.

"Giving me the comfort of a few answers doesn't cost you aught, Drostan. I...I only aim to comprehend what you have planned for me. Surely you have known me long enough to grant me that."

In truth, Elisead didn't know Drostan at all, but she wasn't above appealing to any shred of decency he might still possess.

"What...what do you hope to accomplish in this?" she prodded tentatively.

The long silence that followed sent defeat sinking into Elisead's stomach like a stone. But then Drostan spoke.

"I am doing what is best for our people. Just as your father, my Chief, taught me."

Elisead fought the sickness that washed over her. What kind of deranged madman would justify what he was doing by invoking the honorable tutelage of the man he'd just killed?

She choked back the bile in her throat. She had to press on, no matter how revolting Drostan's perverse logic was.

"What do you mean? What is best for our people?"

He turned in his saddle and pinned her with his gaze. Under the war paint, his face was a mask of disgust. "To rid ourselves of those filthy Northmen once and for all."

She inhaled and shied away from his glower, but there was nowhere to go unless she flung herself from her horse's back again.

"Once and for all?" she managed.

"They are like a pestilence," he muttered, turning forward in his saddle once more. "Seven years ago we weeded them out—or so we thought. But now they keep coming. Your father was a fool to think that allying with them would solve his problems."

Elisead swallowed, letting his words wash over her. "So you have been working against the negotiations, trying to force the Northmen out with subterfuge and veiled threats."

Drostan's fist tightened around the two horses' reins. Elisead held her breath, fearing she'd gone too far.

"I tried to convince Maelcon that he was taking the wrong course of action," he said through clenched teeth. "But my advisement fell on deaf ears. It would have been simpler my way, swifter. We should have attacked the Northmen when they first arrived at the fortress, not invited them in."

Elisead thought back to that first day Alaric and the others had appeared on their shores. Drostan seemed to have completely forgotten that her father's men were outnumbered and that the Northmen hadn't even wanted to raid or attack the fortress.

Suddenly a memory flickered across her mind. Drostan's family had been trapped in the village when they'd closed the gates against the Northmen seven years ago. He'd had a mother, a younger brother, and a handful of cousins living in a few of the huts beyond the fortress walls.

Elisead remembered Drostan's singlemindedness in leaving the gates open a few more moments. But her father had given the order to have the gates sealed against the onslaught of Northmen. It had been for the protection of all those within the fortress, but the decision had cost dozens of innocent villagers their lives. Drostan never spoke of his family after that, though perhaps that was the moment when he'd decided to one day kill Maelcon.

Drostan seemed to believe that the Northmen's arrival this time was the same as it had been seven years earlier. But it wasn't—Alaric and his men had always intended to stay and join her people in living on the land, not raid and kill. And now that she knew Alaric, she was certain he wouldn't have been deterred no matter how many times Drostan tried to thwart his mission.

Drostan's memory was clearly colored by the desire to have a simple solution—kill the Northmen. But Elisead had sat in on the many rounds of negotiation between Alaric and her father. Peace was much more difficult than war. Drostan, however, had the simple mind of a killer.

"And...and since you didn't convince my father to change course, you thought you could force the Northmen away by ending their negotiations?"

He waved one hand dismissively. "Those were acts of desperation, poorly conceived. I should never have wasted so much time on such foolish, small attempts to be a thistle underfoot to their plan to settle."

"Then what should you have done instead?" She feared she already knew the answer, but she would hear it from Drostan's traitorous lips.

"I should have sent for Domnall sooner, and not let the fool's pride get in the way of my plans. The Picts must stand together against the plague of Northmen who threaten to blot us out."

Elisead quickly checked the position of the moon through the trees overhead. She'd been vaguely aware when they'd left the fortress that Drostan was guiding them southwest. Though the moon had crossed a fair portion of the sky in the few hours they'd been traveling, they still bore southwesterly. Toward Dál Riata. And Domnall.

"And that is where we are going now. To secure Domnall's aid in vanquishing the Northmen from my father's fortress."

Drostan glanced back at her. "Clever girl. Only it isn't your father's fortress anymore. It is yours."

Pain and nausea washed over her at the reminder spoken flatly by her father's killer. But before she could swallow her anguish, Drostan went on.

"Though soon enough it will be my fortress, for I plan to have us wed."

At his calmly spoken declaration, the moonlit forest spun around Elisead. The ground seemed to be closing in on her. Suddenly Drostan's hand was once again gripping her arm. He pulled her back into her saddle, from which she'd apparently nearly toppled.

She regained her seat, but his hand lingered on her arm, tightening painfully.

"I know you let that savage rut with you," he said, his voice soft. "I have no desire to make you my wife knowing that the barbarian's filth may grow within you. However, I can wait until your next bleeding to ensure that you do not carry the savage's spawn. And then I shall have my own heir on you." His jaw ticked behind the blue paint. "I will overcome my own disgust at your whorish ways and wed you."

"Why?" she breathed at last.

"I already told you—I am doing what is best for our people."

"You are mad."

"Silence," he snapped, leveling her with his dark, widened eyes. "It is you who are mad to open your legs to a Northman barbarian. And Maelcon must have been crazed to agree to let you marry him. Only I can see the depths to which our people would have sunk under Maelcon's misguidance. And only I can save us."

"You and Domnall," she bit out, no longer checking her tone.

"Aye, he will provide the soldiers necessary to reclaim the fortress. He'll not dirty himself with a Pict girl used by a Northman, so I will bear that burden. And then at last our people will be strong again."

This time Elisead didn't hesitate. She wrenched her arm free of his grasp and threw herself from her horse's back. Blessedly she landed on a bed of moss. She rolled to her feet, her ankle screaming in protest, and bolted through the trees.

Even before she'd made it ten steps, she heard Drostan closing in on her. She pushed herself to the limit, for she now knew that she was in the clutches of a madman who would stop at naught to enact his twisted version of rule.

He tackled her, crushing the air from her lungs. Even if she could have cried for help, there was no one to hear her.

Drostan dragged her to her feet once more and flung her onto her mare's back. But this time, he produced a length of rope. With deliberate slowness, he bound her hands to her saddle. The rope bit into the flesh of her wrists, but the pain was distant.

Might anyone come to her aid? Surely her father and Alaric's bodies had been found by now. Would Madrena come after them? Or perhaps when they reached Domnall, she could persuade him somehow to free her from Drostan's clutches.

Even as the sky began to lighten as dawn approached, blackness descended upon her.

There was no point in fooling herself.

No one would come to her aid.

43

———————

How much of a lead did they have on him? And how long would it take them to meet up with Domnall as he made his way to his holdings in Dál Riata?

The two questions twined into a hard knot of fear and urgency within Alaric's mind as he rode hard in the direction he prayed was correct. It had been too dark when he'd set out to pick up any tracks Drostan might have left, and Alaric wasn't familiar enough with this land to know aught beyond the general southwesterly direction of Dál Riata.

Instead of dulling him, the pain at the base of his chest made him all the more sharply aware of his surroundings—and the stakes that balanced on the knife's edge of fate.

Elisead's life.

His people's future.

The fortress and the villagers, for whom he now felt responsible.

Alaric forced his attention back to the present. Though he hoped to one day count himself a good leader and strategist, he was born a warrior, a man of action. All he could do was drive his horse a pace, then a pace more through the forest, which was now brightening with the first beams of the radiant morning sun. When he caught up to Drostan—not if—he would know what to do. He had to have faith in himself and the gods in that.

As the sky had lightened first to pale blue and then to the yellow of dawn, the forest around him had thinned. The rolling hills that surrounded the fortress had turned increasingly jagged and steep.

Alaric sent up thanks to Dagur, God of day, for lighting his path over the ever-rockier terrain. The old nag he rode was slower than he liked but surefooted even as they began to climb.

The trees suddenly fell away completely and Alaric was at last able to assess his surroundings. Rough, rocky peaks rose sharply from every side, with only a few patches of moss to blunt the stones here and there. Far below the rocky outcropping upon which he and his horse were perched, a river wound its way through the barren terrain.

A distant roar filled the air. Though the sky overhead was a clear and brilliant blue, a low mist clung close to the ground. As Alaric's eyes continued to search the landscape, he realized the source of the mist and the distant thundering sound.

His gaze traveled up the length of the crooked river to his right and landed on an enormous waterfall in the distance ahead. Spray frothed at both the waterfall's top, where the river cascaded over rocks and fallen logs, and from the churning pool at its base far below.

A flicker of movement to the left of the falls snagged his eye.

Two specks of color dotted the bare rocks. They had cleared the tree line and were slowly making their way up to the top of the falls.

Elisead.

It had to be her and Drostan.

Alaric had overshot their path too far to the north-west, yet he was so close to Elisead now.

He spurred on his mare, but the steeper they drove, the looser the rocks under the nag's hooves grew. Her strength was flagging, even though he tried to push her ever harder.

Alaric squinted at the rocks ahead. The two specks were still picking their way slowly up the craggy mount from which the waterfall spilled. He'd hardly gained any ground on them since he'd spotted them not long ago.

At least they hadn't pulled farther away. Their horses were likely just as tired as his, and the animals still had to pick their footing carefully as they climbed.

Without thinking, he threw himself from the mare's back. He landed on both feet, but the impact sent jarring pain shooting straight to the wound in his chest. He grunted and pressed the bandages down into the wound. His palm came away damp and red with his blood.

He didn't have time to check the injury or to properly secure the nag. She was wise enough not to wander off the ridge atop which they were perched. If he survived, he could come back and find her.

Alaric forced his legs into a stiff run. As he scrambled higher up the ridge, the frothing mist from the waterfall began coating everything in a thin sheen of moisture. He slipped, then slipped again. The rocks seemed all too eager to give way under his boots. But still he pressed onward.

Every few scrambling paces, he allowed himself to look farther up the craggy ridge. The dots at last seemed closer, but so too were they closer to the top, where the waterfall spilled over. Was Drostan fool enough—or desperate enough—to try to cross the river in the span before it fell away over the steep cliffs?

He pushed his legs to the limit, his breath ragged in his throat, but still he had to climb higher. His eyes locked on the smaller of the two figures ahead. Elisead. Her flaming hair glinted like copper in the sunlight. No matter what it took, he would reach her.

The two horses and their riders disappeared as they crested the top of the ridge. With a new burst of energy, Alaric drove himself the remaining several dozen paces. Rocks slipped out from under his feet, clattering down the ridge the way he'd come, but the roar of the waterfall, which was deafening now, drowned out the noise.

Just before he crested the ridge, he paused, flattening himself against the rocks. The waterfall crashed through the air and down into the pool far below to his right. To the left, the ridge sloped off more gradually into the forest below.

Alaric dragged in a few misty breaths. He didn't have a plan aside from reaching Elisead. He would have to trust his instincts beyond this point.

He eased himself over the crest of the ridge, body tensed and ready to attack.

A dozen paces away, Elisead sat atop a spritely mare. Drostan rode Maelcon's warhorse. Both of their backs were to him, their eyes fixed on something to the right and across the river just before it tumbled into the waterfall.

His eyes followed their line of sight. A twist of dread knotted in his belly, just below the aching wound Drostan had delivered.

On the far banks of the river, a band of warriors approached.

One man rode in front of the others, sitting proud and straight in the saddle. His jeweled hilt glinted in the morning sun.

Domnall.

Drostan stood in his stirrups and waved. Domnall returned the gesture, but they were still too far apart to be heard over the roar of the waterfall. Domnall pointed farther upriver and motioned to Drostan and Elisead.

So, Domnall thought they'd be able to cross and join him on his side of the river further up. Alaric's gaze traveled up the coursing waterway. It rushed powerfully from higher still in the mountain range they all sat in. The river was full of debris—fallen logs and enormous boulders spoke of the water's power.

At least neither Domnall nor Drostan was fool enough to try to cross in such a dangerous spot as they were in now. But Alaric doubted from the raging waters that the river was docile at any point. Blessedly, the river provided a natural barrier between himself and Domnall's army. He silently thanked the gods as he crouched in preparation to attack.

Upon receiving Drostan's signal of comprehension, Domnall rode back to where his small army, the remains of the men with whom he'd attacked Alaric's camp, marched upriver.

Alaric was alone with Drostan at last. But just as he launched himself from his crouch, Drostan turned his head. His eyes landed directly on Alaric.

44

———

Drostan's dark eyes widened behind his blue war paint. He yanked his horse and Elisead's around, giving Alaric his first full glimpse of her since he'd said goodbye forever.

Her hands were bound to her horse, her eyes rounded with fear. Dirt marred her skin and tunic. Her hair was wild and filled with twigs and leaves.

By all the gods, Drostan would pay.

His window of surprise now closed, Alaric bellowed a battle cry, drawing his sword. He ignored the stab of pain in his chest from the motion of pulling the blade free. It didn't matter now if he lived or died, as long as he could make Elisead safe.

Drostan spurred his horse on, but just as Alaric was about to close on him, he yanked on Elisead's mare's reins, pulling her in front of him like a shield.

Alaric jerked back his sword just as it would have descended on Elisead. She screamed, but tied as she was to the saddle, she was unable to move out of the way.

With the telltale hiss of metal against leather, Drostan unsheathed his own sword.

"I thought I killed you, Northman," he said.

Elisead's eyes seemed to focus on him for the first time. She cried out wordlessly again, her desperation rending him.

"You can't get rid of us quite so easily," Alaric shot back. He began circling, but Drostan continually repositioned Elisead's horse so that she was between the two men.

"You prove yourself a coward yet again by hiding behind a woman," Alaric snarled, darting his head to keep his eyes on Drostan.

Drostan's face darkened. A flicker of movement caught Alaric's attention. His gaze fluttered to Elisead. She was working her wrists against the rope that bound them. The rope had already turned blood-red from her efforts, but she kept pulling.

"But you have already chosen the path of dishonor," Alaric said, his gaze returning to Drostan. "I shouldn't be surprised that you'd rather ally with a snake like Domnall than shake the hand of an honorable Northman."

How much longer would Elisead need to free herself? How much longer could Alaric keep Drostan occupied before his opportunity to strike ran out?

Drostan bared his teeth at Alaric's words. "I'll make sure you're dead this time."

A faint pop was all the warning Alaric had. Elisead

suddenly flung herself from her saddle, landing in a pile at her horse's hooves. She sprang to her knees and slapped the mare's flank as hard as she could.

The animal reared in fright. For a long, terrible instant, it appeared as though Elisead would be crushed under the mare's hooves. But at the last second, she rolled out of the way. The mare bolted, yanking its reins free of Drostan's hand and giving Alaric a clear target at last.

"Go!" Alaric barked at Elisead, never taking his eyes off Drostan as he lunged for him.

Barely in time, Drostan blocked the blow with his sword. But Alaric grabbed a fistful of the man's tunic and dragged him from his horse's back.

Drostan fell in a heap at Alaric's feet. Alaric rammed the tip of his sword downward, but Drostan rolled out of the way. He came up standing, his sword poised in front of him.

Out of the corner of his eye, Alaric saw Elisead scrambling away from the river and the two men. She could take one of the horses and get safely back to the fortress, he thought with a flood of relief. Still, the need for Drostan's blood surged within him.

He launched himself at Drostan once more, blade flashing in the sun. Drostan blocked and the two were locked together, swords straining against each other. Drostan began to circle, pushing Alaric with him. Then with a mighty surge, Drostan shoved Alaric backward.

Alaric's boots slipped against the mist-dampened stones and he landed on his back.

The blinding flash of metal was his only warning.

On instinct alone, he threw up his blade, just barely catching Drostan's sword before it cleaved his head in two. Drostan pushed down with all his might, leaning his weight against his sword. It inched closer to Alaric. His grunt of exertion turned into a bellow of rage as he fought to fend off Drostan's sword, but still his enemy gained another inch, then another.

Alaric's hands trembled on his hilt. Drostan's blade was now hovering just over his face.

Drostan lifted a booted foot and rammed his heel into Alaric's chest—directly on his still-bleeding dagger wound. Alaric roared in pain, his vision dimming around the edges. As waves of agony washed over him, he could feel his strength flickering. His sword slipped a hair's breadth in his grip.

Suddenly Elisead flung herself onto Drostan's back with a scream, her arms tightening around his neck. Drostan growled in rage as she tried to pull him back. With one hand, he ripped her from around his neck and hurled her aside.

It was all the opening Alaric needed. Drawing on the last threads of strength he possessed, he thrust Drostan's sword away with his blade and rolled to his knees. Drostan stumbled back, his sword pulling him sideways and exposing his middle.

Like lightning, Alaric grabbed the dagger he'd tucked into his belt at Rúnin's insistence—Drostan's dagger. With a lunge, he buried the dagger in Drostan's unprotected side.

Though the tip was bent back, Alaric drove with

such force that the dagger pierced Drostan's flesh and rammed in to the hilt.

Drostan staggered, his sword dropping from his hands. He turned dark, disbelieving eyes on Alaric.

"Nay," he hissed. He fell to his knees, then slumped to the ground.

"I'll not make the same mistake you did," Alaric said lowly. He crouched over Drostan, watching the eyes of the man who'd tried to take everything from him.

Drostan sputtered and coughed. Blood came to his lips. At last, after several shuddering exhales, his breathing stopped. Slowly, the light faded behind his still-open eyes.

"Keep your traitor's dagger," Alaric said, standing over Drostan's now-motionless form.

It was over. At least for Drostan.

The fog of bloodlust receded, to be replaced with utter fear as his eyes landed on Elisead's crumpled form nearby.

"Elisead!"

He sprinted toward her, fearing the worst. She looked so small and frail lying where Drostan had thrown her to the rocks. But just before he slid onto the ground next to her, she stirred.

He reached out to her but was afraid that if he pulled her to him, he'd hurt her further.

"Elisead, are you all right? Speak, my love."

She pushed herself into a seated position. Though he saw no blood, his heart still hammered with panic.

"Aye," she said, her voice shaken. She reached for

him, her trembling fingers touching his face. "You are alive."

"Ja," he breathed, leaning into the hand on his cheek. "I would defy death to protect you."

"And Drostan is—"

"He will never hurt you again."

"He thought to marry me, to take control of my people and drive you away with Domnall's army."

"But he is either in your God's underworld or Hel's realm—whichever one, he is paying the debt of a coward and traitor."

She nodded, her bottom lip trembling. "I thought…I thought I would never see you again. I thought all hope was lost."

This time he couldn't resist dragging her into his embrace. But he was careful not to squeeze her as hard as he longed to. She shook silently in his arms, but he knew the shuddering exhale that fanned his neck was a sigh of relief. At last, the nightmare was over.

A loud whistle sounded from across the river, causing Alaric's head to snap up. He leapt to his feet, putting himself between the noise and Elisead.

Domnall must have grown weary waiting for Drostan farther upriver. The man now rode back toward the falls, his eyes locked on Alaric. He reined his horse to a halt on the far side of the river, eyeing the scene before him. Drostan lay dead, the horses were scattered, and Alaric stood protectively over Elisead.

"Are you fool enough to try to ford this river and face me?" Alaric shouted over the noise of the waterfall.

Domnall considered him again for a long moment.

"Drostan told me to meet him here when he drove us away from your camp," he said at last. "It seems as though he had some grand plan to bring me back into the fold."

"He killed Maelcon and thought to drive out my people," Alaric said flatly. "He failed. Would you like to try your hand against me and my Northmen again?"

Domnall sneered, baring his teeth, but then he took on an air of indifference. "Maelcon's petty fights never interested me," he said with a wave of his hand toward Drostan's body. "I want naught to do with you filthy Northmen. You can keep the bitch as well."

Now it was Alaric's turn to bear his teeth in a low growl. But he knew what Domnall was doing—he was trying to save face while escaping Alaric and the Northmen's wrath.

"Very well," Alaric said evenly. "Then I suggest you and your father keep to your lands, and we'll keep to ours. There is no need for further contact between us."

Domnall fluttered his hand as if he was granting Alaric a reprieve. Without another word, he reined his horse around and rode back toward where his men had gathered behind him. With a sharp gesture of his hand, Domnall and his small army began moving away from the river.

Alaric stood watching for a long time, until the sun was hot overhead and Domnall and his men were just specks far off in the hills to the southwest. At last, he turned and helped Elisead to her feet.

He tucked her under his arm and they hobbled down the slope toward the tree line, where the horses stood cautiously. He didn't look back at Drostan, whose body was for the ravens now.

He carefully placed her on her mare's back and took Maelcon's war steed. After a bit of searching, they found the old nag chewing contentedly on the underbrush not far away.

As they pointed their horses back toward the northeast, Alaric stilled her hands on the reins and leaned toward her. Their lips met in a kiss that communicated more than words ever could.

He loved her and would protect her all of his days.

With the sun shining down on them, they spurred their horses into motion.

Toward home.

EPILOGUE

"The Northmen are coming!"

Alaric's head snapped up from his morning meal of porridge, cream, and berries.

He darted a glance at Elisead, who sat next to him at the table on the raised dais. She had a berry halfway to her mouth, but she'd frozen at the sudden appearance of one of the wall guards.

But instead of terror at the words, the great hall erupted into merriment. Alaric rose, but Madrena, who sat on his other side, was faster. She had leapt from the dais and was halfway to the great hall's double doors before Alaric could help Elisead rise.

Elisead maneuvered carefully down the dais's steps, never letting go of Alaric's arm. She had begun to have trouble with her balance now that her belly was rounding with their babe. But Alaric didn't mind the excuse to be ever at her side, her arm tucked under his.

The two followed in Madrena's wake through the

double doors and across the yard, which was filled with sunlight and activity. The fortress's gates were open, and Pict villagers and Northlanders streamed in and out freely as they went about their daily tasks.

He was once again attentive as he led Elisead up the rough-hewn stone stairs to the top of the wall. Madrena already stood next to the guard who'd burst into the great hall with the news. The guard was pointing off toward the bay. Since the sky was vibrant blue, with nary a cloud to obscure the view, Alaric immediately spotted them.

Two ships, long and shallow of keel.

Their sails, striped red and white in Eirik's distinctive pattern, stood out clearly in the morning sun. They had already entered the bay and were making their way toward the mouth of the river.

Madrena whooped in excitement and dashed from the wall.

Alaric turned and directed his attention to where many villagers, Pict and Northmen, gazed up at him from the yard in eager anticipation.

"In honor of our guests, tonight we shall feast!" Alaric boomed.

The gathered crowd cheered in excitement. Several people dashed away to prepare the copious amounts of food and drink that would be needed to satisfy so many more Northmen. Luckily, the growing season already promised to be bountiful. The land under the care of their united people was thriving.

"Shall we greet them here, or at the water?" Alaric said softly to Elisead.

Her amber eyes flashed with that forest spirit he loved so much. "I would greatly enjoy a walk through the woods."

"Very well," he said, guiding her back down the stairs. With each step, his heart squeezed in anticipation. After nigh a year of hard work, Alaric would finally be able to present his successes to his Jarl.

They strolled through the gates and past the village. When they reached the woods separating the fortress from the bay, Elisead's eyes danced and a wide smile stole over her face.

He carefully guided them around the old site where the Northmen's bodies had been burned so many years ago. Alaric had ordered the remains of the bones destroyed and the sand churned. He'd also removed the stone with the runes, which still disturbed Elisead. She'd breathed a sigh of relief to know that at least in the case of that particular stone, her work had been erased.

By the time they reached the shoreline where Alaric's old camp had stood, the two ships were only a stone's throw away. Madrena stood in the bay waters up to her knees, nigh shaking with impatience.

"This is where I first laid eyes on you," Elisead said, drawing them to a halt at the tree line.

"And I thank all the gods every day that a wild forest spirit was haunting these woods that morn," he said, drawing her even closer.

She laughed and leaned her head against his shoulder.

The camp had long ago been broken down and the materials stored away in the fortress, but evidence still remained of his presence on these shores nigh a year ago. The fire pit was still black with ash, and the ground was still tamped down and clear of underbrush.

How long ago those days seemed to Alaric, when he held Elisead as a hostage, and when he was still a stranger to this land, which was now his home.

Madrena's shriek of joy interrupted his musings. The Northmen were beginning to leap from their ships into the shallows. Alaric spotted Rúnin, a dark head among many blond and red ones, just as he hoisted himself over the gunwale of the smaller of the two ships.

Practically before Rúnin had gained his footing in the water, Madrena launched herself at him. The two collided in a hard embrace. They stumbled, then fell backward into the shallows, still bound together.

Alaric chuckled. It had only been a little more than a fortnight since Rúnin had left, taking a small crew and one of Alaric's two ships to give word to Jarl Eirik that all was well at their settlement. Though Alaric had insisted that the voyage not take place until the seas were reliably calm, Madrena had been prickly as the thistles that grew so abundantly in these lands to be separated from her mate.

At last the two rose from the water, to the amusement of the other Northmen leaping from the ships and pulling them toward the shoreline.

"I trust it was a safe voyage?" Alaric said as Rúnin and Madrena strode, dripping wet, onto the sand next to him.

"Ja," Rúnin said. "Aegir the sea god smiled on us.

And Feitr had already set out for his home village without issue by the time we left Dalgaard."

Alaric nodded, satisfied. He'd now completed his promise to Feitr to allow him to return home. The former slave could have a new start back in the Northlands as a free man.

"Hail!" Eirik's booming voice drew Alaric's attention to the longships once more.

Eirik, as hearty as ever, hoisted himself into the water, then turned to carefully lift Laurel, who held their young son Thorin in her arms, down from the ship. Laurel set Thorin down in the shallowest waters, and the boy, so much bigger at a winter and a half than Alaric had last seen him, immediately began splashing and squealing with joy.

"Hail, Jarl!" Alaric called in response. Eirik strode toward him, a grin plastered on his face.

Just in time, Alaric released Elisead to receive Eirik's fierce bear hug.

"It is good to see you," Eirik said, pounding Alaric on the back.

"And you must be Chieftainess Elisead," Laurel said as she approached, holding a squirming Thorin in her arms.

Elisead went to curtsy to Laurel, but Laurel placed Thorin in Eirik's hands and caught Elisead up in a hug instead.

"If you have captured Alaric's heart, you must be a truly special woman," Laurel said into Elisead's ear even as she shot a wink at Alaric.

Laurel stood back and took in the gentle swell of

Elisead's stomach. "And you," she said to the babe who grew within, "you are the link between our peoples, just like Thorin."

"Aye," Elisead said, her voice suddenly choked with tears. "It is an honor to meet you and to welcome you to our home."

"Let us show you all that we've accomplished in the last year," Alaric said.

Just as he was turning to guide them toward the fortress, he noticed that Laurel had turned and was looking out at the water. In the bright morning sun, tears shone in her eyes.

"Are you well?" Alaric asked, coming to Laurel's side.

"Aye," she said with a smile. "I just...I never thought I would set foot on this land again."

"Alaric tells me you are from Northumbria," Elisead said, approaching Laurel. "It is less than a sennight's journey south of here on horseback if you wish to visit your home once again."

"Nay," Laurel replied, shifting her gaze toward Eirik. "Dalgaard is my home now. I simply never expected to again see the sun rising over the North Sea instead of setting into it." She laughed and wiped her eyes. Naught but happiness remained there when she removed her hands.

As the two crews worked to drag the longships onto the sandy shore and unload the chests holding their personal effects, Alaric put his arm around Elisead again and led Eirik and Laurel, who scooped up Thorin once more, toward the fortress. Rúnin and Madrena trailed behind them, their heads pressed together and their arms interlocked.

They made their way through the forest edging the river. As the river ducked behind the hill upon which the fortress stood, they reached the clearing where the village sat.

"Oh! What is this?" Laurel stopped abruptly right where the tree line ended and the village appeared.

Her dark brown eyes were locked on the large stone which had once been meant as Elisead's bride gift to Domnall. After she'd wed Alaric, she took her time in carving it the way she wanted to—the way she felt it was always meant to be.

Laurel circled the stone, which stood upright in the ground even taller than Alaric. It had taken a dozen of Alaric's strongest men to lift the slab and place it into the hole he'd dug. But it had been worth it, for now the stone stood proudly at the village's foot.

"I made that," Elisead said, smiling shyly.

Both Laurel and Eirik pinned her with wide-eyed stares.

"I...I carve stones," Elisead went on. "This one represents the entrance to the village. Here—" Elisead circled to where Laurel stood, "—here is the cross, since my people and I are Christians."

Laurel nodded, her eyes clouding with emotion for a moment as she gazed at the intricately carved cross, which took up almost the entire back side of the stone.

"And on this side," Elisead said, walking around the stone. "This was to be me, as the Virgin Mary, traveling to my betrothed." She touched first the woman

340

riding sidesaddle, then the mirror and comb symbols. "Now I suppose it is me when I traveled into Alaric's camp while he negotiated with my father." Her eyes flickered to Alaric for a moment, then back to the stone.

"These are my people." She pointed to the rows of men standing below the woman. "And these are Alaric's." Her finger traveled down to where she'd added the Northland longship, its rectangular sails seeming to flutter in an imaginary breeze. "And this is the land that binds us together," she said, running her fingertips along the border, which was filled with vines, leaves, and animals in motion.

An awed silence stole over their group as they all gazed at the beautiful stone.

At last, Laurel darted a glance at Alaric. "A truly special woman, indeed," she said, her eyes twinkling. Then she turned back to Elisead. "You'll have to explain how you create such fine details, Chieftainess."

"Please, just call me Elisead," she replied, her cheeks pinkening in a blush.

Laurel's dark brows drew together. "But Rúnin said that among your people, women can inherit the role of leader. I wouldn't want to disrespect you by not using your title. Did Rúnin misunderstand?"

"Nay," Elisead said quickly. "He was correct about my people, I just…"

Sensing her shyness, Alaric jumped in. "Elisead isn't accustomed to the use of formalities."

She shot him a grateful look, for the title once held by her father still brought up painful memories of his death. "We are both the leaders of the people here," she said, holding Alaric's gaze.

It was true, for at first there had been lingering tension between the Northlanders and the Pict warriors who'd served under Maelcon—and Drostan.

But there was always plenty of work to do, and united in the common goals of farming, building huts, making cloth and tools, and all the other tasks necessary to thriving on the land, the two peoples had grown at first accepting, and then downright friendly with each other. Both Picts and Northlanders alike respected Alaric and Elisead as their leaders. The announcement of the impending birth of their first child had only knitted their peoples together tighter.

"Very well, Elisead," Laurel said warmly. "But I still insist that you tell me how you carve like that. The animals are nigh leaping from the stone!"

"Aye, I will," Elisead said, a soft smile growing to match Laurel's.

Alaric motioned for them to continue on to the village.

"The number of huts has doubled in the last year," he said as they walked through the collection of buildings. "The Picts showed our men how to make them in this style, which is suited to the winters as well as the summers here."

"How was your first winter away from the Northlands?" Eirik asked as he admired the tightly thatched rooves and wattle and daub walls.

Alaric snorted. "Child's play," he said. Elisead swatted his shoulder, but her amber eyes were merry.

"Compared to the Northlands, the winters are mild here. We never completely lost the sun. And the growing season is longer though not quite as intense as in Dalgaard."

Eirik nodded, stroking the blond stubble that had accumulated over the sennight's journey across the North Sea.

"The fields are beyond the village to the northwest," Alaric said, motioning. "We've expanded those as well to support all our people. Barley and rye grow well here, just as in the Northlands. Many things are the same, actually."

Just then, several of Alaric's original crew began to stream out of the open fortress gates. They all bore wide smiles to behold their Jarl and his wife. As they each bowed to Eirik and Laurel, Eirik drew several of them up into a hearty hug.

"How do you like this new land, Olaf?" Eirik said with a pound on the red giant's back.

"Very well indeed," Olaf said, his eyes slipping toward a dark-haired widow who stood outside her hut watching the Northmen. "It is a land of great...opportunity."

Alaric shook his head and chuckled. Though Olaf's recovery had been slow, he was now as good as ever during training and had apparently caught the eye of the Pictish woman who gazed at him with a small smile.

When the greetings were complete and the North-landers were sent back to their tasks, Alaric led Eirik and Laurel into the fortress.

Eirik's eyes widened in respect at the thick stone

walls and the wooden great hall within. "A clever design," he said as he turned in the yard, taking in the smaller buildings and the guards along the walls.

"Ja, they have fewer natural defenses in this land," Alaric said. "So they built their own—the wall, the gates, the iron grille. This fortress is a powerful asset indeed."

Alaric led them into the great hall and called for ale, bread, and meat to be brought.

"And have you had to make use of its defenses much?" Eirik asked as they all took seats at the high table.

Alaric exchanged a glance with Elisead. "There was some...trouble when we first arrived."

"Rúnin mentioned it, but said he'd let you explain."

"Ja. All has been quiet since last summer, blessedly. Perhaps I can tell you more tomorrow, once you are settled."

Eirik raised an eyebrow but nodded.

"How many of the crew you landed with will be staying on?" Alaric said as the food began to arrive.

"Perhaps half—so a score. We will leave you with the two ships you sailed with last summer and return with only one."

"So you don't plan on staying?"

Eirik glanced at his son, who squirmed in Laurel's lap. "Nei. Dalgaard still needs their Jarl, though the village is smaller now that so many have chosen to settle here."

"And how does the village fare?"

"In truth, we had another hard winter, but with

fewer people, the small harvest was not as much of a burden. Even with the promise of a new land, I think there will always be those who wish to stay—it is their home."

"Ja," Alaric said. "Someday I hope to show Elisead —and our children—where I grew up."

"It is only a sennight's sail in good weather," Laurel said with a smile.

As the others turned their attention toward the food, Alaric spoke only loud enough for Eirik's ears.

"Now that you have seen the settlement, have I honored you, Jarl?"

Alaric rarely used Eirik's title, for they had been friends since childhood. But he invoked it now to make clear just how seriously he took the responsibility with which Eirik had entrusted him.

Eirik must have sensed Alaric's earnestness, for he grew sober. "You have done more than honor me, Alaric. You have honored yourself and the gods with all you have achieved."

"Thank you," Alaric said, extending his arm toward Eirik. "I will work hard to continue to do right by your people."

Eirik took Alaric's proffered arm in a firm grasp. "They are not my people anymore, Alaric," he said with respect shining in his blue eyes. "They are yours now— yours and Elisead's. In my eyes you are a Jarl now, my equal, not my subject—or whatever the equivalent to a Jarl is in Pictland."

Alaric's chest swelled so greatly with pride that he feared it would burst. Eirik released his forearm and lifted his wooden cup of ale toward Alaric in a little salute.

Elisead's small, callused hand fell on Alaric's arm where Eirik had just shared their grip. Though he'd thought Eirik and his voices had been too low to overhear, Elisead's eyes shone with understanding and pride as she gazed up at him.

He was most blessed indeed.

The End

AUTHOR'S NOTE

One of my favorite things about writing historical romances is, well, the history! In doing research for this book, however, I learned just how little we know about the Picts. It made for a fascinating treasure hunt for information!

Very few examples of Pictish writing remain, but they are thought to be ethnically and linguistically similar to the Celts. They appear in others' written accounts even before Roman occupation of Britain. The Picts were considered fierce and wild because they resisted all outside conquest, both from the Romans and later from the Northumbrians with their victory in the Battle of Dun Nechtain in 685.

They were, however, influenced by Christianity by way of the Celts in the sixth century. Conversion from Pictish polytheism to Christianity was probably gradual, and involved a delicate balance between the Picts' old ways and the new. I tried to portray this fluid perspective on religion in my story.

The Picts lived in loose bands and confederations, though in the eighth and ninth centuries they began united under kings of increasingly large areas. Causantín mac Fergusa (Domnall's father, who is referred to in this story as the King of Picts) reigned from 789 to 820 as king of Fortriu. Fortriu was the most powerful of all the kingdoms within Pictland, and Causantín was therefore considered the King of all Picts. Fortriu was likely located in what is today the region of Moray, Scotland, just east of Inverness.

Causantín mac Fergusa did indeed have a son named Domnall, whom Causantín made King of the lesser kingdom of Dál Riata (what is today the western coast of Scotland and the northern tip of Northern Ireland) likely in the year 811. Other than Domnall's role as Causantín's son and the future king of Dál Riata, his portrayal here is fictionalized, since so little is known of him.

Causantín probably lived in a fortress in what was once called Torridon and is now called Burghead Fort. The fort, built on a promontory overlooking the Moray Firth, was the main stronghold of Fortriu. It was built in phases starting before the third century, possibly by the Picts, or perhaps by even earlier peoples in the area. It had a thick stone wall and two inner courtyards, probably containing a great hall and private chambers. The fort was sieged by an onslaught of Viking raids in the ninth century, and in 884 Sigurd the Powerful captured Torridon. The remains of the fort were uncovered in a nineteenth-century excavation, and you can see some of the stones used for the wall today in Burghead.

Eventually, the Picts fell to the constant waves of attack from the Vikings in the middle and late ninth century. The Picts seemingly disappeared from history after the tenth century, but in reality they merged with the Vikings and the Gaels to become the Scots.

Although part of the Picts' "disappearance" had to do with the Vikings' relentless attacks on their shores, the Vikings did more than simply raid and slaughter, as is the common perception. In the early ninth century (when my story takes place), Vikings began "overwintering" in what are now France, Ireland, England, and Scotland. This is because they went sailing for more than just loot.

Historians hypothesize that Vikings were also looking for arable land and less harsh climates, because farming was incredibly difficult in Scandinavia and their population was outstripping their resources. While Vikings did attack and raid many lands, they also settled and blended with the locals, working side by side, intermarrying, and eventually melding their cultures.

Now on to a few more specific elements I included in my story. In researching Viking tents (I know, my job is strange), I stumbled across a wealth of knowledge that came mostly from the Oseberg ship remains. The Oseberg ship was found in the early twentieth century in Norway. It was a Viking burial ship from around 850 that had been almost perfectly preserved due to soil conditions. The ship was full of artifacts from everyday life, since the Vikings believed that a deceased person must be sent into the afterlife with everything he or she would need to continue living in one of the nine realms.

One such object was a tent. As I described in this story, a Viking tent was basically a giant A-frame construction. The tops of the leaning poles were decorated with the same dragon heads that adorned many a Viking longship prow, and the wood was painted. Though the material used for siding had decomposed, it is fair to guess that it might have been similar to the finely spun woolen sails the Vikings used on their ships. Today, there is a small but dedicated community of people who spend their free time building replicas of these Viking tents—what a conversation starter!

A note on how I portrayed women in Viking society, and specifically their freedom in choosing a husband or leading the life of a warrior. I have stretched the truth a bit here. In reality, Viking women were similar to most other women in the Medieval period in Europe—their marriages were arranged for the financial and political betterment of their families, and they often had little say in the matter.

However, Viking culture is known to be more egalitarian *compared to others of its time*. As I discussed in my note accompanying *Shieldmaiden's Revenge* (Viking Lore, Book 2), there is debate among scholars about whether or not Viking women could be warriors, or if it is just a mythical construct in the Sagas. Because of recent discoveries of weapons in female Vikings' graves, it is very possible that some Viking women were in fact warriors.

Regarding courtship, since most marriages were

arranged, little wooing was involved. But just like couples for all of time, Vikings fell in love and courted, sometimes in secret. It was, however, considered a grave offence to compose poetry praising a woman—it would indicate that the speaker had intimate knowledge of the woman in question, which could lead to generations-long blood feuds over the insult.

And although marriage was arranged by one's parents for financial and political reasons, the Sagas make it clear that it was best for parents to secure their daughter's blessing and consent when picking a husband. In that way, Viking women had more power and choice than many other women in Europe at the time.

Perhaps my favorite aspect of researching for this book was getting to learn about Pictish stone carving. I aimed to portray the process as accurately as possible. Masons would sketch the designs they wanted to create with charcoal, then chisel dots along the charcoal lines. Using various sizes and shapes of pebbles, they'd connect the dots—literally—with the pebbles, or with a chisel and mallet if less detail was called for.

Such artistry was highly valued, and skilled stone masons likely would have been in demand. They may have travelled with their tools, just as Elisead's teacher Una did in this story. They may have held their designs in their head, or they may have had plans for them. Many of the stones that still exist today have a common language of sorts when it comes to reappearing symbols. The comb and mirror, for example, were added next to a human figure to indicate that it was a woman.

Carved stones from the time of the Picts vary widely. Some, dating back as early as the fifth century, are simple designs or animals, incised into unshaped stones or boulders. As Christianity was introduced in the sixth century, many stones began bearing the symbol of the cross.

As time passed, carving techniques grew more sophisticated, so that rather than a simple incision on the face of a freestanding stone, stones were quarried and shaped, then carved so that figures stood out in relief. By the eighth and ninth centuries, these stone carvings were incredibly detailed, complex, and symbolically rich. Often, one side of the stone would bear Christian symbols, while the other would bear Pictish symbols and patterns evocative of Celtic designs.

I based my depiction of Elisead's bride gift on the Hilton of Cadboll stone, which was originally found less than thirty miles (forty-eight kilometers) east of where I set my story. The Hilton of Cadboll stone is thought to have been carved around the year 800. On one face is a Christian cross, and on the other are secular Pictish designs. It stands over seven and a half feet (2.34 meters) tall.

Scholars have two main interpretations of the non-cross side. Some think that it is an aristocratic hunting scene—a woman riding sidesaddle (with comb and mirror to indicate her gender) is accompanied by many men riding below her. Others, however, hypothesize that the woman represents the Virgin Mary, since she was often portrayed riding sidesaddle.

The Hilton of Cadboll stone does not bear a longship on the bottom—that was my addition. However, some carved stones from this period depict ships with the distinctly long, shallow keel of the Vikings. I liked considering the ways that these Pictish carved stones would have changed to reflect tumultuous times, including the appearance of Vikings on their shores.

Thank you for journeying with me to the time of the Vikings and the Picts!

Make sure to sign up for my newsletter to hear about all my sales, giveaways, and new releases. Plus, get exclusive content like stories, excerpts, cover reveals, and more. Sign up at www.EmmaPrinceBooks.com

THANK YOU!

Thank you for taking the time to read *Desire's Hostage* (Viking Lore, Book 3)!

And thank you in advance for sharing your enjoyment of this book (or my other books) with fellow readers by leaving a review on Amazon. Long or short, detailed or to the point, I read all reviews and greatly appreciate you for writing one!

I love connecting with readers! Sign up for my newsletter and be the first to hear about my latest book news, flash sales, giveaways, and more—signing up is free and easy at www.EmmaPrinceBooks.com.

You also can join me on Twitter at:

@EmmaPrinceBooks.

Or keep up on Facebook at:

https://www.facebook.com/EmmaPrinceBooks.

TEASERS

FOR EMMA PRINCE'S BOOKS

Viking Lore Series:

Don't miss a heart-pounding moment of the Viking Lore Series. Step into the lush, daring world of the Vikings with *Enthralled* (**Viking Lore, Book 1**).

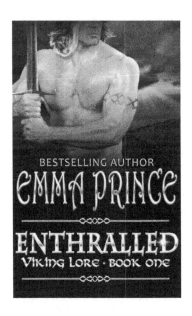

He is bound by honor...

Eirik is eager to plunder the treasures of the fabled lands to the west in order to secure the future of his village.

The one thing he swears never to do is claim possession over another human being. But when he journeys across the North Sea to raid the holy houses of Northumbria, he encounters a dark-haired beauty, Laurel, who stirs him like no other. When his cruel cousin tries to take Laurel for himself, Eirik breaks his oath in an attempt to protect her. He claims her as his thrall. But can he claim her heart, or will Laurel fall prey to the devious schemes of his enemies?

She has the heart of a warrior...

Life as an orphan at Whitby Abbey hasn't been easy, but Laurel refuses to be bested by the backbreaking work and lecherous advances she must endure. When Viking raiders storm the abbey and take her captive, her strength may finally fail her—especially when she must face her fear of water at every turn. But under Eirik's gentle protection, she discovers a deeper bravery within herself—and a yearning for her golden-haired captor that she shouldn't harbor. Torn between securing her freedom or giving herself to her Viking master, will fate decide for her—and rip them apart forever?

Travel into the heart of the dangerous, sensual North-lands with *Shieldmaiden's Revenge* (**Viking Lore, Book 2**).

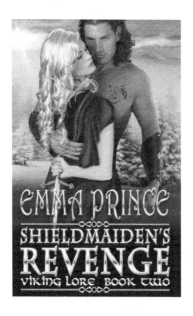

Madrena burns hot for revenge against the man who attacked her village and shattered her life five years ago. When a dark-haired stranger named Rúnin washes ashore in her village, he promises to be her guide in exchange for his freedom. Though Rúnin knows the man Madrena seeks, his life depends on keeping her at a distance, lest her sharp gray eyes discover the secret he must protect at all costs.

Despite the danger, Madrena risks trusting Rúnin. The two travel deep into the Northland wilds, only to be entangled in a world of secrets and peril. Even as they resist the heat that crackles between them, the fires of desire rival those for vengeance. But when Madrena's plans are threatened, will the fierce shieldmaiden choose love over war? And can Rúnin save them both from their pasts?

Taste the sweetness of blooming first love in *The Bride Prize* **(Viking Lore Novella, Book 2.5)**!

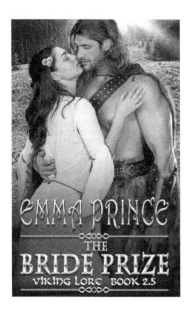

With his family lost to illness, Tarr leaves the only home he's ever known with nothing but a dream—to sail across the North Sea to the mysterious lands in the west. In order to earn a spot on his Jarl's voyage, he must compete against his fellow Northmen in games of strength and skill. But when he learns that the prize for winning the competition is the hand of the dark-haired beauty he met only days ago, will he be forced to choose between his dreams and his heart?

Eyva wants nothing more than to train as a shield-maiden, but her parents refuse, hoping to yoke her to their Northland farm forever. When they put her up as the bride prize for their village's festivities, she fears she will never escape the fate of a grueling life on her parents' farm. But Tarr's longing gaze and soft kisses just might give her the courage to fight for herself—and for their budding love.

Join Thorolf and Bridget for a daring escape from the Northlands to Pictland in ***Thor's Wolf* (Viking Lore, Book 3.5)**—a Kindle Worlds novella.

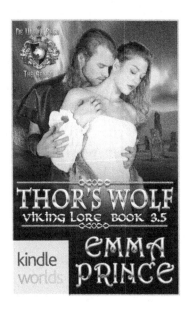

A shadowed past...

To avoid questions about his shameful secret, Thorolf has carefully constructed a life as a roving shipbuilder. But when entrancing Pict thrall Bridget falls into Thorolf's arms begging for help, Thorolf cannot resist the golden-haired beauty's pleas. He risks his life to spirit her safely back to her homeland, despite vowing never to return to Pictland. Now he must choose between guarding the truth of his past or giving his heart to the brave woman who heals him with her merest touch.

A fated future...

After being shunned by her people for possessing the gift of Touch, Bridget resigns herself to a solitary life on the outskirts of her village. When Viking raiders capture her and deliver her to their cruel Jarl, she fears that this new nightmare may never end. Yet within Thorolf's protective embrace, Bridget lets herself hope for not only the shelter his strong arms promise, but also the acceptance her own people denied her. But when the truth of both of their pasts comes to light, will fate rip them apart forever?

The Sinclair Brothers Trilogy:

Love Highlanders as much as Vikings? You won't want to miss the complete Sinclair Brothers Trilogy, starting with *Highlander's Ransom* (**Sinclair Brothers Trilogy, Book 1**), available now on Amazon.

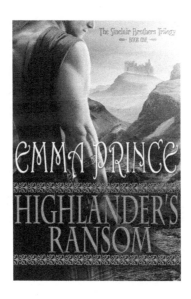

He was out for revenge...

Laird Robert Sinclair would stop at nothing to exact revenge on Lord Raef Warren, the English scoundrel who had brought war to his doorstep and razed his lands and people. Leaving his clan in the Highlands to conduct covert attacks in the Borderlands, Robert lives to be a thorn in Warren's side. So when he finds a beautiful English lass on her way to marry Warren, he whisks her away to the Highlands with a plan to ransom her back to her dastardly fiancé.

She would not be controlled...

Lady Alwin Hewett had no idea when she left her father's manor to marry a man she'd never met that she would instead be kidnapped by a Highland rogue out for vengeance. But she refuses to be a pawn in any man's game. So when she learns that Robert has had them secretly wed, she will stop at nothing to regain her freedom. But her heart may have other plans...

Highland Bodyguards Series:

The Lady's Protector, the thrilling start to the Highland Bodyguards series, is available now on Amazon!

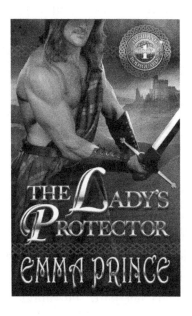

The Battle of Bannockburn may be over, but the war is far from won.

Her Protector...

Ansel Sutherland is charged with a mission from King

Robert the Bruce to protect the illegitimate son of a powerful English Earl. Though Ansel bristles at aiding an Englishman, the nature of the war for Scottish independence is changing, and he is honor-bound to serve as a bodyguard. He arrives in England to fulfill his assignment, only to meet the beautiful but secretive Lady Isolda, who refuses to tell him where his ward is. When a mysterious attacker threatens Isolda's life, Ansel realizes he is the only thing standing between her and deadly peril.

His Lady...

Lady Isolda harbors dark secrets—secrets she refuses to reveal to the rugged Highland rogue who arrives at her castle demanding answers. But Ansel's dark eyes cut through all her defenses, threatening to undo her resolve. To protect her past, she cannot submit to the white-hot desire that burns between them. As the threat to her life spirals out of control, she has no choice but to trust Ansel to whisk her to safety deep in the heart of the Highlands...

ABOUT THE AUTHOR

Emma Prince is the Bestselling and Amazon All-Star Author of steamy historical romances jam-packed with adventure, conflict, and of course love!

Emma grew up in drizzly Seattle, but traded her rain boots for sunglasses when she and her husband moved to the eastern slopes of the Sierra Nevada. Emma spent several years in academia, both as a graduate student and an instructor of college-level English and Humanities courses. She always savored her "fun books"—normally historical romances—on breaks or vacations. But as she began looking for the next chapter in her life, she wondered if perhaps her passion could turn into a career. Ever since then, she's been reading and writing books that celebrate happily ever afters!

Visit Emma's website, www.EmmaPrinceBooks.com, for updates on new books, future projects, her newsletter sign-up, book extras, and more!

You can follow Emma on Twitter at:

@EmmaPrinceBooks.

Or join her on Facebook at:

www.facebook.com/EmmaPrinceBooks.

Made in the USA
Monee, IL
10 November 2020